6.87

# Holiday *Spice*

DISCARD

# SAMANTHA CHASE

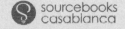
sourcebooks
casablanca

Published by Sourcebooks Casablanca, an imprint of Sourcebooks, Inc.
P.O. Box 4410, Naperville, Illinois 60567-4410
(630) 961-3900
Fax: (630) 961-2168
sourcebooks.com

Printed and bound in Canada.
MBP 10 9 8 7 6 5 4 3 2 1

*For Kathy. Thank you for keeping me organized and focused. Thank you for being a sounding board when I need it. But mostly, thank you for being a friend.*

*xoxo*

# Prologue

*Christmas morning*

EVERYTHING WAS IN PLACE, AND IAN SHAUGHNESSY yawned broadly as he looked around the living room. It was barely five a.m.—much too early to be up—but he relished the time alone on this particular morning.

Christmas Day.

Lily had loved all the holidays, but Christmas had always been her favorite. She loved shopping and decorating and making sure she had gotten all the kids what they most wanted and putting it under the tree for them. Part of her fun came from placing wrapped gifts from her and Ian under the tree and then having the biggest item on each child's list set off to the side unwrapped—except for a big red bow—from Santa. It didn't matter how old the boys had gotten; they loved the tradition.

Glancing over at the row of Santa gifts, he smiled. A new toolbox for Aidan, a set of luggage for Hugh, new racing gloves and a helmet for Quinn, a stereo recorder and microphone for Riley, a new telescope for Owen, and a dollhouse for Darcy.

That's where his gaze locked, and he felt tears burn his eyes.

Lily had never experienced a Christmas with her daughter. As much as she had loved her boys, she'd been simply over the moon about Darcy. He chuckled as he remembered how she had started buying Christmas gifts for their daughter as soon as she was born. That first Christmas without Lily, he was thankful for the chance to put those precious gifts under the tree. Darcy wouldn't know the difference, but he did.

Darcy.

His normally chatty and excitable child had been rather subdued lately—which was odd. The fact that it was so close to Christmas made it doubly so.

Her Christmas list had been short—a dollhouse, a doll, a dress, and roller skates. Ian had expected a much longer list, but since she was only six, he supposed she'd get to that stage eventually.

But then there was her behavior.

She'd been good. Really good. *Extra* good.

Her room had been spotless for weeks. She helped out around the house and went to bed on time without giving him any trouble at all. She was polite to everyone. And while these were all wonderful things, they weren't completely normal for Darcy.

"A little early for you, isn't it, Dad?"

Ian turned as his eldest son walked toward him. Seeing him in flannel pajama pants and a T-shirt, it was hard to believe Aidan was a college graduate already making plans to start his own construction company. Right now, he looked like…well, a child. Ian's child.

"You know I wanted to make sure everything was set up and ready. Besides, it's not often I get to enjoy this much alone time."

Aidan chuckled. "I'm going to start the coffee."

"Already ahead of you." Together, they walked into the kitchen, poured themselves mugs of coffee, and sat at the table. Ian decided to run his musings by his son. "Have you noticed anything odd about Darcy lately?"

"In what way? She's six. There are a lot of odd things about her."

Ian shared his observations and then waited. Aidan was his most level-headed child, and if he noticed anything, Ian might feel a little bit better.

"It's Christmastime, and she's probably being good for Santa so she won't get coal in her stocking." He shrugged. "If you're lucky, she'll keep it going long after Christmas."

"I don't know. Sometimes I feel like I'm failing her."

"Why?"

"Aidan, she's already figured out that she's different from all her friends because she doesn't have a mom."

"She *has* a mom," Aidan replied fiercely.

"You know what I mean. My heart breaks when I watch her with her teachers at school or her friends' moms…hell, even watching her with Mary Hannigan. Mary was your mom's best friend, and she's done so much to make sure Darcy has a female figure in her life, but…"

"But?"

"Mary has children of her own. Bobby and Anna are growing up, and I've noticed how Darcy gets jealous when Mary can't spend time with her or if she finds out Mary's doing something with Anna and she's not invited. How do you explain to a six-year-old that Mary and Anna are mother and daughter and can't always include her in their plans?"

"Dad, she'll have to get used to it. Mary's great, and we all appreciate everything she does, but she's *not*

Darcy's mom. It's not up to her to take on that role, and
Darcy will learn to deal with it."

"I don't know. She doesn't talk about it. I do my
best to be both mom and dad to her. We all dote on
her and make sure she's not missing out on anything.
If anything, she's probably a little overindulged." He
paused. "That's what makes this whole pattern of
behavior so strange."

"I still think it's a Santa thing. She'll be back to her
old self by the time we finish breakfast."

Ian wasn't so sure. They sat in silence and finished
their coffee.

"The stampede should begin any minute," Aidan
said as he rinsed out his mug. "It's funny how we never
could get up on time for school, but on Christmas morning, everyone's up and ready at six o'clock on the dot!"

Ian chuckled softly. "It's one of the great things about
being a kid. Even as an adult, you can't help but get
excited on Christmas morning. There's something special about it."

Aidan nodded, looking at the floor. "It was Mom's
favorite."

"Yes, it was." He was about to say more, but he heard
footsteps overhead. "And so it begins."

"I see you're already prepared in here too with everything ready to go for breakfast."

"Can't break tradition. Belgian waffles. I know I don't
make them quite the way she did, but I'm getting better."

Walking over, Aidan put an arm around his father's
shoulders and hugged him. "You do great, Dad."

Within minutes, everyone was gathered in the
living room and began tearing through their Santa

gifts. Ian watched the smiles on each child's face as they opened their presents—and he was thrilled with their reactions.

Happiness.

Surprise.

Anticipation.

And Darcy was looking a little perplexed. He was about to ask her if she was all right, but Aidan began handing out more gifts, and it distracted her, and she was smiling again. Every few minutes, however, that look was back.

Had he missed something?

Had he somehow forgotten something from her wish list?

Lost in his thoughts, he missed most of the craziness of the rest of the gift exchange, and then it was time to start breakfast.

"Okay! You know the rules. You all are in charge of getting this wrapping paper and extra boxes cleaned up. We'll be eating in twenty minutes."

One of the great things about his kids—they were cooperative.

Most of the time.

Well, especially on Christmas morning.

Soon they were seated, and everyone was talking excitedly about what they had gotten. Beside Ian, Darcy was daintily eating her waffle—*graceful as a princess,* he mused. "It looks like Santa saw what a good girl you've been," he said, reaching over and stroking her dark hair.

She nodded. "Mmm-hmm."

"How's your breakfast?"

Looking up at him, she flashed him her most precious smile. "It's wonderful, Daddy. You make the best waffles in the whole wide world."

His heart filled with pride and love and...just more of everything. "Thank you, sweet pea."

Around them, the boys were all talking and making plans to try out their new gadgets after breakfast. Ian had to remind them about one last round of cleanups before they could go, and once everyone finished eating, they all jumped up to help.

"May I be excused for a minute, Daddy?" Beside him, Darcy stood.

"You okay?"

She nodded. "I'll be back in a minute," she said excitedly. "I promise!"

Before he could comment, she was running from the room.

"What's with her?" Quinn asked, reaching over and picking up his sister's empty breakfast plate.

"Not sure," Ian replied, slightly distracted. "C'mon. Let's get this mess cleaned up so we can make an even bigger one later with dinner."

They all laughed and began to move the dishes to the kitchen. With that room under control, Ian wandered to the living room and saw Owen and Riley picking up the last of the discarded wrapping paper.

"Hard to believe it was such a mess an hour ago, right, Dad?" Riley asked with a chuckle.

"You boys do great work!"

"Can I take my microphone upstairs?"

"Can I take my telescope outside and test it out on my stand?"

Ian was about to answer when Quinn and Hugh walked into the room. "We're going to set up a video game tournament upstairs," Quinn said to the twins. "Either of you want in?"

Aidan sauntered in and smiled at them all. "Did I hear video game tournament? I think you should all prepare to lose!"

They were so busy laughing and talking smack to one another that at first, Ian didn't notice his daughter coming down the stairs. Out of the corner of his eye, he caught a glimpse of the red velvet dress she had just gotten, and he could only stop and stare.

Her hair was brushed neatly, and she had put a white ribbon in it.

The dress was pristine, and she had already put on tights and her best shoes.

And she descended the stairs as if she were doing it for the queen herself.

At once, conversation stopped as all six Shaughnessy men stared.

Darcy stopped on the landing and looked at them and then beyond them to the living room. The smile she had been wearing dropped ever so slightly. "What's everybody doing?" she asked.

"Um, the boys are going to play video games and—"

"But they can't!" she cried. "We're not done! All the presents aren't done!"

Ian looked nervously at his sons before turning to his only daughter. "What are you talking about, Darce? We opened all the presents. Santa was here and gone last night and left all the gifts."

Tears welled up in her big eyes, and for the life of

him, Ian had no idea what had brought this on or what he was supposed to do.

"But…but I sent Santa my letter," she said, her voice trembling. "And…and he brought me everything else that was on my list. Everything! There's only one more!" Tears rolled down her cheeks in earnest.

Crouching beside her, Ian wrapped an arm around her tiny frame. "Sweetheart, I'm sure Santa remembered everything. You gave me your list too, remember? And everything you had on it—"

She shook her head. "I sent him a special letter. A secret one!" she cried. "It was supposed to be just for Santa to read!"

"O-kay," he began cautiously. "What was in your letter?"

And for the first time that morning, Ian saw the uncertainty. The self-awareness. His normally confident daughter suddenly didn't seem so sure of herself, and he had a feeling it was because they were all standing around watching her. But when he was about to ask his sons to go and let them have a little privacy, Darcy spoke.

"I asked Santa for a mommy," she said finally. Then she looked up at him pleadingly. "Why didn't he bring her for me?"

# Chapter 1

THERE HAD BEEN A LIGHT DUSTING OF SNOW OVERNIGHT, and as Benjamin Tanner watched the sunrise, he realized this scene never got old. This was where he was meant to be—to live and breathe—in the mountains of Washington.

That didn't mean he didn't want to travel or see some of the rest of the world, but this was always going to be where he called home. His brothers had both moved away once they'd finished college, and while it meant he didn't see them very much, Ben understood the need to forge your own path.

The forests, the mountains, and working with actual wood had never appealed to either Jack or Henry. For as long as Ben could remember, his brothers had been athletes and intellectuals, and neither had any interest in anything remotely artistic that required working with their hands. And he was fine with it. Really. Growing up, it had meant Ben got to spend a lot of quality time with his grandfather that his brothers never got to experience. It meant that all of his grandfather's hard work had led to something—to leaving a legacy that was now Ben's to pass on someday.

Some. Day.

Maybe.

If he didn't start getting his priorities in order, there wouldn't be anyone to leave this legacy to, and that made him sad. Turning away from the window, Ben looked at the open floor plan of the home's main floor. At one time, this had been a simple three-room cabin his grandfather had built. Over the years he'd expanded, and when his grandparents had died and left the house to him, Ben knew he'd make improvements on it. And he had. Some were out of necessity, and others were… Well, everyone should live in a space they enjoyed.

The property was magnificent, and his grandfather's workshop was still standing. There was a lot of new equipment and upgrades out there too, but for the most part, Ben preferred working with the same tools his grandfather had used. Of course, over the years, so many of them had needed to be replaced, but he did his best to stick to the basics and stay away from the newer power tools.

Anyone could work with those.

It took time and patience and skill to do it all by hand.

Speaking of… He took a minute and flexed his left hand. It still hurt like a son of a bitch, and he knew it would continue to feel that way for a couple of days—not enough to make him stop working, but it was going to slow him down. And right now, that wasn't necessarily a bad thing. There was nothing worse than the sting of a sharp metal blade cutting through skin, no matter how many times it happened.

Looking over at the kitchen table, he saw the letter that had turned his perfectly peaceful world upside down. He'd committed to doing a book on his art and sculptures, and he was supposed to do a fair amount of writing—including a very lengthy foreword and introduction—and he hadn't done jack shit to get it done.

And now he was out of time.

As much as it pained him to admit, he needed help. Fast. He needed to find someone who was organized and had a basic knowledge and appreciation for art—specifically the kind of art that he did. On top of that, they needed to be able to write about it in a way that would make readers both intrigued and excited about his work. There was only one person he could think of to fit the bill, and that was Savannah Daly—well, Savannah Shaughnessy now. She'd interviewed him about three years ago, and even though he'd been vehemently against it at the time, she'd been fairly easy to work with—not intrusive, and she didn't waste time. She came and got on with the interview and was gone without it being too incredibly awkward. And in the end, she'd done a kick-ass article that had garnered him enough new clients to keep him working well into the next decade.

She'd kept in touch since then, sending him cards or notes when she'd seen or read something about his work. Honestly, if he had to have someone here in his house for a couple of days to get this whole book thing off his plate, he couldn't think of anyone else he'd want to do it. He considered her a friend.

And he didn't consider many people that.

So he'd called her, and after talking to Savannah, he had reluctantly agreed to her version of helping him out. She couldn't come personally, but she was sending someone to help him—someone she trusted and assured him would be an asset. Right now, he wasn't so sure. It was no different from his publisher sending someone, but at least this way, he had a personal reference from a friend.

Darcy Shaughnessy. Over the last several years, Ben had heard Savannah mention her sister-in-law, but he'd never had the opportunity to meet her himself. He was going to. Soon. But he still wasn't sure she was going to be of much help to him. After all, she wasn't a writer like Savannah, and that was what Ben had wanted. Ultimately, he had accepted the offer because Savannah had assured him that Darcy had brilliant office skills and a creative mind—all the things combined she swore would help him finish this project.

With a stretch, he walked into the kitchen and poured himself a second cup of coffee and contemplated his day. There wasn't any reason to be up this early; it was just the way his internal body clock worked. And with his hand still throbbing, he knew going to the workshop right now wasn't wise.

"Looks like a paperwork day," he murmured and then realized the paperwork was everywhere. A muttered curse was his first reaction and then a more vicious one when he raked his bad hand through his hair and rubbed it the wrong way.

"Okay, so clearly it's going to be *that* kind of day. Great."

Yeah. Things weren't looking too good for him to make much progress on anything right now. Darcy was due to arrive this evening, and he'd already invited her to join him for dinner, so he was going to have to attempt to clean up. Not that the house was dirty, but there was stuff everywhere. Like paperwork. Newspapers. Tool catalogs. The first thing to do would be to do a quick sweep of it all and throw away the junk he didn't need.

That took over two hours, because there were a lot of

tool catalogs he'd forgotten about, and now he had a list of items he wanted to order for some projects he wanted to do in the spring.

"Still progress," he told himself as he began—in earnest again—to weed through the junk mail and minimize the piles.

By the time lunchtime rolled around, Ben was beginning to wonder if maybe he should have offered to go to LA and work with Savannah there. It probably would have been a whole lot less stressful and aggravating than this nightmare. But on the upside, the living area looked good. Small piles of magazines and catalogs were fanned out on the coffee table, and he could totally live with that. He dusted off the newly uncovered surfaces and then ran the vacuum and felt a sense of accomplishment.

Maybe it wouldn't be so bad after all.

---

Six hours later, the steaks were ready to go on the grill.

The salad just needed to be dressed.

The potatoes au gratin were in the oven.

And there was a platter of assorted cheeses and crackers on the counter along with a bottle of wine and glasses. He might not entertain much, but he hadn't forgotten how to be a good host.

Off in the distance, he heard a car door close and smiled. It seemed weird that he was actually looking forward to this night. It was possible that Darcy would want to wait until morning to get started, but hopefully—with a few strategically placed hints—she'd see there was no time like the present. After all, the sooner they got started, the sooner they'd be done. And if she felt half as awkward about this unconventional situation as he did, she'd see his thinking was right.

He opened the front door and was heading down the steps just as she was pulling her purse from the backseat. He was about to call out a greeting, but words simply escaped him.

Dark chestnut hair that seemed to caress her shoulders. Fair, flawless skin that had a hint of rose from the cold. And wide green eyes that seemed to sparkle as she looked over at him with a smile. Ben noticed how she moved with grace and ease and confidence. Medium build, with trim legs encased in well-worn denim and... He had a feeling he was staring and forced himself to stop.

Stepping forward, he closed the distance between them and held out his hand. "Darcy? Hi, I'm Ben."

Darcy smiled brightly at him as she shook his hand. "Hi! It's a pleasure to meet you. Savannah's told me a lot about you."

Ben forced himself to keep his eyes on hers and not to look as shaken as he felt. She had a firm handshake— one that in a professional meeting he'd appreciate—but right now, he found it hard to ignore how small her hand felt in his or how soft her skin was. He noticed the odd expression on her face and realized he hadn't responded to her.

Part of him wanted to ask if it was good or bad stuff she'd heard, but he figured it would sound too corny. "Likewise," he said instead. "How was the trip?"

"My flight was great, but I had a little trouble getting here from the airport," she said, but it didn't come off like a complaint. "You're certainly not close to any major cities. I was beginning to think I'd never get here."

He chuckled. "Sorry. I guess I should have warned you."

She laughed with him. "Savannah mentioned it, but I thought she was exaggerating." She paused. "The scenery was amazing. Seriously, with the little bit of snow on the trees, it felt like I was driving into a Christmas card scene or something."

They stood there for a moment, and Ben realized he still had her hand in his. It would seem weird just to drop it, so he kind of casually slid his palm against hers until he could simply put his own hand in his pocket.

"Thank you so much for doing this," he said as they pulled apart. "I don't know how much you know about this project. Savannah said you were there visiting and on vacation, so..."

"Well, you caught me at a good time. I think I would have gone broke if I'd stayed much longer."

"Broke?"

"Savannah and I did a lot of shopping," she said. "With Halloween coming up, I bought Aislynn a couple of costumes."

"Does she need more than one? She's a baby, right?" he asked with mild amusement.

Darcy nodded. "She is, but all the more reason for her to need multiple. Babies are messy."

"Makes sense."

"Then I started Christmas shopping—"

"It's October," he stated, figuring she might need the reminder.

"I know, but the stores already had Christmas stuff out—I swear it gets earlier and earlier every year—and that got me all excited because it's Aislynn's first Christmas."

"Do babies know it's Christmas?"

She giggled, and just the sound of it made him smile.

"She may not, but I bought her the cutest little elf costume." Then she stopped and blushed. "Sorry. Here we are standing out in the cold, and I'm yammering on about my niece."

"It's quite all right," he said, enjoying the color in her cheeks. "But now I kind of feel worse about taking you away from all of that. It sounds like you were having a great time."

"It was a lot of fun, but this work you need help with intrigued me. I'll admit it seemed like an odd request when Riley told me."

"Riley?"

Darcy nodded. "He was the one who initially told me." Ben was about to ask why, but she was one step ahead of him. "I had been teasing him earlier in the day, and I guess he thought it would be funny to throw me out."

Ben's eyes went wide. "Throw you out? That seems a little harsh."

She shook her head and laughed. "Trust me, that's not it at all. Like I said, this sort of hit at a good time. I've been job hunting for what seems like forever. I'd love to work at an art gallery or an art magazine, but those jobs are few and far between. My job back home is only a temporary one, so I'm kind of looking at other options. So really, I should be thanking you," Darcy said with a smile.

"What can I help you with?" Ben asked, looking over at the car. "Can I carry anything?"

She shook her head. "Savannah mentioned that you offered to let me stay here, but..." She shrugged. "It's nothing personal, but I'm more comfortable staying at a hotel."

"I understand," he said and took another step back, because he felt himself wanting to move in closer just to be near her. He knew he was going to have to be careful if he was already feeling this drawn to her.

"I promise it won't interfere with our work time. I'm not a super early riser, but if that's what you need from me, then that's what I'll be," she said with a wink.

"No worries. I'm sure we can come up with a schedule that works for both of us." He motioned for Darcy to precede him up the front steps. All twelve of them. Which was a mistake. With nothing to do but admire the soft sway of her hips as she moved and how snug the denim was across her—

"Great cabin!" Darcy said, interrupting his thoughts.

Ben had done a lot of renovations and updates on his home, and he found himself curious about what Darcy saw when she walked inside. He'd done his best to keep the original feel of the cabin, but he'd wanted more rustic elegance than just rustic. So he'd added more windows along the rear of the house for a better view of the lake and for the natural lighting. Vaulted ceilings and exposed beams along with a stone fireplace made the living room one of his favorite rooms in the house.

Unable to help himself, he mentioned some of the newer aspects of the house as they made their way inside. He talked about the improvements and what he still had planned for future projects. She smiled and nodded until they walked into the kitchen.

His domain.

This was the room that stepped away from the original rustic charm his grandparents had aimed for. Gone were the simple-yet-functional cabinets and butcher block counters, and in their place, Ben had installed restaurant-quality stainless steel appliances, granite countertops, an additional vegetable sink in the large island, a gas stove, and ebony wood cabinets with undermount lighting.

To him, it was a spectacular space.

"This kitchen is a dream," Darcy said softly as she turned and smiled at him. "I don't cook a lot, but I bake, and the sheer size of these countertops has me feeling a bit envious. I'm imagining how many dozens of cookies I could cool on these surfaces!"

He couldn't help but smile at the look on her face—he could almost see the wheels in her head spinning as she tried to figure out how she'd utilize the space.

"I'm not much of a baker, unless you count boxed mixes. And even that's only when I absolutely have to have something sweet to eat and I don't want to drive the forty minutes into town." They both laughed softly at that. "So what's your specialty?"

"I am a whiz at cookies and gourmet brownies, but other than that, it depends on my mood."

"I get it. That's how I am with cooking. I love to do it, but it's certainly more fun when I'm making something I really want."

And for a brief moment, all he could think of was how he wanted *her*.

Clearing his throat, he offered her something to drink and then decided to get their dinner started.

"You have quite the view," Darcy commented as Ben started gathering the steaks and grilling utensils. "I bet when the snow really comes down, it's mesmerizing." She looked over her shoulder at him. "Probably have a white Christmas every year too, huh?"

He chuckled. "I'm noticing a trend here—you sort of have Christmas on the brain."

"I know. We live in a coastal town and don't get a lot of snow. Most of the time, I only see it in Christmas movies or cards or that sort of thing. But when I look around here, that's what it reminds me of." She paused and reached for a cracker. "And I love Christmas. Like, seriously love it. And this view and all the shopping I just did…it has me in that frame of mind. Plus, I bought a ton of holiday romances. So yeah, just in case I didn't say it enough, I totally love Christmas. Don't you? It's my favorite holiday."

She was so passionate about what she was saying, and her smile was beautiful and beguiling, but… He sighed. He wasn't going to start out their working relationship by lying to her. Not knowing what to say to that, he simply nodded and walked out onto the deck, sliding the door closed behind him.

His parents had died two weeks before Christmas.

Even thinking of it now caused his heart to squeeze painfully in his chest.

Still.

They had been away on a vacation—just the two of them—when it had happened. It was something they had started doing once he and his brothers had gotten old enough to stay home alone. Ben had never begrudged them their time together. They'd worked hard for so many years to provide a good life for their kids, and he felt they deserved the time away.

On that particular trip, they had gone to Mexico. Ben remembered how excited his mother was to be going somewhere tropical. After living in the cold Northwest her whole life, going someplace warm and sunny for vacation was her idea of heaven.

As if it were yesterday, he could remember what he'd been doing when the phone rang that day. He'd been helping Henry cook dinner because Jack wouldn't. They had been arguing about it. The phone had shut everyone up for a second, and Ben had grabbed for it distractedly.

As he listened to the voice on the other end telling him about the boating accident, he thought he was going to be sick. His head had begun to pound, and his stomach lurched.

*There was an accident…*

*Drowned…*

*We've recovered the bodies…*

He had wanted to scream for the man to stop. To shut the hell up and stop lying to him. His parents weren't dead. They were on vacation. They were coming home for Christmas. The tree was up, and presents were already wrapped and waiting under it.

But they didn't come home. Not alive. And Ben's world had never been the same.

And since then, he had stopped celebrating the holiday.

It was too painful—brought back too many bad memories.

And Darcy loved Christmas.

When she had admitted that to him, he had gone a little bit cold.

It didn't take long to get the steaks on the grill, and rather than go back inside, Ben took the time to get himself—his emotions—under control. Turned out, freezing cold temperatures worked well on that sort of thing, and by the time he stepped back inside and joined her at the table, he felt more like himself. Maybe now would be a good time to start to get to know each other—break the ice, so to speak. They sat in companionable silence for a moment before Darcy spoke.

"So tell me about this book," she said enthusiastically. "Savannah told me about your work, but I guess I'm having a hard time envisioning why you would need a writer to describe your own work."

*Okay, not so much with the breaking of the ice,* he thought. And while he had been hoping to learn a little bit more about her, he knew he needed to focus on the book.

For the next few minutes, Ben went over the concept and explained the pictures, files, and paperwork he had. "I've got all the proofs back, and honestly, I hate it. All of it. Nothing's right with the wording, and I'm just too busy to deal with it."

"I'd love to look at it, if that's okay," Darcy said. "I mean, I know you're cooking and everything, but I'm really curious."

With a nod, Ben stood and went to get the pile of stuff he'd put to the side in preparation. It didn't take long to put it all out on the kitchen island, and Darcy stood and began sorting through it. When he watched her, she gently shooed him away. He took the hint and began to work around her to get dinner on the table.

Their conversation flowed, and even as he served the food, he watched as Darcy moved around to help him while still eyeing the assortment of photographs and notes.

"Do you have anything in mind for the intro?" Darcy asked, interrupting his thoughts, and he instantly gave her his full attention.

"The intro?"

She nodded. "I made sure I got as much info as I could out of Savannah before I left, and from everything she said and what you just told me, what you need help with is the writing portion of the book—the acknowledgments, intro, describing your work with stories about your inspiration or funny anecdotes. Now I'll admit, I'm not a journalist—"

"*That* was why I reached out to Savannah," he said with a hint of exasperation. "She's excellent at what she does, and since we had worked together in the past, I knew she'd be able to help me with this better than anyone else."

As soon as the words were out of his mouth, Ben wanted to take them back.

She looked deflated.

With little more than the slightest of nods, Darcy put her attention on her plate, and that made him feel even worse. How could he have messed up this soon? And it wasn't as if he was saying that Darcy *couldn't* help him, it was just… Okay, that was kind of how it came out. All he had to do was take his foot out of his mouth and try again.

"I know you haven't had a chance to look at everything yet, but after your first glance, what do you think?" he asked, hopeful it would be enough to turn this whole thing around.

Darcy finished chewing, took a sip of her wine, and looked him square in the eye. "As I was saying, I'm not a journalist, but I do feel confident that I can help you. Previously, I interned for *ArtView* magazine, and I worked as a receptionist at a small gallery in Myrtle Beach. In college, I used to work with the art department, helping them hang and display work for their shows, and I worked in the Contemporary Art Museum office." She paused and took a steadying breath. "So as you can see, I'm familiar with the arts, and it's something that I'm passionate about. If it's all right with you, rather than work with what they wrote for you, I'd like to start from scratch. And really, the key is to get you organized."

That was it? That was her suggestion? Organization? Hell, if she had been here earlier, she would have seen that he could master that task, and it hadn't brought him any closer to knowing what to do with this book.

"I don't see where—"

She held up a hand to stop him. "A writer may very well be able to phrase things more eloquently," she began, "but people who will buy this book aren't looking for that. It isn't as if this is the great American novel. They're interested in your work and—therefore—you. So you need to make sure the words on the page are yours."

"That's all fine and well," he countered, "but that's the problem. I can't seem to *get* my words and thoughts on the page."

She grinned at him, and damn if it didn't hit him square in the gut.

"That's because you're not organized," she replied with a hint of sass. "I'm telling you, Ben, once we start working and we get this pile organized and in order and we talk it through, you're going to find those words coming to you."

Honestly, he wasn't convinced, but rather than argue, he went back to listening to Darcy talk about layout, wording, and tone.

Everything made perfect sense. And it was all

obvious. Listening to her made Ben feel a little bit stupid for not having been able to figure it out on his own. However, Darcy seemed confident in what she was saying and had an excitement and enthusiasm about her that was starting to make him feel the same way. She knew how to put it all into perspective for him, and now it didn't feel quite so overwhelming.

They finished eating and began cleaning up together. It seemed like the perfect time to take a break from talking about work and start getting to know one another. If they were going to be spending so much time working closely with each other, he wanted them to feel comfortable. He couldn't speak for Darcy, but he thought it could be helpful.

Plus, he was curious as hell to know more about her.

"So, you're from North Carolina," he said casually.

She nodded. "Born and raised. Although I did live out in California for one semester of college, and I've traveled a bit because my brothers were all living in different states or working in different states at one time or another, so…"

"But the East Coast sounds like your home base. Ever think about moving? Trying out the West Coast?"

"If the right job came along, I'd probably be okay with moving." She turned and looked at him as she rinsed off a dinner plate. "Although I have to admit, normally when I think of the West Coast, I think of California, but I don't know if I could live there full time."

"Really? Why not?"

"Well, remember how I told you all the Christmas stuff was out in the stores already?"

He nodded.

She shook her head and laughed softly. "I just don't know if I could handle such a warm and green

Christmas. I mean, they put Christmas lights in the palm trees, for crying out loud!"

Why did everything come back to Christmas with her? And rather than change the subject, he found himself asking, "Isn't it warm and green where you live? You're in the South."

"We still get all four seasons, and trust me, we may not get a lot of snow, but it definitely gets cold." Then she turned and looked out the window over his sink. "I would love to have a view like this on Christmas morning. I bet it's amazing when you have the lights hung outside and…"

"Um, yeah. Sure," he said gruffly and grasped for something to say to get them back on track. Again. "So you're not overly attached to North Carolina. That should be helpful in your job search."

"Definitely," she agreed. "There's not a big art district or art scene where I live, so I'm keeping my options open. What about you? Have you always lived in Washington?"

"Born and raised," he said with a smile, grateful to move on from holiday chatter. "I can't imagine ever living someplace else. This is just…it's home for me."

"I get it." She paused. "What about your family? Are they all here?"

*Ugh.* Why hadn't he thought about this part of the conversation? He hated getting into this with anyone. With a sigh, he said, "I have two brothers, and they both moved to the East Coast—northern East Coast."

"Are you close?" she asked as she loaded the last plate into the dishwasher and got it started. "When was the last time you saw them?"

"They were home for a visit about three months ago,"

Ben said, smiling fondly at the memory. "It was just for the weekend, but we fished and hung out, and it was good. Really good."

"Nice! Do you ever take time off and go to visit them—you know, like for the holidays?"

"Um…"

"Because you know it's safe to leave the mountain, right?" she teased. "I know you love it here, and it's beautiful and all that good stuff, but there is no crime in getting away for a little while."

"Wait, what?"

She laughed. A deep, rich, throaty laugh, and if it wasn't an erotic sight—as was everything with her—he might have gotten ticked off at how she was mocking him.

"Savannah told me of your attachment to this place," she said, still grinning. "Sorry. I didn't mean to tease, but it just came out."

"Yeah, well, I did offer to go to LA to work on this book," he said, sounding a little more defensive than he wanted to. "Savannah teased me about taking me to snooty restaurants and galleries while I was dressed in my jeans and flannels. She said I'd get banned from Hollywood for being a fashion no-no."

Darcy began laughing uproariously again, and he couldn't help but join her.

"A fashion no-no?" she repeated. "Seriously?"

Doing his best to look serious, he deadpanned, "True story." Wiping the countertop, he looked around and saw everything was in order. "I wasn't sure if you'd want dessert or not, but I do have some ice cream if you're interested."

Darcy's face lit up. "Chocolate?"

"Like there's any other kind," he said with a

conspiratorial grin and immediately walked over to the freezer. "We can wait a little while if you'd prefer. I know we just got done eating."

"I'm actually kind of tired from the trip and was hoping to get to the hotel and crash before it got too late. This way, I can get up early tomorrow, and we can start fresh." She looked at him as he put the carton of ice cream down. "If that's okay with you."

Ben was feeling hopeful—they were off to a great start, and he was confident they could put the work aside for the rest of the night and simply focus on socializing now. Maybe he'd get to talk with her a little bit and hear about her and her hobbies and interests. Maybe he could show her his—

"I might work on a draft for the introduction tonight—you know, in case I can't sleep or something. You know how sometimes it's hard to sleep in a strange bed and all that," she went on. "What I'd like from you is a list of any acknowledgments you'd like to include and a dedication, that sort of thing. Then when I get here tomorrow, we can get right to work."

She was rambling. Or at least it seemed like she was rambling. Was she nervous about something, or was this the way she normally talked?

"You really don't need to do that, Darcy. You should just relax tonight, and we'll get started in the morning. It's not a big deal."

She instantly waved him off. "It's rare that I can just sit and relax. My mind is always going. Sometimes it's annoying, but sometimes it really comes in handy."

"Like when you're working on a project?"

"Exactly."

He put their dessert down on the table and waited as she took her seat again.

"So if Savannah were here helping you, how do you think this would be going?"

He looked at her oddly. "What do you mean?"

"Well, I want to make sure I'm helping, so I need to know if I'm off to a good start or if I'm just mucking up the works here."

"You weren't—"

She laughed and took a spoonful of ice cream. "I'm kidding. But I'm curious about what you were hoping Savannah would be able to do for you if she came."

It was an easy question to answer because he had put so much thought into it before he had even picked up the phone to call her. For the next fifteen minutes, he talked about exactly how he envisioned Savannah helping him and how much he respected her and liked her and considered her to be a great friend. Hell, after a little while, he began to feel like he was running for the president of Savannah's fan club.

During it all, he shared about how Savannah had helped him during their first interview and how it was one of the reasons he wanted her to be the one to help him with this project. It wasn't until Darcy stood to put her bowl in the sink that Ben realized how long he'd been talking. He stood and put his bowl in the sink as well. He was just about to finally ask her some questions about herself when she turned and walked toward the living room.

"I should get going," she said, picking up her purse as she made her way across the room. "I really am tired, and the thought of navigating these mountain roads in the dark is a little unnerving."

Damn. Why hadn't he thought of that? "I…I can drive you to the hotel and pick you up in the morning if that would help. And my offer for you to stay here still stands."

Darcy shook her head but never made eye contact with him. She slipped her coat on and was opening the front door before he even realized what she was doing.

Damn, she moved fast! Ben followed her out the door and to the car. She had the driver's door open and tossed her purse in. When she stepped back, she straightened and gave him an odd look.

No, not odd.

Annoyed.

*What the hell?*

Deciding he wasn't going to accept her attitude, Ben stepped in close and smiled. "It was a pleasure meeting you, and I'm really looking forward to working with you, Darcy," he said. "I think we're going to work well together."

"Thanks for dinner," she said, shaking his hand. Her words were void of emotion, and she dropped his hand as if she'd been burned. "What time would you like me to be here in the morning? Is nine okay?"

*What's happening?* he wondered to himself. *What changed from our casual conversation to right now?* "Nine is okay with me," he said carefully. "Are you sure you're okay to drive? The roads can be kind of tricky. There's ice and—"

She nodded. "I'm fine. Just tired. I'll see you in the morning."

"I've got all the makings for omelets, so bring your appetite," he said, hoping to coax a smile out of her before she left.

He got one.

Barely.

Making his way toward the front steps, Ben watched as she climbed into the car and still wondered what had happened. He waved as she pulled away and stayed rooted to the spot until her taillights were out of sight. His breath was visible as he let it out. It wasn't normally this cold in early October, but not completely unheard of either. He shivered a little as he sat on the front steps and replayed the events of the night.

He'd been a good host.

No signs of the arrogant jerk that he could be. Hell, he'd been out-and-out charming. So what had happened to cause Darcy to go arctic on him? No matter how much he tried, Ben could not think of anything to cause her sudden change.

Rising, he turned and looked toward the house and realized how dark it was. There was only one small exterior light by the door and two motion-sensor lights that lit the property. Other than that, it was just dark. He thought of Darcy's comments about the Christmas lights, and for a moment, he remembered how his grandparents always lit up the house for the holidays.

Shaking his head, he pushed the thought aside. That was then, and it was a long time ago—when there was something to celebrate. Slowly, he walked up the steps and made his way into the house, and it was quiet again.

Too quiet.

Especially after having the place filled with female laughter not that long ago.

He wandered around the house looking for something to do but couldn't find anything. He didn't want to watch television, wasn't interested in reading a book. He stopped in front of the wall of windows and looked out at the property. It was dark out, but he'd turned on the outside lights earlier so he had a limited view.

Off in the distance, he saw his workshop. Flexing his hand, he tested it. Going out and working probably wasn't the smartest thing to do if he wanted his hand to heal properly, but right now, it was the only thing he wanted to do. There were several projects he was currently working on, but he had a desire to pull out a fresh piece of wood and create something new.

Something different.

Something inspired.

A slow grin spread across his face as he quickly made his way to the master suite to get changed. It was the only bedroom on this level—another new addition—and as he stripped along the way, he was thankful for its proximity. Later on, he'd lie in the massive king-sized bed and admire the stone fireplace he'd put in. Or he'd appreciate the luxury of the spa-quality bathroom as he stood under the rainfall shower as wall jets beat on his tired skin. It would be glorious.

But right now, all he wanted was to grab a pair of old jeans and an older sweatshirt and go and get his hands dirty.

~~~

Darcy seethed all the way to the hotel.

Several times, she had wanted to scream in frustration, but what was the point?

Benjamin Tanner was not at all what she'd expected.

Damn him and his stupid Christmas-esque cabin!

The rat bastard had practically been gushing over Savannah. She understood that the two of them were friends—Savannah had shared some nice stories about Ben as well—but something in the way Ben had talked just seemed like he felt more than friendship for her sister-in-law.

And holy *crap*, did that make her feel awkward.

Up until their last round of conversation, she'd felt fine. Ben was... She sighed. He was attractive. *Way* more attractive than Savannah had let on. So attractive that when Darcy had first climbed out of the car and seen him, her knees went weak.

And her knees never went weak.

Then he'd dazzled her with his smile, his home, and his cooking, and... Hell, she had started to question whether it was even smart of her to stay and work with him, because she was seriously crushing hard on him in a matter of minutes.

That hadn't happened to her since high school, when Jimmy Nichols had flirted with her at their homecoming game.

She was a woman now, dammit, and she didn't... well, she didn't *do* crushes.

Or at least she hadn't in a while.

Once she checked in at the hotel and got to her room, she tossed her suitcase on the rack and let out a long sigh.

Then she put on pajamas and paced.

"*Gah!*" she cried in frustration. "Why is this such a big deal? I'm here to work, and just because I *thought* I was interested in Ben doesn't mean—" She stopped. "Hell, I don't know what it means."

So maybe Ben had a crush on Savannah.

So maybe she—Darcy—had a crush on Ben.

That didn't mean they couldn't work together, did it?

"I really need to talk to somebody, because I think I'm losing my mind," she murmured.

Anna.

She could call Anna.

Anna had been like a sister to her for her entire life. In all of Darcy's earliest memories, Anna was there. It wasn't until she had started kindergarten that she'd realized Anna was her neighbor—her friend—and not an actual sister. That was right around the same time she'd realized Mary Hannigan—Anna's mother—wasn't someone she could have as a mother figure either.

"Focus, you idiot," she huffed. "We'll get back to these mommy issues later. Right now, I have to figure out what I'm supposed to do here." Stomping over to her purse, she pulled out her cell phone and pulled up Anna's number. She'd text her first, just in case she was still up.

The phone rang while in her hands, and she let out a small screech and watched it fly out of her hands and on to the bed. With her heart racing, she reached for it and saw Savannah's name on the screen.

"Hey!" she said, trying not to sound breathless. "What's up?"

"Just checking in," Savannah replied. "The last time you texted, you were leaving the airport, so I've been worried."

Darcy couldn't help but let out a playful snort. "God, you are such a mom now."

"I know, I know, but I sent you up into the wilderness, and then I didn't hear from you."

"I'm sure Ben would have called you if I didn't show

up," Darcy said with a soft laugh, and an image of Ben instantly came to mind.

She pushed it away.

"So what did you think of him?" Savannah asked.

"Think of him? Um, he's nice."

"And?"

"And I got a look at the stuff he has for the book, and it's majorly unorganized. I think once I have time to sort through it and get it all in order, he's going to have a much easier time getting this done."

"Oh."

"Oh? What's so oh?"

"He was a jerk, wasn't he? Dammit, I told him to be nice," Savannah muttered.

"What are you talking about? Ben wasn't a jerk."

"Oh. Okay. Whew!"

"Care to expand on that?" Darcy deadpanned.

"Ben can be difficult. He's not a real people person. Like, at all. I know he said he was going to be nice, but I was afraid he was just saying that to appease me."

"And would he do that? Say something just to *appease* you?" Okay, it was a stupid question—childish, really—but Darcy had to know if she was the only one getting the vibe that Ben was crushing on Savannah.

The instant bark of laughter answered her question.

"Normally, I'd say no. From what I know, Benjamin Tanner does *not* go out of his way to appease anyone. If anything, he makes things as complicated as possible!" She was laughing as she said it. "Trust me when I tell you that Ben likes things his own way and really doesn't seem to know the meaning of appeasing others." She paused, and her tone grew serious. "However, I know he's in a tight spot right now, and I thought maybe he was just sort of saying what he had to in order to get the help."

That didn't sound at all like the man Darcy had spent the evening with. "I don't know about any of that, but he was very nice tonight—accommodating. I looked over the stuff, and we had dinner and talked, and he seemed easy enough to work with."

"Okay. Then...good. That's good," Savannah said cautiously.

"But?"

"I'm not trying to scare you off the job or anything—after all, you're already there—but just know that he *can* be difficult."

Darcy chuckled. "So can I."

That had Savannah laughing too. "Oh lord, I can only imagine what this week is going to be like!"

"It's going to be fine, I'm sure. Don't worry. We know what needs to get done, and we'll get it done. Then I'm flying back to you to finish my vacation where it's warm. It's cold here. Did you know how cold it was here?"

Savannah laughed again. "I did warn you. And gave you warm clothes to wear."

"Yeah, well, it was still a bit of a shock. A few days ago, I was walking around in shorts and a tank top."

"You're probably wearing that right now. Stop complaining."

"To sleep in!" Darcy cried. "Two completely different things."

"Okay, okay, don't go getting all snippy. You'll be back here in the California sunshine before you know it."

"I am already counting down the days. And not

because of the job, but I miss the weather. I'd love a white Christmas, but it isn't even Halloween yet."

"And I promise we will totally make this up to you." She paused. "Seriously, Darce, I really do appreciate you doing this. I know it was all kind of thrown at you, and I had offered up your help without asking you first."

"It's okay. You know I'm looking to find a career, and this is really kind of in line with what I want to do. Not that working on Ben's book is going to turn into a career, but I can see if being an assistant to someone other than my brother is something I'm interested in."

"Well, you've been a really good sport about it. And the pay's not half bad either."

"Yeah, yeah, yeah."

"I know it's late, and you're probably tired, so go and get some sleep. But promise you'll call if you have any questions or just to let me know you're doing okay."

"Again with the mom mode?"

"What can I say? I'm a mom." And Darcy could hear the smile in Savannah's voice.

"I promise to call. Happy?" she asked with a smile of her own.

"Very. Night, Darce."

"Night."

Putting her phone down, she pulled the pillows off the bed and considered her options.

"Oh, right! Text Anna!" Walking across the room, she picked up her phone and quickly tapped out a message to Anna to call her in the morning—or now if she was up.

Fifteen minutes later, Darcy was under the blankets, and no matter how much she stared at her phone and willed it to ding with an incoming message, it didn't.

*Dammit.*

With nothing left to do, she placed it on the nightstand and picked up the television remote. Even though she was tired, it normally took an effort to fall asleep. Most nights, she'd read or watch a movie. She had picked up four Christmas romances at the airport bookstore, but they were in her satchel over on the chair in the corner. Her Kindle, also loaded with all the new holiday romances, was on the desk all the way on the other side of the room, so it was TV by default.

Making herself more comfortable, Darcy scanned the channels and stopped on the local news when she saw the weather report.

"No. No, no, no, no, no." She paused and listened a little more and then groaned.

The temperatures were going to drop, and there were snow flurries in the forecast.

"Seriously?" she murmured. "I was poolside yesterday. Gloriously warm in the California sun, and now I'm going to be stuck in the snow?"

She listened to the report and relaxed. The forecast was only calling for a few inches or less, so she figured they were going to be fine. It wasn't too unusual for this area, so she felt pretty safe knowing no one was going to get upset over it.

Except her.

"Moving on," she said with a small yawn, hoping to find something else to watch to help her relax. Getting worked up over the weather wasn't the ideal way to make herself fall asleep, that was for sure.

More channel surfing.

The crystal-blue waters caught her eye, and Darcy's

hand instantly froze on the remote. It was some sort of travel show, and they were clearly in Hawaii. She sighed longingly. A couple talked about how this was their dream destination and how after living all their lives in Canada, they felt it was time for a change.

"I hear ya," she said softly. "I wouldn't mind being there right now." And as if on cue, she got a chill and shivered. Snuggling a little more under the blankets, a helpless moan escaped. "Note to self: next time you want to go on a vacation, skip the family."

"Who wouldn't want to live in a tropical paradise year-round?" the perky voice on the television said.

For some reason, that question struck her. Would she want to live in a tropical paradise? Back home in North Carolina, she lived on the coast, but it was far from tropical. But was tropical something she really wanted?

"I wouldn't exactly say no to it," she murmured as she watched the couple frolicking on the beach with palm trees gently swaying in the background. The guy picked the girl up and swung her around before putting her back on her feet and kissing her soundly. Darcy heard herself sigh longingly.

Right now, she wouldn't mind being on a beach somewhere with a sexy guy swinging her around and kissing her.

Someone like Ben.

"Ugh. I so need to *not* have Ben on the brain right now."

Before she knew it, it wasn't the cute couple on the TV she was seeing but her and Ben on the beach. She envisioned him being muscled under all those layers of flannel, and with a smooth chest.

*Mmm…*

He wasn't tan, but he certainly didn't have a fair complexion, either. Darcy imagined he would look good with a tan—and even better with her rubbing some sort of lotion all over him.

"Who could say no to paradise?" the perky television voice asked again.

Flipping off the television, Darcy tossed the remote aside.

Who indeed.

# Chapter 2

FOR TWO DAYS, THEY WORKED NONSTOP.

Ben had to give Darcy credit—she was prompt, and she really was a whiz with getting things organized. Once they had gotten through the basics of the book layout, she had talked him through the acknowledgments and the dedication and found a way to write them both up so they sounded more like him than a generic statement.

She asked a ton of questions about his work, but rather than letting him take her to his workshop, she opted to stay focused on the work laid out on the table. And no matter how much he tried to explain that she'd have a better grasp of it all if she saw the work in person rather than in a photograph, she wouldn't be swayed.

So they worked.

And worked.

And worked.

They ate breakfast while they worked, as well as lunch, and other than the first night, she hadn't stayed for dinner again.

Several times, Ben had tried to ask her if she was all right or if she wanted to take a break, but she always managed to turn the question around and bring it back to the work in front of them.

It was maddening.

*She* was maddening!

He knew he had asked her to be here—or he'd asked *Savannah* to be here—but he was starting to lose his mind. The constant chatter, the way she questioned everything he did, and the way she was always moving things around under the guise of "organization" was killing him. They'd argued—out-and-out raised voices argued—multiple times. She never backed down, but he'd walked out to cool off more than once.

Right now, Darcy was furiously texting back and forth with someone about something, and Ben was almost afraid to ask what was going on. She'd hardly gotten any messages or calls in the last two days, but this one seemed to have her tensing up. He was all set to mind his own business—because she was finally quiet—but then she began cursing under her breath.

"Is everything all right?" he asked, secretly hoping she was just annoyed with the disruption. Like he was.

"Can we turn on the television and find the weather channel or local news or something?"

"What's going on?"

"Savannah just forwarded me some information about a fast-forming storm that's coming our way. It looks like they're predicting over a foot of snow three days from now, and that's going to mean my flight will more than likely be canceled and—"

"Okay, okay," he said, doing his best to sound soothing. "Give me a minute, and I'll see what I can find." Ben turned on the television and immediately went to the local news channel. They were on a commercial break, so he decided to explain the local weather.

"This time of year, it's not unusual to get some snow. I'm sure that forecast is a little off. We don't get that kind of accumulation this early in the season. But we know how to handle it, and there's minimal disruption. It might not even come, so I'm sure you'll be fine."

Ben could tell she was only half listening to him, because she nodded, but her focus was still on the phone in her hands. "Uh-huh."

Sighing, he walked over to her. "I'm sure your flight won't be affected at all." Then he caught himself. They had worked hard and gotten a lot done in a short amount of time. He was just telling himself how annoyed he was with her, so why was he arguing with her wanting to leave earlier? "You flew into Seattle, right?"

"Uh-huh."

That was over a hundred miles away. "Maybe you should—" He stopped talking when the weather report came on, and he noticed Darcy looked up from her phone as well. Silently, they listened to the grim forecast. Ben wasn't normally prone to paying attention to these predictions, but he had to admit it didn't sound good.

When the news broke away to another commercial, he muted the TV. "So…"

"I've got to call the airline and get an earlier flight. I'm going to try for tomorrow. I know we still have so much to do, and I promise you I am going to continue to help you but from home."

"Darcy, it's all right. Really."

She waved him off as she stood and began looking around for something. "No, it's not. I hate that I started something here that I can't finish. It makes me crazy. But we have a good foundation, and I'll be able to do the rest remotely. If I have any questions, I can call you. Right?"

Forcing a smile, he said, "Of course."

That seemed to relax her a bit.

"Make your calls, and let me know if there's anything I can do to help."

"Thanks, Ben."

For the next twenty minutes, Ben listened as Darcy talked, begged, and pleaded with whoever was on the other end of the phone to find her an earlier flight out of Seattle to Los Angeles. For the life of him, he couldn't imagine it being this difficult. Judging from the exasperation in her voice, it was. When she finally hung up the phone, she put her head on the table and lightly banged it.

"That good, huh?" he asked.

Looking up at him, she looked defeated. "I'm not the only one wanting to move up a flight. Even without the weather, there weren't many open seats. I found that out from booking my flight here on such short notice. The best they can do is put me on standby."

"Is that what you're going to do?"

"I don't have a choice," she said wearily. "I hate it because it's a whole lot of hanging out at the airport and a chance of not getting on a plane. And all that not knowing makes it even more stressful."

"Darcy," he began. "You don't have to freak out and rush out of here. So you stay a couple of extra days. It's not a big deal. Hell, you can stay here if it's better for you."

*Are you crazy?* he admonished himself. *Help her pack and get to the airport now!*

"Ben, I appreciate the offer. I do. But it's important for me to get home or at least back to LA. I don't want to get stuck here indefinitely, and I've got things planned for next week with Riley and Savannah." She looked at him apologetically. "I'm sorry."

"It's fine." Stuffing his hands in his pockets, he did his best to give her a smile. "Why don't you call Riley and let him know what's going on? Maybe he can find a way to get you home."

Her eyes went wide. "You're right! Why didn't I think of that?" Walking over, she gave him a loud, smacking kiss on the cheek. "You're a genius!"

Of that, he wasn't so sure, but at least she seemed to perk up. And maybe she didn't mean to kiss him but that stupidly worked to perk him up too.

With nothing to do, Ben went and made himself a cup of coffee before walking over and looking out the wall of windows. The sky was gray, and as much as he wasn't an alarmist, it certainly looked like the kind of weather that promised some heavy snow.

If it were just him, he wouldn't mind. The house was well-stocked with food, and he had a generator and an abundance of firewood. Getting snowed in would not affect him in any way, shape, or form. Getting snowed in with Darcy? That was a whole other story. It would affect him in *every* way, shape, and form.

A sigh came out before he could stop it. None of it mattered. He was never going to know, because he wasn't going to see Darcy Shaughnessy again, and it was probably for the best. It had been obvious she had an issue with him, and to be honest, he had one with her. She was bossy and outspoken and irritating as hell. And even though they had worked well together for the last couple of days, it was very different from the easy camaraderie they had shared on her first night here.

He knew what his issues were with her, but for the life of him, Ben couldn't figure out what he'd said or

done to make her so against him. He'd replayed that
night at least a dozen times in his head and came up
empty every time.

Not that he wasn't used to this sort of thing. He
wasn't exactly a warm and fuzzy guy. People had been
telling him for years he came off as cold and standoff-
ish. Savannah had been the only one to try to push past
that—and succeeded. For the most part, Ben was fine
with being viewed that way. It was who he was.

Except this time he didn't want to be seen *that* way.

He had put in an effort that night. He'd worked hard
to prepare a nice dinner and made sure he was polite and
kept up the conversation. Hell, he'd been the perfect host.
So what was her deal? What the hell did he say or do?

"For crying out loud," he murmured, "obsess much?"
Behind him, he heard Darcy saying goodbye to Riley.
He turned and gave her a smile. "Any luck?"

"He's making some calls," she said with a sigh.

"I'm sure Riley could charter a plane."

It was Darcy's turn to laugh. "He's going to look into
that too. I hate to think of spending that kind of money.
It seems too frivolous."

"It's not frivolous," he corrected. "It's important to
him that you get home safely. I'm sure Riley would do
anything to make that happen." There. That sounded
nice, right?

She took it for the compliment that it was. "Thank
you." After a minute, she said, "Let's try to get some
more work done. I think if we make some notes on each
picture, I can take them with me, rewrite it once I'm
home, and get it all together for you."

And there was something different in her tone as

well. Maybe they could finish out her time here on better terms. If he looked at the big picture, she was helping him, and she'd be leaving soon. He knew he could hang on and get through it.

"You have no idea how much I appreciate your help, Darcy." Unable to help himself, he reached out and took her hand in his and squeezed it. "There is no way I could have gotten this done without you."

She squeezed his hand in return before walking toward the kitchen table. "You would have done just fine with whoever your publisher sent to work with you. You might not have liked it, and I'm sure you would have given them hell like you've been giving me, but you would have gotten it done."

With a small laugh, Ben followed her. "Maybe."

She gave him a smile and then went back to sorting through her notes.

"Can I ask you something?"

"Sure."

"Did I do something wrong the other night?"

She looked at him oddly.

"I thought everything went well. We had a nice dinner, we talked and laughed, and yet by the time you left, you seemed to have a definite problem with me."

Those big, beautiful eyes went wide at his bluntness. "Did I? I honestly don't remember."

Seriously? Was he making more out of this than there was?

"Are you telling me that we're good? That you don't have some sort of issue with me? Because you seem to be acting a little distant. You won't stay for dinner and—"

"Ben," she began patiently, but he noticed she

wouldn't look at him. "I'm here to help you with this project, and we're on a short timeline. I'm just trying to keep us on track. If we sit here and hang around or goof off, it's not going to get done."

It sounded reasonable, and yet… "Then why not stay for dinner? By that time of day, we're done working."

"Seriously? You're getting this bent out of shape over dinner?"

"I didn't say I was bent out of shape."

"Back at home when I'm at work, I get to leave for lunch and then leave for the day at five. That's how a job works." She paused, and this time she did look at him, but her expression seemed almost sad. "And that's what this is. A job."

And that's when it hit him—he had gotten too involved in his own mind where she was concerned. Saw things that weren't there. Of course she had been pleasant to him—she was trying to make a good first impression, and it had nothing to do with him personally.

And this was why he preferred to work alone.

Less chance of awkward misunderstandings.

———— ~~~ ————

"Everything is packed up and loaded in the car," Darcy said to herself the next day. "It's already starting to flurry, and I need to get going." She looked around the hotel room one last time as she ran through her mental checklist of what the rest of the day held in store for her.

"I should have left earlier," she murmured as she pulled out of the parking lot a few minutes later. "If I have to do the standby thing, I would have had a better chance with an early morning flight." Talking to herself wasn't something she normally did, but right now, it was keeping her calm as she faced the long drive to Seattle.

"I can't believe I overslept."

She had been driving for about twenty miles with the radio playing softly when her phone rang. The rental had Bluetooth, so she could answer it safely.

"How's it going?"

"I overslept," she admitted.

"Are you on your way to the airport?"

"I can't believe Riley couldn't get me on a flight. His celebrity status is getting less and less impressive, Savannah," she teased.

"He tried, Darce. He really did. We couldn't get a charter on such short notice and with the threat of the storm. No one was willing to risk it. We need to be optimistic."

"Somehow, I don't think optimism is going to get me on a flight," Darcy said skeptically.

"Be positive! Please!" Savannah cried, a hint of frustration in her voice. "I feel horrible that you're in this situation. I hate how you're there alone and...ugh! Maybe you should see if you can stay with Ben and avoid all of this."

"Please. Good riddance," Darcy mumbled.

"Excuse me?"

"What? Um, nothing. I just meant it's going to be good to get away from this cold weather. I'll be happy to be back in LA."

"I'm sure," Savannah agreed. "Do you want to get off the phone, or would you like someone to talk to for a little while?"

"Are you kidding me? I'd love the company. I was

starting to go a little crazy talking to myself!" she said
with a laugh.

Over the next hour, she drove toward the Seattle airport amid flurries that were getting heavier. There was
already accumulation, and as much as Darcy hated to
admit it, she had a sinking feeling she wasn't getting
out of Washington today — or anytime soon. Rather than
mention it to Savannah, she kept up her end of the conversation with stories about all the things she wanted to
do when she got back to North Carolina.

"I want to move out and get a place of my own,"
she said.

"Have you talked to your dad?"

"I haven't mentioned it yet. And he's been busy. He
and Martha are closer than ever, and they seem to be
going away every weekend. I think if I weren't still at
home, they wouldn't have to."

Savannah laughed softly. "You may have a point. But
you should still talk to him. Maybe they like traveling."

"I'm sure that's part of it. Dad didn't go anywhere or
do anything for years, so it's nice to see him enjoying
his life."

"But…"

Darcy couldn't help but laugh. "But I don't know. It
still seems weird."

"In what way?"

"I was probably more excited than anyone to see my
dad start dating. And Martha seemed like the perfect
woman for him."

"O-kay…"

"And I was…" Pausing, Darcy realized what she
was about to say wasn't going to make her come off

sounding so great. Instead, she decided to go the safe route. "And now I'm glad they worked things out."

"How about you tell me what you were going to say?"

"I don't know what you mean."

"I mean that last part was total bullshit. You thought Martha was perfect for him, and then you were going to say something else. So spill it."

She could play dumb, but what was the point? "Fine. She was—*is*—perfect for Dad. She's everything I could ever want for him."

"So again I say, *but…*"

Darcy rested her head back and sighed. "I thought if she was perfect for him, she'd be perfect for us. All of us."

"And she's not?"

"It's not there."

Savannah was quiet for a moment before asking, "What's not there?"

Dammit, she was not going to cry. Taking a preemptive strike, she wiped at her eyes for any moisture. "She's great, but she's not…I don't feel…there's no…"

"Use your words."

"She's not my mom." Her tone was quiet and a little bit trembly, and she hated that more than anything.

On the other end of the phone, she heard Savannah sigh softly. "Oh, sweetie. I don't even know what to say to that."

"My whole life, I kept thinking if I found the right woman for Dad, she'd be not only a wife, but a mom. I've had people like Mary Hannigan—or teachers and counselors—who've been like a mom to me, but in the end, they're not. They have families of their own, and I always found out I was more like a project or someone they felt bad for. I thought my mom—Lillian—would send someone to me. To all of us. And then our family would be complete."

"Your family is complete," Savannah said softly. "You have a father and five brothers who love you. There isn't anything any of them wouldn't do for you. And now you have five sisters who think you're awesome and adore you. There is so much love in this family, Darcy. We're very lucky. *You're* very lucky."

But she wasn't buying it. "It's not the same. And I know it's something you can't understand. Your mother is alive and well, and she's always been there for you. You have no idea what it's like to not have that."

"You know if she could have been here…"

"I know. I know. It's not like she abandoned me on purpose."

"So you don't feel any connection to Martha?"

"I do. Some. She's nice and she's kind and funny, but when I'm with her, all I can think is she's a nice woman. She's good to my dad. I have no overwhelming urge to confide in her or to bond."

"I hate to say this, but maybe that's more on you than Martha."

"What do you mean?"

"Maybe you're holding yourself back because you have an unrealistic expectation about how something's supposed to feel to you where Martha—or any mother figure—is concerned."

"No. Trust me. I've been searching my entire life. Mary was a constant figure in my life since I was born, and by the time I started school, her life was changing because Anna and Bobby were older, and she started pulling away. And I resented it at first. But I moved on. There were teachers I adored, but then the school year would end." She paused. "Everyone leaves. They all walk away."

Savannah said softly, "Have you talked to anyone about this?"

"You mean like a therapist?"

"Uh-huh."

"About a dozen of them. I've been to every kind of therapy there is. Dad thought it would help, my teachers thought it would help…hell, everybody everywhere thought it would help. But it didn't. Unless you've lost a parent—or never had one—you can't possibly understand."

"So maybe you find a group setting for kids who've—"

"Did that too. It was depressing. I'm not a victim, Savannah. I know that. I'm just a girl who missed out on having a mom. And I know my dad did a great job, and he did everything he possibly could to fill the role of both mother and father, but…"

"It's not the same."

"No. It's not." She pulled off the highway at the exit for the airport, and Darcy knew she wasn't going to have any great revelations, especially not here and now when there were so many other things she was going to have to focus on, but she couldn't help but be mildly disappointed. "Sometimes, I wish I could talk to her. Just once."

"I wish you could too. I wish she could see what an amazing woman you turned out to be."

Now she *was* going to cry. Swiping at her eyes, she looked out the window as she passed all the long-term parking lots where cars were covered with snow. And off in the distance, there were planes lined up but not moving.

Not a good sign.

Pulling up to the rental car drop-off, she sighed. "Okay, this is where I need to get off the phone," she said to Savannah. "Thanks for talking to me. It made the drive a lot more bearable."

"Let us know the minute you find out about a flight, okay?"

"I will. I promise."

"Good luck!"

Shutting off the car, Darcy did her best to sound positive. "Thanks!" And it wasn't until after she hung up that she added, "I'm gonna need it."

---

Three hours later, Darcy heard the words she never thought she'd hear. "Good news! There is a seat available on this flight. You got lucky. There's only one left."

Relief swamped her. Almost overwhelmed her as she sagged against the ticket desk. Whipping out her license and her phone, she gave the ticket agent her information. If all went well, she'd be leaving Seattle behind within the hour. *Hallelujah!*

There was a line of at least twenty people behind her, and part of her wanted to jump with victory that she was getting out of Dodge and would be in the land of sunshine in a matter of hours, but she didn't.

"Bear with me," the agent said. "The computers are all running a little bit slow."

"No problem," she replied as she started to put her items back into her purse. The noise around her was almost deafening, but the conversation behind her caught her attention.

"What would you like me to do, Cathleen?" the man

behind her said wearily. "We're all in the same boat here. Everyone is trying to get out ahead of this storm."

Darcy glanced over her shoulder and noticed the baby in the woman's arms. A tiny baby. Like a newborn.

"I hate this," the woman said quietly. "The customer service person I spoke to last night said we shouldn't have a problem getting on a flight. My mom is waiting for us at LAX." As she spoke, her tone got more and more disheartened. "This was not the homecoming I envisioned for us. I wanted us all to go home together."

"Me too," the man said as he stroked the baby's tiny head.

Dammit.

Dammit. Dammit. Dammit.

Before she could change her mind, Darcy turned around and faced the couple. "Um, excuse me. Hi. I couldn't help but overhear you're trying to get on a flight to LAX."

"Ma'am?" the ticket agent began. "I need your ID one more time, please."

Ignoring her, Darcy kept her focus on the couple. Now that she could really see them, she saw they both looked exhausted. "You're trying to get home too, right?"

The woman—Cathleen—nodded. "This was an unexpected trip," she said, her voice a near sob. She looked at her husband. "We got the call that there was a baby for us, so we hopped on the first flight we could get and came here. We had no idea there was a storm moving in. Now we want to get our son home to the nursery we prepared for him and introduce him to our family."

It was a no-brainer. Turning toward the ticket agent, Darcy said, "I want you to give my ticket to them. To

her and the baby. You said there was one more seat
available after mine, right? They need to get home."

The couple gasped. "Oh, no," Cathleen said with
tears in her eyes. "I'm sure you need to get home too."

Darcy couldn't help but smile even as she shook her
head. "Not like you do," she said softly. "Sometimes
I'm a completely selfish brat. And other times…" She
shrugged. "It's not a big deal for me to hang out in the
airport. I'll find a hotel or something."

"All the area hotels are booked," the agent said without looking up.

"I've never camped out in an airport then," Darcy
said cheerily. "It will be like an adventure."

Maybe if she kept telling herself that, she'd believe it.

"You're not selfish," Cathleen said. "You're one of
the most giving people I've ever met."

"Well, then you should know that I have to do this.
That sweet baby needs to go with both of his parents
and meet his family," she said and felt herself getting
emotional. She forced a smile. "Now let me get out of
the line so you can get your tickets home."

The couple embraced her and thanked her over and
over again. She wished them luck—both with getting
home and with their new lives that were just beginning—
and turned to walk away.

Making her way through the crowd, Darcy couldn't
help but sigh. This was going to be her home away from
home for at least the next twenty-four hours. She had a
feeling it was going to be longer, but she refused to let
her mind go there right now.

Finding a quiet corner, she called Savannah and told
her what had just happened and how she wasn't going

to be getting back to LA today. "You're not mad at me, are you?" she asked.

"Are you kidding me? I'm practically bawling over here with pride. That was an incredibly selfless thing you did."

"Yeah, well, they needed to go home as a family." She looked over her shoulder and saw the couple hugging each other, and it made her smile.

"They are going to remember you forever, you know that, right?" Savannah paused. "So now what?"

"Now, I try and find a place to hang out away from the gate areas and just chill. I'll keep asking around and checking online for a hotel room, but I'm not going to hold out much hope. I don't want to venture too far away from the airport, because the first flight I can get on, whether it takes me to LA or North Carolina, I'm taking."

"We didn't even check on North Carolina flights."

"That's going to be my project this afternoon." She was going to say more, but the flight to LAX was being called, and the noise level went up. "I should go."

"I hate the thought of you being there by yourself."

"It was my choice, and I'm going to be fine. I'm choosing to think of this like a little adventure."

"Your brother is going to freak out that you're there alone, you know."

"Nah, he'll be thankful he doesn't have to deal with me right away. But make sure you tell him I was a hero, and he should feel bad for treating me the way he did," she said with a grin. "I love you guys, and hopefully I'll have some good news soon."

"My fingers are crossed for you!"

Anything else she might have said was drowned out

by the stream of announcements coming over the PA system. She said a quick goodbye and moved into the crowd to find a place to set up camp.

An hour later, she had snagged a corner table at a wine bar. No kids, and it was much quieter than being out in the terminal. Her phone was charged, and she had her tablet out so she could search all the travel sites for a hotel room. She'd struck out with a flight to North Carolina, but she was feeling hopeful about finding a room.

Two hours later, she had polished off a plate of assorted meats and cheeses—and two glasses of wine— and was feeling more than a little relaxed. And more than a little hopeless. After searching every travel site and calling a dozen different hotels, she was done. She had no choice but to accept her fate.

She was stuck at the airport.

Knowing she was going to have to find another place to hang out—there was only so much wine and cheese she was willing to purchase to secure her table—Darcy began putting her things in her satchel. She paid her bill and walked out to the terminal when she heard her name paged.

Did someone find her a seat on a plane? Was she finally going to get to leave Washington and get to LA? How awesome would *that* be?

With a renewed pep in her step, she quickly made her way to the gate area and cut to the front of the line.

"Excuse me! Excuse me!" she called out until one of the agents looked at her. Ignoring the angry glares of all the people in line, Darcy smiled brightly. "Hi, I'm Darcy Shaughnessy, and I heard my name paged."

The ticket agent looked at her oddly for a moment

and then looked at her computer screen. "Okay, yes, Miss Shaughnessy, you need to go to the baggage claim office. It's on the lower level."

"But I thought you found a flight to LAX for me?"

The look on the agent's face bordered on disbelief as she stared at Darcy for an awkward minute.

"So…um…"

"Lower level by the baggage claim carousels. Someone will be able to help you. Next in line!"

Fine. No flight. But what would anyone want with her in baggage claim? With no other choice, she secured her satchel, grabbed her suitcase, and made her way through the crowds, ignoring annoyed looks from the people in line, and to the escalators.

With her mind racing, she wondered if Riley had found a plane to charter. That would be amazing. She would totally forgive him for being such a jerk and forget her plans for payback and spa treatments.

Maybe not the spa treatments, but she'd be totally willing to let the rest slide if he got her home on a private jet.

She was good like that.

Weaving her way through the masses, Darcy spotted the baggage claim office and picked up her pace. The sooner she could get to the chartered plane, the better. She was totally going to kiss Riley when she got to LA and proclaim him her favorite brother. It was goofy, but for some reason, each of her brothers loved when she did that for them. Who was she to buck tradition?

There was a line coming out of the office, and she hated how there wasn't a way to cut to the front. They only allowed a certain number of people through the door, though there was a security guard standing beside it, so maybe…

"Excuse me," she said sweetly, flashing him a brilliant smile. "I was paged and told to come here, but I'm not sure who I'm supposed to see."

He looked at her blankly.

"Is there, like, a customer service desk or a supervisor I can talk to?"

"You'll need to wait in line," he finally said. "If they told you to come here, this is the only office there is."

There were easily a dozen people ahead of her, and all she wanted to do was scream how it didn't matter if their luggage was lost, no one was getting home anyway! She walked to the back of the line. Arms folded, foot tapping, she waited. She huffed, she sighed, and she shifted.

Why? Why did everything have to be so damn difficult? She let her head fall back. "Come on, come on, come on. Seriously, I just want to go home!"

"I can't get you home, but I can get you out of the airport," a deep male voice said from behind her.

Darcy was ready to turn and slug the perv, but when she turned around, all she could do was gasp.

It was Ben.

---

It had been tempting to watch her for a little bit longer. Everything about Darcy was so expressive that even though Ben hadn't heard one word of her exchange with the security guard, he had been able to imagine the entire conversation based on the look on her face.

It was highly entertaining.

"What are you doing here?" she asked, her expression one of total confusion.

"Savannah called me and told me you weren't able to get on a flight. So here I am," he said, offering her a small smile.

She frowned.

Seriously? Even when he came to save her, she was still pissed at him?

"What if I had gotten on a flight between the time Savannah called you and the time you got to the airport?"

He shrugged. "Then I would have made a very perilous trip for nothing. I would have gotten here sooner, but people don't know how to drive in the snow. I passed a bunch of accidents."

"You could have been one of them."

Another shrug. "I have a truck that happens to be exceptional in the snow, and I'm used to driving in it. It wasn't a big deal. You need to drive slowly, and you'll be all right."

Darcy looked around and made a noncommittal sound. "So you just got here, huh?"

"No, I've been here for a while. I couldn't get past security, and it took some time to page you. I tried calling you several times, but I kept getting a message that all circuits were busy. I guess with the storm moving in and all." He paused and gave her a lopsided grin. "Anyway, I saw you when you were on the escalator, but you didn't see me."

"There's, like, a million people here," she said with a hint of sarcasm. "And I wasn't looking for, well, you."

He frowned at her tone. "What did you think you were coming here for?"

"Honestly? I thought my brother had been able to charter a plane for me."

He couldn't help but chuckle. "Sorry to disappoint you. But the only charter you have is me—in the form of a truck and a trip back to the lake."

"Oh. So I guess I'll get a room at the hotel," she said, and he noticed she wouldn't look directly at him.

"I just planned on bringing you to the cabin until the storm is over and flights are back to normal. It won't be more than a couple of days. No need for you to have to go to a hotel or anything."

Now she did look at him. "No, really, it's okay. I'd prefer to go to the hotel."

She was looking at him with a hint of defiance, and he figured he'd let her have her way for now. The sooner they got on the road, the better. There was already a very real possibility they weren't going to get home until after dark. It would be pointless to drag this out.

"That's fine. No problem." He motioned toward her suitcase. "I'll take that for you. Let's get going."

"Oh."

Ben could hear the relief in her voice and smiled to himself. For right now, he was happy to have a truce with her. They had a long drive ahead of them, and he'd rather it be peaceful than tense and awkward.

He waited while she pulled her coat on and got herself together, and then they made their way out to the parking garage. The traffic was insane, and he prayed it wasn't going to be as bad as he was fearing.

It was.

And it was tense and awkward.

By the time they hit the highway, it was almost

whiteout conditions. They were driving at a near crawl, and he figured Darcy could tell he wasn't into doing the chitchat thing, because she stayed blessedly quiet beside him, tapping away on her phone. It was well over an hour later when he finally felt like he needed to break the silence.

"Did you text Savannah and let her know you're with me?"

She nodded. "Uh-huh."

His lips flattened in a grim line as he fought not to snap at her and demand to know what her problem was. If anyone else had ever been this rude and unreceptive to him, Ben would have simply blown them off and moved on. But he was stuck with her for now, and out of respect for his friendship with Savannah, he was determined to not be a jerk.

No matter how much she provoked him.

Rather than make any other attempt at conversation, Ben turned on the radio. At the first words from Eric Church's "Record Year," he immediately felt some of the tension leaving his body. Country music was the only music he listened to. And as they made their way slowly down the interstate, he felt the first glimmer of hope that he was going to get through this trip without giving in to his naturally irritable nature.

Beside him, he heard Darcy make some noise. Like a snort of disgust or something.

"Is there a problem?"

Maybe they weren't going to make it through.

"Country music? Seriously?" she asked, turning to face him.

"What's wrong with country music?" he asked.

She gave him a look of disbelief. "Where do I even begin?"

"You do realize country music is just as popular as the mainstream stuff your brother plays, right?"

Now she rolled her eyes. "First of all, I don't base all music on my brother's, so don't go there. All I'm saying is I'm not a fan."

"Have you ever really listened to it? Especially the newer artists? This isn't the country music that was around when we were kids."

"Um, no. Doesn't matter. It's not my thing."

He sighed, because she was seriously trying his patience. "What do you listen to?" He had a feeling she was going to say something like Taylor Swift or Beyoncé.

"I have eclectic taste in music," she began. "Don't get me wrong, I listen to all of Riley's stuff and love it, but I don't think he's the be-all-end-all in music."

"So what music fits under this eclectic category?"

Biting her lip, she thought about it for a minute. "I listen to a lot of Coldplay, Foo Fighters, Twenty-One Pilots…um…and Mumford and Sons."

"Sounds like the same old same old. Not very eclectic at all."

"I love some classic rock too—Aerosmith, Bon Jovi, and Cheap Trick. But then I listen to a lot of Elton John—his early stuff—and Billy Joel." She gave him a smug smile. "See? Eclectic."

He shrugged. "If you say so. All seems the same to me."

"And you think country music is so unique? Isn't it all sad crap that happened to someone—like his girlfriend left him and took his dog? That kind of stuff?"

Ben couldn't help it. He laughed out loud. "Damn. Where did you get that from?"

And for the first time since the night they'd met, he saw Darcy smile. She chuckled, and her eyes lit up a bit and… *damn*. His gut tightened, and he wanted to tell her never to stop smiling, but he knew he couldn't. If anything, saying that would probably make her defensive and snippy again, and he was hell-bent on enjoying the moment.

"I don't know," she said, still laughing softly. "Any country music I've ever heard just seemed to have corny lyrics like that."

"Well, it's not all like that. I mean, some of it is, but don't judge the masses by one or two songs."

"It doesn't matter. It's just not my thing. I like my music with a little more…I don't know…I like it a little heavier. Does that make sense?"

"Sure. But you do realize there are a lot of rock stars who are also playing country music now, right? I mean, Dave Grohl of the Foo Fighters did a song with the Zac Brown Band. Darius Rucker used to play with Hootie and the Blowfish, and now he's country. Bon Jovi did some crossover stuff too, and so has Steven Tyler. I don't think you've given it a chance."

"Oh my God. What are you, the country music police?" she said with a hint of exasperation. "Clearly, we're here in your truck, and I have no choice but to listen to your music, so can we just drop it?"

"Savannah mentioned that Riley plays a lot of country music when he's at home. What would you think of it if your brother put out a country album?"

Darcy sighed loudly and stared at him. "You're not going to let this go, are you?"

"We've got some time to kill."

"How far away are we? I feel like we've been in this truck for hours."

He knew the feeling. He'd pretty much give anything he had to be home and off the roads. "If it wasn't snowing, we'd have another thirty minutes. But with these conditions…"

"So at least another hour," she said and sighed again. "Great."

"Yeah, I'm sure it's rough for you sitting there and relaxing," he murmured.

"Excuse me?" That got her attention. Sitting up a little bit straighter, she looked like she had a whole lot of things to say to him but was trying to find just the right one.

"It's much easier being the passenger than the one driving in this mess," he said, not waiting for her to get her thoughts together. "I drove all the way to the damn airport to get you—"

"I didn't ask you to!"

"No, but Savannah did," he snapped and then instantly regretted it. Clearing his throat, he was about to apologize, but Darcy had suddenly found her voice.

"Oh, and God forbid you upset Savannah, right?" Her voice was thick with sarcasm.

"What the… Of course I don't want to upset Savannah. She's my friend. A good friend."

"Right. And you did it all out of the goodness of your heart." She snorted with disbelief.

If he could, he would have pulled the damn truck over and hashed this out, because clearly, there was something going on here that no one had clued him in on. "Believe what you want," he finally said. "But remember this. If it weren't for me doing a favor for Savannah, your ass would be hanging out in the airport for the next two to three days."

He let that sink in for a minute.

"The correct response to something like that is thank you," he added sarcastically.

The words she murmured certainly weren't ones of gratitude, but they were fairly colorful. He wasn't used to a woman being quite so open with her displeasure. He had said it before, and he'd say it again—Darcy Shaughnessy was nothing if not entertaining.

"No need to get snippy about it," he commented mildly and then reached over and turned up the music.

And sang along with it the rest of the way home.

# Chapter 3

THAT DAMN TWANG WAS GOING TO BE STUCK IN HER head all night.

Normally, Darcy considered herself to be pretty open about music, but this was ridiculous. She knew she'd closed her eyes and dozed off, but she had a feeling just having the damn music playing in the background was going to be enough for it to stay with her for a while.

And dammit if some of it wasn't just a little bit catchy.

With a stretch, she sat up and looked around. They had to be close to town—to the hotel—by now, right?

"Oh, good," Ben said from beside her. "You're awake. We're home."

Home? It was dark out, and as he pulled the truck to a stop, she saw they were indeed parking next to his house.

"What the hell, Ben!" she cried. "I thought we decided I was going to a hotel."

"No, *you* decided. I never agreed," he said nicely as he turned off the truck and stretched. "Damn, I didn't think we were ever going to get here. C'mon. I'm sure you're hungry. I know I am."

"But...but..."

"I'll grab your suitcase," he said sweetly and then climbed out of the truck.

*Damn the man!*

When she finally got her hands on Savannah, Darcy was going to strangle her. She had done a decent thing—a

good thing!—and this was her reward? Forced to stay in
the snowy mountains of nowhere with a man who was…
was…*ugh*. There wasn't even a word for him.

But she'd think of one.

Of that, she was certain.

Grabbing her satchel, she carefully stepped from the
truck and out into the snow. There was easily several
inches—close to four—on the ground, and it didn't
seem to show any signs of stopping.

"Great," she murmured. "Just great."

Gingerly, she made her way through the snow—not
an easy task in her cute little leather ankle boots that were
never going to recover from this. The front entrance to
Ben's cabin had a dozen steps to climb to get to it, but
as she looked around, she didn't see any footprints in the
snow in that direction. Where the hell had he gone?

It was dark, and she had no idea where she was supposed to go and… A light on the side of the house came
on, and as she looked a little bit closer, Darcy saw Ben's
trail and immediately followed it. Actually, she used his
footprints to help her protect her boots a little. As she
rounded the house, she found Ben waiting for her at a
ground-level door.

"I was wondering if you were going to follow or not."
He paused and chuckled. "Thought you might be stubborn enough to sit and freeze in the truck rather than
come inside."

"Well, since you were so *gracious* about coming
to get me, I thought it was only right for me to come
inside." She gave him her most syrupy sweet voice and
smile, but she knew he wasn't fooled.

Once they were both inside, Ben closed the door

behind them and locked it. "You can leave your boots and coat here," he said, a no-nonsense tone to his voice now. "I'll go and get a fire started upstairs."

Darcy watched him go up the stairs with her suitcase and sighed. As much as she wanted to be angry—or at the very least annoyed—she knew she had no right to be. She might not like Ben or his obvious feelings for Savannah, but he had seriously come to her rescue today. She wasn't that much of a bitch that she couldn't remember that.

He'd traveled over a hundred miles in the snow—each way—to help her out. Right now, she'd be huddled on the dirty airport floor with hundreds of other people and hating every minute of it if it wasn't for him.

"Great. Now I'll have to apologize to him," she said and sighed. She tugged off her coat and hung it up on the wooden rack he had on the wall. Then she sat on the bench just beneath it and pulled off her boots. They were soaked, and she could only hope they would dry out and not be completely ruined. Just as she was about to go up the stairs, her phone vibrated in her pocket. When she saw it was a text from Savannah, she momentarily thought about ignoring it.

But she couldn't.

Again, as much as she hated the situation, she was thankful.

You okay?

It was a shame there wasn't a sarcasm font she could switch to.

I'm fine. We just got to Ben's.

Savannah's response was a smiley face emoji. And as much as she wanted to go on a little rant, Darcy was hungry and figured she owed it to Ben to help with dinner.

We're looking for dinner stuff. Talk to you later?

Without waiting for a response, Darcy slipped the phone into her pocket and made her way up the stairs. There was already a fire roaring in the massive fireplace, and Ben was in the kitchen.

"How long was I down there?" she asked, hoping she sounded casual and not bitchy.

Ben looked over his shoulder and smiled at her, and Darcy wanted to sigh. He was handsome—sandy-brown hair that was shaggy enough to look sexy, and the kind of dark eyes a girl could get lost in. Add a strong jaw that was a little rough with stubble right now, and Darcy almost had to smack herself to keep from reaching out and touching him.

Not a good sign.

"You weren't down there long at all. I'm just efficient."

*I'll bet you are.*

Ugh. Could there be a worse time to start having sexy thoughts?

"I have to admit, I have a fully stocked freezer, pantry, and refrigerator, but I didn't take anything out to make for dinner before I left for the airport," he explained as he stepped up to the kitchen sink to wash his hands. "There's more than enough options for dinner, but it certainly won't be anything gourmet."

"I'd be fine with some sandwiches. I don't expect

you to wait on me. I'm just glad I'm not going to have to sleep on the terminal floor tonight."

Drying his hands, Ben laughed. "I doubt you would have gotten much sleep."

She smiled and felt even more tension leave her body. He had a great laugh and really great hands. Big hands.

"So that fireplace throws off a lot of heat, huh?" she said quickly, taking a step away from him to fan herself off.

Behind her, she heard Ben moving around in the kitchen, pulling open the refrigerator and then opening cabinets. "It does. It's a great feature to have, especially in the winter."

"I'll bet." Stepping closer to it, she couldn't help but marvel at the stonework—it went from floor to ceiling. Immediately, her mind went to imagining it decorated for Christmas—lots of greenery and twinkly lights, candles, and stockings. It was big enough to hold enough stockings for a family of eight. Stepping back, she continued to admire it, and when she noticed light coming through where the flames were, she crouched to inspect it. "Does this fireplace have two sides?"

"Yup," he replied and then walked toward her. "On the other side is the master bedroom. When my grandfather originally built this place, it was just the basement and this floor, and the fireplace was the primary source of heat. When I did the upgrades and renovations, I redid the stonework on both sides." He smiled and motioned for her to follow him. "Come check it out."

Intrigued, Darcy followed him and immediately stopped short in the doorway.

*Holy decadent bed, Batman*, she thought to herself. It

was huge! Clearly, it was a king-size, but it was high and had this amazing four-poster frame that Ben must have made himself, because it was far too fabulous and unique to be store-bought. Slowly, she stepped into the room, and rather than look at the fireplace, she immediately gravitated toward the bed.

"Did you make this?" she asked softly, reaching out to touch the wood. It was dark in color and smooth as silk. The design that was carved into it was so intricate that all she could imagine was how long he must have worked on it. The hours, the days…months, she imagined, that Ben would have put into this piece. And suddenly, she wanted to see more of his work and cursed the times he had offered to take her to his workshop and she'd declined.

"I did," he said. His voice was a little low and gruff and came from almost directly behind her.

With a shaky breath, Darcy looked over her shoulder at him even as she continued to stroke the bedpost. "How…how long did this take you?" Her gaze locked with his, and holy hell was it potent.

"Two years. Off and on between other projects."

Was it her imagination or did he look at her lips? Self-consciously, she licked them and noticed how his gaze lingered there.

This wasn't good. This was borderline inappropriate, and she needed to put an end to it right now.

"So, the fireplace?" Stepping away from the bed, she switched to a safer topic.

Ben cleared his throat and turned away. "Uh, yeah. The fireplace. It used to be a small, brick facade, but when I redid it, I went with the stacked stone and took it up to the ceiling." He walked over to the fireplace. "And I did the mantel myself."

Wood had never been something Darcy looked at, let alone admired, and for the life of her, she couldn't figure out why she had such an overwhelming urge to touch the damn mantel. But she did.

Like a caress.

Like one would touch a lover.

*Shit.*

"What…what kind of wood did you use for this?" *What?* Did she seriously ask that? What difference would it make? She had no idea what the difference was between any kinds of wood.

"Mahogany," he said.

"Oh, well, it's so smooth and pretty."

*Stop. Stroking. The. Mantel.*

"Thanks." There was a slightly amused look on his face, and Darcy was pretty sure he knew she didn't have a clue what he was talking about.

"Dinner," she blurted out. "We should look into what we're going to make for dinner." And then she high-tailed it out of the room. Between the wood-stroking and the giant bed, her mind was firmly in the gutter, and she needed to stop it. Right now.

Ben followed her to the kitchen, and together they began randomly looking for something to make.

"I can whip up some pasta, or we can do omelets, or even soup and grilled cheese sandwiches," he suggested. "Any preferences?"

"Do you have bacon?"

He looked taken aback for a moment before he nodded. "I believe I do."

"I happen to love bacon on my grilled cheese sandwiches. If you promise we can do that, then I'm completely on board with that and some soup."

"You're on."

While Ben went to work on frying up the bacon and getting the sandwiches assembled, he directed Darcy to where he kept the cans of soup and the pots. While she was in the pantry picking what soup she wanted, she also did a quick mental checklist of any baking ingredients he had on hand.

"You're taking a long time choosing a soup," Ben called out.

Stepping into the kitchen, she raised two cans in the air and showed him. "I'll admit I was a little overwhelmed at the variety. When you said you had a fully stocked pantry, you weren't kidding."

He laughed softly as he flipped the bacon. "I enjoy cooking almost as much as I enjoy eating. So I try to make sure I always have what I might be in the mood for on hand, because there is nothing worse than finding yourself in the mood for something specific and then not having it here."

"Probably because you live so far from the nearest grocery store," she commented. "I don't think I've ever lived more than ten minutes from one."

"I'm used to it, but I know the importance of shopping with a list."

She put the cans on the counter and then pulled out a couple of pots. "Do you like to bake?"

Ben shook his head. "Too much measuring. When I cook, I tend to ad lib. I don't like following recipes. It takes all the fun out of cooking."

Interesting. "See, I'm the opposite. I love to bake. The precision of it and all the measuring…it works for me. But when I cook, I need a recipe. I mean, not for the basic stuff, but if I'm trying something new, I have to have something to follow."

He nodded with understanding. "Were you checking out the pantry for baking supplies?" he asked as he smiled at her over his shoulder.

*Such a sexy smile,* she thought. *Is he even aware of that?*

*Stop it!*

"Busted," she said and then actually felt herself blush. *Seriously, what is going on with me?*

"I know there are cake mixes and cans of frosting in there."

"And you also have a couple of boxes of brownie mix," she added. "But I did notice the flour and the sugar and some other key ingredients I could use to whip something up from scratch. I'll probably have to get creative since you don't have anything other than chocolate chips, but it could be a fun challenge. I've never had to work blindly before—you know, without the traditional ingredients."

"Is that what you want to do? Because I don't expect you to do anything like that."

"Actually, the baking wasn't so much for you as it was for me. It relaxes me, and I just thought, you have this amazing kitchen, and I wanted to check it all out. Besides, I may concoct a fabulous new Christmas cookie!"

"Well, in that case, don't let me stop you. But feel free to use any of the boxed stuff. I bought it, but I rarely remember to use it. So if it doesn't offend you, please go right ahead."

"I might. I know some recipes for cookies that require boxed cake mix. Maybe I'll try them out."

"Cookies *and* a snow day?" he said giddily, and Darcy knew he was being funny. "Ten-year-old me is very excited right now!"

That had her laughing. "I'm not making any promises, because I won't have a whole lot of time to do much after dinner. But maybe tomorrow."

"Beggars can't be choosers, and I'm more than happy to wait."

Ben went back to frying the bacon while Darcy poured their soups into pots and placed them on the stove. "What would you like to drink?" she asked.

"There's beer in the fridge," he said without taking his eyes off the frying bacon. "What about you? What would you like?"

Walking over to the refrigerator, Darcy pulled it open and studied the contents. She could just do water, but that was boring. There was always wine, but she'd had two glasses earlier, and that was her hard limit. She spotted several cans of Coke, a gallon of milk, and a bottle of iced tea. "I'll probably just grab a can of Coke."

And then they were back to the quiet.

Darcy had at least a hundred questions for Ben—about his work, about his cooking, about Savannah—but right now, she was enjoying working beside him to prepare a meal. It was a first for her. Other than her brothers, she had never met a man who enjoyed cooking.

When she noticed him putting the sandwiches together and getting them on the griddle, she turned on the burners for the soup.

"Would you mind if I went and changed before we eat?"

For a minute, Ben didn't say anything, but his gaze raked over her.

She would need to splash some cold water on her face if he didn't stop. "Where's my suitcase?"

"In the guest room at the top of the stairs on your right. There's a full bathroom up there as well."

"Oh. Thanks!" she said with a smile. "I'll be back in a few."

She didn't run up the stairs exactly, but Darcy knew she was moving faster than usual. Why? She had no idea. Maybe it was because she was starving and was anxious to get downstairs and eat dinner, or maybe she just needed a few minutes alone away from Ben.

There was a large sitting area at the top of the stairs with a picture window on the far wall that looked out over the property. Something about this house just... it called to her. In her mind, she envisioned a huge Christmas tree in front of that window that you'd be able to see when you pulled up to the house. It would be fun and festive and—

"There are clean towels in the bathroom," he called up to her, and she snapped out of her holiday trance and remembered she only had a few minutes before their dinner was ready.

Stepping into the bedroom, she smiled.

It wasn't nearly as magnificent as Ben's, but his stamp was here too. The bed had to be one that he made, because it was unique. Again, not quite as magnificent as the one he had in his room, but still impressive. All the furniture in the room was in a lighter finish, and there was a rustic chic vibe that Darcy found oddly appealing.

"You can look and touch all of it later," she reminded herself as she walked over and opened her suitcase. What she needed was to do some laundry. This was supposed to be a short trip, and even though it had been cut even shorter, it would be nice to have options.

Grabbing her toiletry bag, a pair of yoga pants, and a T-shirt, she quickly made her way to the bathroom. The first glimpse of herself almost made her gasp, but she recovered quickly. Her makeup was faded, and her hair was a mess, and she looked more than a little tired.

Awesome.

Stripping off her jeans and top, Darcy quickly swiped on some deodorant before changing into more comfortable clothes. Then she brushed her teeth and put on some lip gloss before contemplating her hair.

The last thing she wanted to do was look like she was trying to make an impression, and Ben had already seen her. With a sigh, she simply finger-combed the dark tresses and called it done.

"Perfect timing," he said when he spotted her walking down the stairs. "Everything's ready."

"Well, damn."

He looked at her curiously.

"I took longer than I thought. I wanted to help you."

"Well, you could get the soup into the bowls if that makes you feel better," he suggested with a grin.

"Done!" Within minutes, Darcy had the table set and drinks poured and was helping him set their sandwiches out. When they sat, she smiled at him. "Thanks. This looks great."

He shrugged. "Just sandwiches."

When she took her first bite, she moaned with pleasure—an eyes closed, head thrown back, holy-shit-this-is-fantastic kind of moan. Realizing what she'd done, she quickly straightened and looked at Ben with a sheepish grin. "Sorry. But this is way more than just a sandwich. What did you do to it?"

Chuckling, he took a bite of his sandwich before he answered. "Like I said, it's just a sandwich."

"No, no, no," she corrected him. "This is not your run-of-the-mill grilled cheese. Trust me. I make them a lot. So spill it. What did you do?"

He shook his head and took another bite even as he continued to laugh.

"Come on! You have to tell me!" she begged, laughing with him. Picking up her sandwich, she shook it at him. "This has ruined me for all other grilled cheese sandwiches." Then she took another bite and did her best to hold in the moan.

Ben took a pull of his beer and studied her. "Fine. Three kinds of cheese—American, pepper jack, and cheddar." He shrugged. "I probably should have asked you before I put the pepper jack on there—some people don't like anything spicy—but I love the combination of the three together."

"And this isn't ordinary white bread, either," she observed. "It's a lot sturdier."

"It's sourdough. With all the different cheeses, standard white bread gets a little too soggy. This holds up much better. Plus, I needed to use it up before it went bad," he added with a wink.

"It's brilliant. Absolutely brilliant. I never thought of

grilled cheese like this. I'm totally going to try this when I get home."

They ate in silence—normally the sign of a good meal—and by the time she had finished her sandwich and was halfway through her bowl of soup, she was stuffed. Pushing away from the table, Darcy placed a hand on her belly and sighed.

Ben was watching her every move. "Done?"

"I don't think I could eat another bite. That was amazing. Thank you."

If she wasn't mistaken, he was blushing.

"I'm glad you enjoyed it," he said, his voice a bit gruff.

"And since you did the bulk of the cooking, I'll clean up," Darcy said as she rose.

"That's not necessary."

"Oh please, you've done enough for me today. Just say thank you and let me do this." In truth, she hated doing the dishes. Always had. She didn't mind making the mess in the kitchen, but she preferred someone else cleaning up. But what she'd just said was true—Ben had gone above and beyond for her today. And although she had a feeling it had more to do with him trying to impress Savannah, that was no reason for her to be an ungrateful guest.

Damn.

She'd gotten so caught up in his sexy smiles and his incredible talent that she'd almost forgotten about that agenda of his. Well, good thing her brain kicked into gear. While she was stuck here with him, she was going to have to start a campaign to get him to leave Savannah alone. There was no way she was going to let Ben—or anyone—mess with her brother's marriage.

———

One minute, she was laughing and smiling, and the next, it was like someone had flipped a switch, Ben thought.

Darcy had an extremely expressive face, and he knew when her thoughts shifted from doing the dishes to something else. She didn't say a word, but the irritated glare spoke volumes.

Standing up, Ben picked up his plate and bowl and followed her to the sink.

"I said I'd clean up," she said, and although it wasn't said through clenched teeth, there was a definite edge to her voice.

"Well, I can't help it. I'm used to cleaning up after myself," he replied.

"Fine. Whatever."

They worked together, and it took less than ten minutes for the kitchen to look pristine again. He noticed her looking around—for an escape or something to do, he wasn't sure.

"Would you like to watch TV? I'm sure we can find something that isn't a weather report," he joked and noticed she didn't even attempt to grin. Okay, new tactic. He walked into the living room and simply turned on the television as he sat. "Personally, I enjoy home improvement shows or a good documentary, but I'm open to suggestions. Maybe we can find a movie or something."

"I think I'm going to head upstairs. It's been a long day," Darcy said.

"It's seven o'clock," he said, his patience all but gone. Shutting off the TV, he stood and advanced on her, determined to get to the bottom of things.

They were stuck together for at least the next couple of days, and he'd be damned if he was going to put up with her attitude. He didn't care if he pissed her off or if Savannah would be disappointed in how he was handling this. He was done bending over backward to be nice to this woman.

Darcy's eyes went as wide as saucers as he got closer, and she reached behind her to grab the newel post.

"Did I say something wrong at dinner?" he demanded and was surprised at how level his tone was.

"No, why?"

He had to fight the eye roll that was threatening. "Have I done something to offend you? And I'm not just talking about today or tonight, but since I met you? Because I have to tell you, this whole attitude you keep throwing my way is getting old."

Her mouth opened and immediately shut.

So there *was* something.

"Look, I have been racking my brain for days, and I have no idea what it is that I said or did, but whatever it is, I'm sorry. Can we move on?"

Her eyes narrowed as she looked at him, and he was certain she was going to let him have it—Darcy seemed like the kind of woman who wouldn't hold anything back. But in the blink of an eye, her expression changed and went completely neutral.

"Would it be all right if I did a load of laundry?"

That was pretty much the very last thing he expected her to say. "Laundry?"

She nodded. "Uh-huh. Laundry. I have stuff I need to wash, and if it's all right with you, I thought I'd do it now."

"Now," he repeated.

She nodded again. "If you don't mind."

To say he was confused was an understatement. She hadn't accepted his apology, and she hadn't told him what he'd done wrong, and until she did one or the other, there was no way he was going to let this go. He couldn't. If there was one thing that irritated Ben more than anything, it was people who weren't honest. And right now, he wanted her.

*No!* Not her. Her honesty.

Dammit.

He wanted her honesty!

"As a matter of fact, I do mind," he said mildly and walked to the couch and sat back down. He knew the instant his smug expression got to her, because she stomped across the room after him.

"You mind? Seriously? It's laundry! And I'm not asking you to do it for me. Hell, if you have some stuff you need washed, I'll do it for you. And dry it. And fold it!"

Tempting offer. He hated doing laundry.

"I just did a load last night. But thanks."

*Fascinating.* Again, it was the only word that came to mind when he watched her battling with whatever was going on inside her head. So many emotions played across her face as she towered over him and tried to look intimidating. He had no doubt she had honed this skill on her brothers, but he wasn't buying into it.

And he certainly wasn't intimidated easily. If anything, he could probably teach Darcy a thing or two about the art of doing it properly.

Slowly, he rose to his feet and watched as she refused to move except to let her head fall back so she could hold his gaze.

So maybe he was a little impressed.

"I want to know what your issue is with me," he said, his voice low and deep.

He had to give her credit; she didn't react. Hell, she barely blinked.

"You can deny it all you want, but I'm not a moron, Darcy. You were fine with me when you first showed up here, but by the end of that night, you had a definite attitude, and I want to know why."

Still nothing.

"I'm not opposed to calling Savannah and asking her. I'm sure she'll tell me."

And there it was. The chink in the armor. Her shoulders slouched a bit, and her expression fell.

It was both rewarding and made him feel bad. Why couldn't she just talk to him?

"Fine," she finally said. "I have a problem with you."

"Care to tell me what it is?"

"I'd rather not."

He sighed as his head fell back. The woman was killing him. When he straightened and met her gaze, he said, "Look, you're stuck here—in my home, might I add—for the next several days. Wouldn't it be better for both of us if we cleared the air now? I mean, why not get it out in the open?"

She seemed to consider that for a moment before answering. "Look, can't we just say we don't... I don't know...gel? Or get one another? And then move on? I mean, it's crazy to expect everyone to like each other and get along or be instant friends. That's not realistic."

Now it was his turn to study her for a long moment

before speaking. "I see what you're saying, but here's the thing. I think you and I *did* gel. And there have been several times where we got one another. You seem to be picking and choosing when you like me and when you don't. Maybe that's your thing."

"Hey!"

He didn't let her go on. "But I'm here to tell you that I think it's bullshit. It's a childish way to behave, and I'm not going to stand for it."

Her eyes went wide again. "You're not going to *stand* for it? Who the hell are you?"

"I'm the guy who saved your ass today and opened his home to you rather than letting you sit and stew in a crowded airport for days. And besides that? My house, my rules." He crossed his arms over his chest and waited to see how she'd respond to that.

The obvious reaction was going to be outrage. Possibly name calling. Ben was prepared. Hell, he even welcomed it. The sooner she got out what was pissing her off, the sooner he could relax and focus on the things he needed to—like the book and the backlog of work waiting for him in the workshop.

"I'd tell you what I think of your rules, but you're a smart guy, Ben. I'm sure you can figure it out." And with that, Darcy turned and walked down the stairs to get her satchel.

*Um, what just happened?* he wondered. How was it possible that she somehow managed to get the last word without answering him? Again?

He could follow her, but that would be so obvious, she was probably expecting it. So he quickly thought outside the box.

And went up to the guest room to wait for her.

He didn't have to wait long. Five minutes later, Darcy came strolling in, looking at her phone. It was obvious she didn't see him reclining against the pillows on her bed at first, but when she did, she screamed.

"What the hell?" she cried, her hand fluttering to her chest.

"We weren't done talking," he said, tucking his hands behind his head and grinning. "So I figured I'd wait for you."

Hanging her head, she sighed. "Are you always this stubborn?"

"Yup. Just ask Savannah. When we first met—"

"You know what?" she quickly interrupted. "I believe you." Tossing her phone on the corner of the bed, Darcy moved around the room plugging in chargers and getting her devices hooked up. It didn't take long, and soon she was back to staring at Ben.

"There's a simple solution to all of this," he reminded her.

Whatever it was, she really didn't want to talk about it. Maybe that's why it was bothering him so much, because it was obviously a big thing for her, and for the life of him, he didn't remember doing anything that would cause this strong of a reaction.

Finally, she straightened and looked him in the eye. "Fine. Just remember, you asked."

Ben instantly sat up and swung his legs off the bed.

"For starters, I am very good at what I do."

He looked at her as if she was crazy. He didn't remember critiquing her—out loud—about her work skills.

"Before I even had the chance to get started, you

implied that I couldn't possibly be qualified for this since I'm not Savannah."

"That is not what I said, Darcy. You asked me—"

"And I think your crush on Savannah is completely inappropriate."

He instantly jumped to his feet. "Excuse me?"

"She's a married woman. A *happily* married woman with a child, and your feelings for her are wrong!" she shouted.

And then she began to pace.

"And on top of that, they're inappropriate."

"What the hell are you talking about?"

"Seriously?" she asked sarcastically as she stopped and stared at him. "You're going to stand here and deny that you have feelings for her?"

"Of course I have feelings for her! Savannah and I are friends, Darcy. Good friends. If you read anything more into that, then that's on you, not me."

"Spoken like someone who's trying not to look guilty," she said snarkily.

"You know what? You're crazy! Genuinely crazy!" Ben said as he moved away from her. "I don't know where you got any of this, but you're wrong. And honestly, when did I ever say I had a crush on her?" He paused but not long enough for her to reply. "And you want to know what else? It doesn't matter. We're friends. That's it. Nothing more."

"Uh-huh. Sure. Whatever."

Raking his hand through his hair in frustration, he put plenty of distance between them, because he was on the verge of strangling her. "Why don't you tell me what was so *inappropriate*?" he prompted, using air quotes for emphasis.

"It was everything," she said without hesitation. "The way you talk about her... It's just so damn obvious!"

"Really?" he deadpanned. "It's obvious? For who? Because you're the only one who thinks that."

Rolling her eyes, she immediately returned to pacing. "Look, I already knew you were going to deny it, but please stop. Savannah is a married woman and you just...you just need to back off."

"You're infuriating, you know that? You think you have all the answers to everything, and God forbid—" He gasped mockingly. "You're wrong." The bored look on her face told him that he wasn't getting anywhere with her, and knowing that continuing to protest would add fuel to her fire, Ben decided he would go another way. "Have you already talked to Savannah about this?"

The look of surprise on her face told him she was ready for more denials. Good. He enjoyed keeping her on her toes, even if it was over a completely ridiculous topic.

"Uh, no. I had planned to, but then the whole weather thing happened, and I haven't had the opportunity."

He nodded. "And your brother?"

Another eye roll. "Why would I do that?" She huffed with irritation. "Look, can we just do this book thing and then you can...I don't know...go away?"

What happened next couldn't be helped.

Hell, Ben wasn't even sure he would have if he could.

He laughed.

Like an honest-to-goodness hearty laugh.

The look of pure indignation on Darcy's face just made him laugh even harder. Did she have any idea how insane all of this was? How ludicrous?

"What's so funny?" she demanded, and that just made Ben laugh even harder. "Stop it! This is serious!"

Again, he just kept laughing.

Couldn't seem to stop.

His entire body hurt from it.

"Dammit, Ben! Stop!" Darcy stomped her foot, as if that was going to intimidate him enough to calm down. Then she started walking toward him. She wasn't tall by any stretch of the imagination. He'd put her at five foot four tops. And when she looked up at him—and he was six foot—she should have been the one intimidated.

But she wasn't.

He was all set for her to start yelling at him again, and this time, he did try to stop laughing. It was almost down to a chuckle when she shoved him. Hard.

"Hey!" he yelled, and then it struck him as funny again.

"You want to keep laughing? Well, you can laugh someplace else. I'm done."

Another shove.

Actually, she was pretty damn strong for being so small.

"And if you think for one minute I'm going to let someone like *you*—or anyone—break up my brother's marriage, you've got another think coming," she was muttering behind him.

And that's when it stopped being funny.

Although she did manage to get one more shove in before he could turn around and say anything.

"You know what?" he snapped. "That's enough."

She didn't look the least bit fazed.

"It doesn't matter what I say, you're not going to listen, and you're certainly not going to believe me. Obviously, there's nothing I can do about it, and honestly, there isn't anything I *want* to do about it. You think you know something? Fine. Go call Savannah and talk to her, and when you realize you were wrong, you can apologize. But for now, we are going to have to agree to disagree."

"No, we're—"

"Yes, we are," he interrupted. "I'm not going to keep having this argument with you for the next couple of days. I refuse. So if you want to keep it up, then you can do it alone, because I've got nothing left to say on the subject."

"Because you know I'm right," she said smugly, crossing her arms over her chest.

"Agree to disagree," he said just as smugly, mimicking her pose.

He could practically see the steam coming from her ears.

"I...you..."

"The way I see it," he began reasonably, "you can stay up here and pout for the rest of the night. No big deal to me. But it's still early. We could go downstairs and watch some TV and relax and put all of this behind us. That's what I'm voting for. And you did mention wanting to bake." He gave her a lopsided grin in hopes of lightening the mood. "You can make as big of a mess as you want, and I'll do the cleanup."

For a minute, he thought he had her. Her entire body seemed to relax, and there weren't daggers shooting out of her eyes anymore.

She took a step toward him, and it was just enough that he took a step back. And before he knew it, he was out in the hallway, and she was in the guest room and...

The door was slammed in his face.

—〜〜—

It had been a long time since a door slam had felt this satisfying, Darcy thought. But she didn't allow herself the luxury of relishing the victory. Instead, she marched over and grabbed her phone as she plopped on the bed. Doing a quick scroll through her contacts, she stopped and hit Send.

"Hello?"

"Three days! I have been waiting to talk to you for *three* days! Didn't you get my text?"

Anna Shaughnessy yawned loudly before answering. "Yes, I got your text, and I'm sorry I didn't call. Kaitlyn has the flu, and Quinn is freaking out about getting it, and I think I'm teetering on it. It's a whole… fluey thing."

"Ew."

"Tell me about it," Anna said wearily. "Let's just say I didn't know such a small person could vomit that much."

"I could have gone my entire life without *that* image in my head."

"Sorry. So what's going on? What are you freaking out about?"

Darcy told her everything, and by the time she was done, she was breathless. Falling on the bed, she sighed. "And can you believe he had the nerve to stand here and deny it? To my face? I mean, why? Why would he do that?"

"Um, maybe because he's telling the truth?"

That had Darcy sitting straight up again. "What? How can you even say that? Weren't you paying attention to what I told you? He was practically *gushing* as he talked about her!"

Anna was quiet for a minute. "Question—do you have any friends who are guys? And who are just friends?"

"Of course I do. What does that have to do with anything?"

"Do you laugh with them?"

"Sure. I mean, sometimes we joke around and get silly and—"

"And when you talk about them or describe them to people, do you maybe, you know, compliment them? Say only good things? Or perhaps gush?"

*Uh-oh. Um...* "I do. But this was different. I'm telling you—"

"Darcy, I believe what you're telling me. And I think maybe you just took it all a little out of context. They're friends and you're her sister-in-law, so he was maybe just praising her because the two of you are related."

"Maybe..." *Oh. No.*

"Did you even talk to Savannah, or did you just pounce on Ben?"

"I kind of hinted at it, but she was pretty oblivious."

"Then why are you obsessing about this? Is Ben a pain to work with?"

"Yes!"

"Really? How?"

"He refuses to listen to my suggestions, he argues with me a lot, and...and I can tell he was annoyed with the whole thing!"

Anna sighed. "Didn't Savannah warn you of this? That he wasn't easy to work with? I mean, even I remember her saying that about him a time or two."

"Okay, fine. Yes. She warned me, but—"

"Has he been rude to you in any other way?"

"No."

"Okay. And it sounds like you cleared the air with him tonight."

"Sort of."

"If you haven't, then you need to. He opened his home to you, and he came and helped you out so you weren't stranded at the airport."

"I would have survived."

Anna chuckled. "Let me ask you something. Where are you right now?"

"Um, at Ben's."

"No, more specifically, where are you right now in Ben's house?"

"In the guest room."

"And where are you sitting?"

"On the bed."

"Did you take a shower yet?"

"No." It didn't take a genius to see where she was going with this. "Okay, fine. This is a million times better than being stuck at the airport. I won't be sleeping on the floor, I can shower, and I have privacy. I get it."

"Have you even thanked him?"

"Believe it or not, I did." Or at least she thought she did.

"Darcy…"

"I think in one of our conversations I did. But there's been a lot of things on my mind."

"Where is Ben right now?"

"Downstairs. But it doesn't matter where he is. I'm going to stay up here tonight and maybe—"

"Start fresh in the morning?"

Sighing, Darcy said, "Yes."

"Good girl."

"But what do I do, Anna?"

Anna sighed. "You know you may have to face the fact that you're wrong here, don't you? There's a good chance his comments were innocent, and you read more into it than there is. And then what are you going to do? Are you going to apologize to Ben? To Savannah?"

Maybe.

Or not.

"I don't know," she replied honestly.

"Sleep on it. And keep away from Ben for tonight. I think that's best. A good night's sleep will put everything into perspective. Personally, I..." Anna paused and then cursed. "Darce? I have to go. Kaitlyn's throwing up and Quinn just ran by me with her."

"Gross. Fine, go, and I'll talk to you soon. I hope she feels better."

"Me too. Thanks. Bye!"

Turning the phone off, Darcy put it on the nightstand and sighed.

And then cursed.

*What if I'm wrong?* she wondered. *What if I misinterpreted the whole damn thing? What if I've been acting like a crazy person to a really nice—and attractive—guy?*

*Maybe this is why I can't seem to find Mr. Right—because I'm crazy.*

These were questions she just couldn't answer right now. So rather than sitting there obsessing, she decided a nice soak in the tub sounded like the perfect thing to do.

Standing up, she stretched and walked across the

hall to check out the bathroom again. Flipping on the light, she saw it was a fairly standard soaker tub. No jets or anything special, but the thought of just sitting and relaxing made her very happy. She started the water and then went to get her things.

Five minutes later, she had a pair of pajamas and a clean pair of underwear with her, a book, and two amazingly fluffy towels. Closing the bathroom door, she stripped, clipped up her hair, and tested the water. *Perfect temperature*, she thought, and groaned with pleasure as she settled in.

It felt glorious, and it was doing wonders in helping her release some of her tension. The last thing she wanted to do was move from this position. It had been a stressful day, and this was the first time she felt herself relax. If the tub had jets, she'd contemplate sleeping in here. But it didn't and she couldn't.

She wondered if Ben's bathroom had a soaker tub. His bedroom had been pretty spectacular, and she wished she had gotten a glimpse of the rest of his space.

*Stop thinking about Ben!* she admonished herself, because it opened the door for all kinds of thoughts, and in her current position, most of them were sexy. With a sigh, she forced herself to carefully pick up her book. It didn't take long to realize that it was a mistake—*a couple who hadn't seen one another in years find themselves snowed in together over Christmas…*

"Great. What is the universe trying to tell me?" Part of her wanted to chuck the book across the room, but she really was a sucker for a holiday romance. And under normal circumstances, she'd find the whole snowed in together trope to be very romantic.

"Screw it. I'm reading."

When she felt the water starting to cool, Darcy forced herself to pop the drain and climb out. Within minutes, she was out and dried off and slipping into her pajamas. She pulled the clip from her hair and shook it out. Tomorrow morning, she'd take a shower to help wake herself up, and then she could put the effort in to look decent. But for tonight?

Why bother?

# Chapter 4

IT WAS STILL SNOWING.

As Ben sipped his coffee the next morning, he stared out the window and cursed. The longer the snow continued to fall, the longer the delays would be for flights to resume their schedules.

And the longer Darcy Shaughnessy would be in his house.

He'd barely slept a wink last night thinking about her accusations. Have feelings for Savannah? Was she crazy? He snorted with disgust as he answered his own question. Of course she was crazy.

Savannah was a friend. A good friend. He'd never had a romantic or sexual thought about her. Not even once. The first time they met, he was openly hostile toward her. And after that? Well, he grew to like and respect her. But that was it. Unfortunately, Darcy didn't want to believe that. If there was one thing that was blazingly obvious about her, it was that she seemed determined to stick to her guns.

And she was a major pain in the ass in the process.

Stepping away from the windows, Ben looked at the clock and knew he should get some work done. Not the kind that he wanted to, but the kind he'd been avoiding for far too long.

Paperwork and returning calls.

Worst. Work. Ever.

He made his way to the lower level where he had a
small office. Inside was a desk, his computer, several
filing cabinets, and—ironically—about twenty-seven
thousand pieces of paper he kept meaning to file.

*Yikes.*

Though he knew he should put a dent in the filing,
he just couldn't muster up the will to do it. Instead, he
sat, booted up the computer, and started going through
his voicemails.

On a normal day, he spent the bulk of it out in the
workshop, working. This stuff? The clerical side of his
work? It was a major distraction and one he tended to
ignore. Occasionally, he caved and would hire an assistant to get it under control, but he hated having anyone
in his home, and by the time he was done explaining
what he needed and how his business worked, he could
have just done it himself.

He'd lost track of the number of assistants he'd fired
in the past three years.

Looking around the room, however, he realized he
needed someone to at least get him back to a decent
starting point. Because right now, as much as he hated
having someone in his home, he hated this clutter more.

He listened to voicemail after voicemail after
voicemail of people requesting a new sculpture, some
for Christmas. Were these people for real? It was the
middle of October, for crying out loud. If they wanted
Christmas, they were going to have to think about
*next* Christmas, and even that was iffy. Looking at
his calendar, Ben knew he was on the verge of being
overcommitted. As it was, he needed a break. An
extended one for his sanity alone. And that meant he

was going to have to call people and let them know he wasn't available.

*Wouldn't having an assistant to do this be so much better?* he asked himself.

And the answer was a resounding *YES!*

"Note to self—call the temp agency next week," he murmured. Sure, he could have written it on a piece of paper, but why add to the pile?

For an hour, he did his best to make notes on who he needed to call, and then he went on to return some emails, and at that point, he was ready to lose his mind. His hands were itching to get out to the workshop and pick up his tools. Unfortunately, he had at least an hour of shoveling just to *get* to the workshop.

"Living the dream," he said as he stood and stretched. It was only eight in the morning, but he figured he might as well throw on his boots and coat and get started. It would get him out of this office and doing something productive and physical, which he needed after sitting around for the past few days working on the book with Darcy.

And then that whole thing came to him again. For the past hour, he'd been able to push it from his mind. Eventually, Darcy was going to wake up and come down from the guest room, and he'd be forced to see her and talk to her and... Hell, he had no idea what to expect. Ideally, he hoped she'd apologize.

Then he realized that was not likely to happen.

Glancing over at his phone, he thought about calling Savannah himself, but it was early. He certainly didn't want to wake her if she had the opportunity to sleep in.

Maybe...

"Oh my God. What happened in here? Were you robbed or something?"

Great.

Darcy was awake.

Turning, Ben saw her standing in the doorway, looking horrified.

*Join the club*, he thought.

"Good morning to you too," he said, forcing a smile. "Sleep well?"

Darcy stepped into the room and looked around, the look of horror still in place. "Um, yeah. Great. That bed was incredibly comfortable—way more than the one at the hotel." Then she paused and looked at the piles of paper on the floor in front of the filing cabinets before looking at him. "Seriously? What is the deal with this room?"

"I'm a little behind on my paperwork," he said simply and shrugged. "Are you hungry? All I've had is coffee this morning, and I could go for something to eat before I tackle the shoveling."

"Ben, how…I mean…all of this…" She stopped and sighed with exasperation. "How can you work like this?"

Fine. He knew it was a mess—okay, a disaster—but he didn't like her tone as she pointed it out to him. "I avoid coming in here, normally," he admitted. "But this morning, I had no excuse, and I was just coming up with a plan of attack."

"And did you?"

He nodded. "Yup. So no worries."

"I wasn't worried," she said quickly. "I was just making an observation."

There was a hint of defensiveness in her voice, but he chose to ignore it. Hell, he knew he was sounding the same way. Either way, if she still wanted to argue with him—about anything—then so be it. He, however, wanted something to eat. Without a word, he walked past her and made his way up the stairs to the kitchen. He heard her footsteps behind him a minute later.

"I can whip up some eggs," he said as he looked in the refrigerator. "I have bacon and sausage if you have a preference." Turning and looking over his shoulder, he saw Darcy standing by the windows and looking out. Closing the refrigerator door, he walked over and joined her. They stood in silence, watching the snow fall.

"It's still snowing," she said quietly.

"It is."

"How much do you think is on the ground already?"

"About a foot, I'd say."

"Damn."

"I know."

Sighing, Darcy turned to him. "So I'm clearly going to be here for a few days."

He nodded.

"And I don't want things to be awkward between us."

Another nod.

"So…"

Was this it? Was she going to apologize? Ben found himself holding his breath.

"I may have…misinterpreted some of the things you said."

That was it? Was she kidding him?

"And to show you that there're no hard feelings, how about I make us breakfast?" she said, interrupting his thoughts. "I know I said baking was more my thing, but I can do some eggs or maybe some French toast or something. What do you say?"

He wanted to say she needed to apologize to him and admit she was completely wrong, but he didn't. Instead, he put another smile on his face—it felt awkward and forced—and replied, "French toast sounds great. Thank you."

Darcy gave him a genuine smile.

And it hit him like a solid punch to the gut.

Yeah. He'd forgotten how her smiles affected him.

"Okay," she said excitedly. "Why don't you go and do…something, and I'll get breakfast going. I know you said you have to go out and shovel, but you probably don't want to go out and get started only to have to come in fifteen minutes later."

"No, but I can assess the situation. So let's say thirty minutes? Deal?"

She nodded, still smiling, and said, "Deal!"

For a minute, he thought she was going to hug him. Something in her body language—she sort of leaned in for a second but then immediately pulled back. The only thing Ben could think of doing was to hightail it out of there and find something to do. Fast!

"Good. Um, I'll see you in a bit then," he stammered as he made his way to the stairs. He fairly sprinted down them and made fast work of pulling on his boots and coat. There was a utility closet off the mud room where he kept a small selection of snow shovels and a blower. He had a duplicate set out in the garage. It made it easier for him, because the winters in Washington meant they could get snow at any time. And when he was in the workshop, sometimes he needed to dig a path to the house. And then the next morning, he'd need to do it all over again. It just made more sense to keep a set in each spot. Grabbing a shovel, he set out to get started.

When he stepped outside, the freezing temperatures felt like bliss on his skin.

"I'm in deep trouble here," he murmured, watching his breath float in front of him.

And he wasn't referring to the amount of snow on the ground.

Darcy Shaughnessy was trouble to, well, just about every aspect of his well-being. He'd been so busy obsessing about how much she annoyed him that he hadn't allowed himself to think about his initial attraction to her. And now that it was out there again, there was no taking it back.

There was nothing he could do about it right now, unfortunately. So rather than stand still and let the snow build up around him, Ben gripped the shovel and began clearing the entryway. As expected, there was at least a foot of snow to deal with. The workshop was about fifty feet away.

He was going to be at this all day.

And for once, that didn't seem like a bad thing.

Then he remembered Darcy was preparing breakfast. But he could eat quickly and get out without it seeming like he was trying to avoid spending time with her. And really, he just needed to focus on getting a path to his workshop. If he could get there, all would be right with his world. He could spend all day out there and not have to see or talk to Darcy at all.

She'd probably appreciate that too.

That was all the motivation he needed to get started.

The first shovelful of snow was always the hardest, but once he got started and found his groove, Ben made decent progress. It was a hard, physical task, but after so many days of being still, it felt good to get his muscles moving. With each pile of snow he tossed aside, he felt invigorated. Every foot closer he got to his workshop, he felt hopeful.

"Ben!" Turning, he saw Darcy peeking her head out the door with a big smile on her face. "Time to take a break. Breakfast is ready."

When he simply stood there and didn't respond, she looked at him curiously.

"Come on," she said cheerily. "I'm just getting ready to plate everything and, if I do say so myself, it all looks and smells delicious." Then she waved before she stepped back inside.

Looking around, he saw he was about ten feet into the path, and even though the snow was still falling, he'd be able to go over his work with relative ease after eating.

Maybe he could just use a broom for that, or the blower, or maybe...

"Ben!" She stuck her head out the door again and laughed. "The snow will still be here after you eat. Come inside and get warm for a little bit before breakfast gets cold too."

And then like a man walking to his execution, he slowly made his way into the house.

———

She was definitely in trouble.

Serious, serious trouble.

Watching Ben shovel snow was just hot. Why the

hell did he have to be so damn attractive? Everything about him was starting to be appealing, and she wasn't sure if it was just her long-dormant hormones coming to life or if the man was just *that* damn sexy.

*Damn romance novels.* All of a sudden, she was having these feelings, and it was starting to get a little disconcerting.

Why couldn't a guy like him be interested in her? Maybe not *Ben* specifically, but...

A small gasp escaped before she could stop it. Was *that* what this was all about? Was she upset because she thought Ben had a crush on Savannah, or because he didn't have one on her? Would she feel this way—be this freaked out—if the whole *gushing* incident hadn't happened? If this had just been a work situation and she had found him attractive but he didn't reciprocate, would she be this worked up? Could she really just be jealous?

"Or is he really that annoying and I've got too much time on my hands and need to think about something else for a little while," she murmured.

Putting the plates on the table, she admired her handiwork. French toast, sausage, warmed syrup, and coffee. She'd set the table and it looked welcoming, if she did say so herself.

She hoped he appreciated it.

From what she could tell about Ben, he seemed to be a bit of a loner who took care of himself. And no one else. There was no evidence around the house that he was involved with anyone.

What kind of woman did he like? Find attractive?

She cursed and was about to let herself get into that stupid mind-set when she heard him trudging up the

stairs. Pasting a smile on her face, she stood next to the
table and waited for him to appear.

And nearly swallowed her own tongue.

The faded jeans, the thermal Henley with a flannel
shirt over it…none of it should have been appealing.
None. Of. It. There was a time when, if she had seen
a guy dressed like that, she would have made a snarky
comment about him looking like a lumberjack. But on
Ben, it looked so damn good.

Too good.

*Sexy* good.

Ben took one glance at the table and then at Darcy
and smiled—and it was a genuine smile. *He has such
amazing eyes*, she thought. And when he looked at her
the way he was looking at her right now, she could feel
herself melting a little bit.

Okay, a lot.

Clearing her throat, she said, "So, um, I hope you're
hungry."

Nodding, Ben began to roll up his sleeves as he
walked over to the sink. With every inch of skin he
revealed, Darcy could only stare. Muscled forearms,
tanned skin… She forced herself to look away. She
heard him wash his hands before he came and sat at the
table. She joined him and felt herself beam with pride
when he said, "Everything looks wonderful, Darcy.
Thank you."

All she could do was nod.

All her life, her family had complimented her when
she cooked or baked, so it wasn't as if she had never
been praised for her efforts, but something about the
way Ben said it—the rich baritone of his voice and the

look in his eyes—made it feel so much more intimate. And that had her melting a little bit more.

They ate in silence, and she racked her brain for something to say that would get her mind off the sexy thoughts. Midway through the meal, she asked, "So is there as much snow on the ground as you thought?"

He nodded. "And it's still coming down. Part of me knows this is going to be a battle to get it cleared and shoveled, but if I don't at least get this first round done, then it's going to be that much harder when it's over."

"Can I help?"

Looking at her with surprise, it took Ben a minute to answer. "You want to shovel snow?"

That had her chuckling. "Honestly? No. I don't have the boots or gloves and all that to be out there, but I'd be willing to come out for short spurts if it would help."

Ben studied her for a long moment. Then he shook his head and looked at his plate. "I appreciate the offer, but I think you'd better stay inside."

She sighed and felt oddly deflated by the rejection. "I don't mind borrowing some boots and gloves from you," she explained. "Together, we could make a dent in getting you a path to the workshop."

He lifted his gaze to hers again. "How...how did you know that's what I was doing?"

Arching a dark brow at him, she said, "Seriously? You mean besides the fact that you were shoveling in that direction when I came to tell you breakfast was ready?"

He laughed softly. "Oh. Right."

"You're probably chomping at the bit to get some work done."

"I am. It's been a few days, and I'm behind. Normally, I'd be out there nonstop until I was done."

"Even in the snow?"

"Especially in the snow. What else is there to do?"

"What if you lost electricity? Does that ever happen?"

Her mind instantly flashed to the couple in the book she was reading last night—they'd gotten snowed in, lost power, and had to snuggle close together with nothing but the heat of the fireplace to keep them warm. Darcy's eyes instantly flicked over to the massive fireplace. No doubt that thing could keep them warm—especially in Ben's bed.

"Occasionally," he said, interrupting her sexy thoughts. "But I have a generator that works on the house and workshop. I don't use a lot of power tools with my work, so I don't need the power for that—it's mainly for the light and the heat. But I have a fireplace out there to help."

"Wow. That's…wow."

He nodded. "I know. I thought it was crazy when I was younger, that my grandfather put one out in the garage. That's what the space was in the beginning, and then he converted it to his workshop. But now I'm thankful for it."

"I'm sure." She turned and looked at the massive fireplace in the living room. "Is it as big as this one?"

"Hell, no. The ceiling isn't nearly as high out there. And this one? Well, this one is sort of like a masterpiece. The stonework and the mantel…it was a labor of love. The one outside in the workshop is your average, run-of-the-mill brick fireplace."

"But it gets the job done, right?" she asked with a grin.

"Absolutely."

They had finished eating, and Darcy stretched. "I am so full," she said, her hand immediately going to her belly. "I think I ate too much. Again."

Ben took his last bite and nodded. "Totally worth it. Although I may need to wait a little while before going outside and doing any more shoveling." He mimicked her pose and then looked at her with a lopsided grin. "Thank you again. That was amazing."

Darcy could feel the heat on her cheeks and averted her gaze. The man could be lethal with his voice and those eyes and just everything.

Afraid he'd be able to tell what she was thinking about him, she immediately rose and began to clear the dishes. Ben's hand on hers stopped her.

Now she'd have to add his hands to the lethal mix. *Dammit*.

Looking at him, she waited to see why he was touching her.

"You don't have to jump up and clean up, you know. There's no rush," he said. "We can sit and relax, can't we?"

Honestly? Darcy didn't think she could. Relax, that is. She felt twitchy and unsettled and so damn mad at herself for thinking she was fine with giving up sex when one touch of Benjamin Tanner's hand had her practically salivating.

"I, um, it's just the way I do things," she said quickly, hating how her voice seemed to squeak. "I know I said I hate cleaning, but I also hate to see a mess just sitting there."

"That's what the dishwasher is for," he countered mildly. "Seriously, sit. Please."

There was no way she could say no, so she sighed and sat. Swallowing hard, she decided to do her best to distract herself. "Your office is a nightmare," she blurted out.

Ben laughed.

And then she noticed the stubbled jaw and the strong column of his throat and thought how much she'd like to feel that—with her hands and her lips.

Brushing against her thighs...

This was hell.

Straightening, Ben looked at her with merriment in his eyes. "I should be offended, but you're right. It is a nightmare, and I don't have the will to care."

"But you should. What if...what if you needed to find something? How do you do it? What if a client needs something from you and you have no idea where it is?"

"My business isn't like that. Most of what's down there are design ideas, bills, and invoices for supplies and that sort of thing. I hate filing."

"But how do you handle the chaos?"

He looked at her oddly. "Chaos? I don't see paper as being chaotic."

Her eyes went wide. "Seriously? It's everywhere! On every surface! How do you not see it?"

"I mean I see it, but I don't look at it and think chaos."

Maybe that was her OCD then. "It would make me crazy. I like order and knowing everything has its place."

"It does have its place. It's just not there yet."

"Ben, it's...I mean, come on!" Her tone was light and teasing, but there was part of her that was totally serious.

He shrugged. "It is what it is. I know my strengths and weaknesses, and paperwork is definitely in the weakness category." Then he studied her for a moment. "I'm sure you have a similar list, so don't even try to deny it."

Right now, she would have Ben at the top of her weakness list. It was as if she was no longer capable of thinking of anything other than him and what she found attractive and appealing about him.

And it scared the hell out of her.

For most of her life, she had been impulsive, doing things before really thinking them through. She thought she was getting over that. It was one thing to do it to antagonize one of her brothers, but it was normally for her own entertainment. But she'd learned her lesson—repeatedly—about doing something crazy and then having to live with the consequences. That part of her life was supposed to be done, and she would have told anyone who asked that she was glad to say goodbye to that girl.

Unfortunately, right now, her impulse vibe was pretty much screaming at her to do something. Her skin felt tight and tingly, her throat was dry, and all she wanted was to climb into Ben's lap and kiss him until neither of them could breathe. She wanted to feel those work-roughened hands on her, feel the scratchy stubble of his jaw abrading her skin... She pretty much wanted him to ease every inch of her that was throbbing.

And that was every inch of her body.

"Darcy?"

*What?* Oh yeah. They were talking about something. Weaknesses. They were talking about weaknesses.

"Oh, um, I mean, yeah. Sure. Of course I do. But even the stuff I don't like to do, I couldn't leave like what you have in your office. It would make me too crazy."

He chuckled and took a sip of his coffee. "That's why my office is downstairs. Out of sight, out of mind."

That was the kind of logic she needed to put into play right now. Get Ben out of sight, and maybe she could focus on something else—anything else—other than hands and skin and getting naked.

This time when she stood, Darcy made sure she was out of his reach.

Instantly, she scooped up her plate and silverware and walked over to the kitchen sink, fairly certain Ben was confused by her abrupt move. But she couldn't let herself linger too long on that thought. Or of turning around to confirm or deny the expression on his face. Nope. It was better to focus on the task at hand—rinse the dishes, put them in the dishwasher, and keep moving with her gaze firmly looking down.

That was safe.

That was smart.

That was not happening.

Turning around from the sink, she bumped directly into a solid wall of man.

*Great.*

Head to toe, Ben pressed up against her, and Darcy wanted to rub along him. There wasn't room for her to move. Her back was against the cabinets and counter, and Ben was all over her front.

*Would it be wrong to purr?* she wondered.

Slowly, she let her gaze wander up to his face, and the intense expression she found there was enough to cause her to go on hyperalert, if that was even possible.

"Um, sorry," she murmured, her voice huskier than she ever remembered it being.

But Ben didn't speak. One arm moved around her as he put his plate on the granite countertop, and when he went to pull it back, his hand skimmed her arm until it came to rest on her hip.

Oh. My.

"I should…I mean…I'll finish…" she stammered and wondered why she wasn't trying harder to move away. Or why he wasn't. Or why…

With his hand on the move again, this time slowly caressing her arm and her shoulder until he was cupping her cheek, Darcy forgot to breathe. His gaze was almost as hypnotic as his touch, and as much as she wanted to keep looking at him, her lids felt too heavy, his touch too good. Slowly, her eyes closed, and she sighed as his thumb caressed her.

At first, she wanted to blame her intense reaction to him on a year of being celibate, but she knew she was lying. Never before had a man's touch ignited so many feelings—such strong, intense feelings—and now that she knew what this little bit of contact could do, she wanted more.

And now.

His hand stopped moving, and for a moment, she wanted to frown and beg him to continue. A small part of her was a little afraid to open her eyes because she knew—she knew!—he'd be able to read her mind.

Ben whispered her name right next to her ear, and she trembled. His breath was so warm and delicious, and how had she not felt him move in that close? And was it her imagination or did his tongue just gently touch the shell of her ear?

"Yes," she sighed, so lost in sensation, she didn't

care that it was a plea rather than an answer to a question. Nothing mattered except getting Ben closer, getting his hand to start touching her again and his mouth on her. Anywhere.

But for whatever reason, he wasn't moving or touching or kissing.

Curious, Darcy leaned back slightly and looked at him. On his face, she saw the same struggle she imagined was on hers. Good to know she wasn't the only one who was in a total state of confusion.

Two minutes ago, they'd been talking and eating and completely casual. How had they gone from that to this?

This was also a little new to her. Sex—the foreplay part of it—was something she normally needed. And it came in the form of all the usual suspects—flirty words, caresses, kisses. Never before had a mundane conversation over breakfast had her ready to throw down on the kitchen floor.

Which, by the way, she'd be totally on board for right about now.

Her eyes scanned his face as she waited to see what his next move was going to be. Or if he even had one. Could he possibly walk away after this?

*After what?* she asked herself. A hand on her hip and a full-body press? Um, she was fairly certain he'd be able to walk away, because it shouldn't be all that she was making it, except…

A slow smile played at her lips, and she arched her back a little and pressed up more *intimately* against him and felt all the proof she needed that this was more than a hand on a hip move. Her smile grew at the sound of the low growl that emanated from Ben at the contact.

*Good to know*, she thought.

So what were they waiting for? What was the holdup? Obviously, he found her attractive. Obviously, he was turned on. What did she have to do to get to the good stuff?

And then she knew impulsive Darcy wasn't going to let this moment pass her by and to hell with the consequences.

With a muttered curse, she snaked her hand around his nape, pulled his head down, and kissed him.

———⁓⁓⁓———

This was *not* what he had planned.

Maybe it was what he had fantasized about, but this was not what he had planned.

But the instant Darcy's lips touched his, Ben was lost. From the first time he'd laid eyes on her, he'd wondered how she'd feel in his arms.

Now he knew. Amazing.

From the first time he'd watched her move, he'd wanted to know how she'd feel moving against him.

Now he knew. Incredible.

From the first time he'd seen her smile, he'd wanted to know what her lips would feel like as he kissed her.

Now he knew. Sexy as hell.

His arms banded around her waist until he made sure there wasn't even room for a breath between them. She went up on tiptoes to press even more intimately against him—which he totally appreciated—and it allowed his hands to linger and cup her denim-clad bottom.

And what a denim-clad bottom it was.

Gently, he squeezed it and even considered grabbing it harder and lifting her onto the counter, but he wasn't ready to let go of the full-body contact just yet.

It was insanity. One minute, she was frustrating the hell out of him in a nonsexual way, and the next, he was so consumed with need for her that he almost didn't recognize himself. This wasn't the man he normally was. He didn't pounce; he didn't even think of initiating anything physical in a situation that was so mundane.

And breakfast was pretty mundane.

When Ben chose to sleep with a woman, there was, well, there was a certain protocol to it for him. There were the required three dates. There was the kiss good night that would build in heat over the course of the dates, and then it was normally at her house. Never here. Never in his bed. His home was just that—his. It was his sanctuary, and he was possessive of it. But right now, all he wanted—almost more than his next breath—was to have Darcy in his bed.

Under him.

Over him.

Another growl escaped before he could stop it.

For a moment, he allowed his lips to leave hers, because he was desperate to taste her in other places. His mouth trailed along the delicate line of her jaw, her throat, and up to nip at her ear, a spot he quickly learned made her knees buckle and had her gasping.

*Good to know*.

But she wasn't having any of it for long. With her hand firmly anchored in his hair, she let him know the instant she wanted to kiss him again, and he went willingly. Over and over, his mouth slanted over hers until he thought he'd simply consume her. Tongue tangled with tongue. Breath mingled with breath. Never had the act of kissing seemed so carnal. So indecent and so damn erotic.

And that's when he knew standing at the kitchen sink

was no longer cutting it. He needed her. Wanted her. And from the sounds she was making and the way she was moving against him, Darcy felt it too.

This time when he reached down and cupped her ass, he lifted her up onto the counter. Stepping in close until he was firmly pressed against the juncture of her thighs, he cursed their clothes. Cursed the fact that the nearest soft surface was so damn far away. And cursed the fact that she tugged at his hair as she pulled away from him.

"Ben, wait," she panted.

Well, shit.

A little dazed, he forced himself to open his eyes and focus on her. Her lips were wet and red and a little swollen, and her skin was flushed.

So. Damn. Sexy.

Resting his forehead against hers, he took a minute to catch his breath.

Was he supposed to apologize? Step away and start shoveling? Hell if he knew, but he was going to stay quiet and let Darcy say whatever it was she was thinking. So he didn't move, and once his breathing was back to normal, he almost felt as if he was holding it.

"What are we doing?" she asked quietly.

Was she serious? Those were some fairly obvious moves going on, on both their parts. How could she be questioning it? And on top of that, she was the one who had initiated it. Lifting his head, he looked at her.

"I thought we were kissing," he said simply.

She blushed, and it was sexy as hell to see. His fingers twitched with the need to touch her cheeks and feel the heat there.

"I…I know, but…I guess I'm just a little confused as to where that all came from."

She was confused? Because now he was a little beyond that himself. Taking a step away, he frowned. "Why don't you tell me?" he began levelly. "Since you were the one who reached up and pulled me into the kiss in the first place."

The blush was instantly replaced by a look of mild annoyance. Darcy jumped from the counter, placing her hands on her hips. "I guess I got caught up in what I thought was a moment. I mean, you came over and crowded me into the cabinets and then started touching me—out of the blue, might I add—so I guess I thought you were into it too."

Oh yeah. He had forgotten about that part. Once she had reached up and kissed him, Ben had pretty much forgotten about his own actions leading up to it. "Fine. Yes. I came over here and—" He stopped and cursed, raking a hand through his hair. "I don't know. I've wanted to do that since you first showed up here."

Her eyes went wide. "Yesterday?"

He shook his head. "No. When you first showed up four days ago."

She blinked at him in confusion.

Taking a step toward her, he said her name. "I mean it. When you got out of the car, and I saw you for the first time, I thought—"

She held up a hand to stop him. "You know what? Don't. You don't need to say something you don't mean. It's okay. Really. It was probably a mistake. We should just forget about it."

"But I do mean—"

"You need to go out and shovel so you can get to your workshop, and I need to get this mess cleaned up." And instantly, she sprang into action. As she fluttered around rinsing dishes and placing them in the dishwasher, she chattered on almost without taking a breath.

"I was thinking of doing some baking while you're outside doing your thing, if that's all right. It will help pass the time. I saw you have all kinds of options for dinner, so if you have a preference, let me know, so I can take that out as well."

"Darcy…"

"Oh, and if it's all right with you, I'd like to do that load of laundry. You'll need to tell me where the laundry room is, and I meant what I said last night. I'll take care of anything else you have to put in as a way of saying thank you and so I'm not wasting the water on such a small load of clothes."

Ben watched in fascination as she moved around, and it seemed that in the blink of an eye, the kitchen was clean, and there was nothing but silence around them. And it was beyond awkward.

"Oh, and I'll probably work on the book stuff too at some point." She paused. "So is all that okay with you?" she finally asked after a long moment.

There was nothing wrong with anything she was asking of him. She wanted to bake? Great. He'd reap the benefits of it. She wanted to take something out for dinner? Wonderful. They were going to need to eat. She wanted to do some laundry? He had a couple of towels, a pair of jeans, and a shirt he could add to the load.

But none of this interested him. At all. He wanted to go back to talking about the kiss. Why was it a mistake?

Why did they have to forget about it? And why couldn't he just haul her into his arms and do it all again?

One look at her face, and he had his answer.

She wasn't comfortable with it.

And as much of a bastard as Ben knew he could be, the last thing he would ever do—ever!—was force himself on her. Or anyone. What had made their kiss so damn incredible was that it was mutual. The heat and the need was on both of them. But right now? The only thing coming from Darcy was a sense of vulnerability and uncertainty.

Not a good combination.

So he'd let this go.

For now.

Swallowing hard, he gave a quick nod. "Help yourself to anything you need." He looked around and let out a small sigh. "As for dinner, there're some steaks in the freezer, and we can do them on the grill like we did the other night. I don't mind using it in the snow. So if you're good with that, they would be my choice."

Darcy nodded.

"And as for the laundry, it's downstairs next to the office. I have some things I wouldn't mind tossing in, and I'll put them in the washing machine on my way out."

And before he did anything like beg and grovel for another taste, he simply walked away.

---

The laundry was going.

She'd made enough cookie dough for several dozen cookies *and* baked a cake.

And she was slowly losing her mind.

Yeah, her usual happy place—baking in the kitchen—was so *not* cutting it right now. She'd used up most of the basic ingredients and knew if she kept going, she was going to have to get creative. Why the hell had she stopped Ben earlier? Right now, she could be naked and satisfied in that amazing bed of his and feeling completely at peace, and instead, her fingers were coated in cookie dough and she was frustrated.

*Good plan, Darce.*

Okay, he'd scared her. Or maybe she'd scared herself. It was all just so intense. So…everything. She felt consumed and hot and bothered, and her heart had felt so damn full that she'd almost had a panic attack over the whole thing.

What the hell was that about?

Sex! She was just supposed to want sex! It would be a great way to pass the time, get out of her slump, and move on. Why had emotions gone and gotten in the way? Or worse, her heart. She wasn't *that* girl.

Or at least she had thought she wasn't that girl.

Rinsing her hands off, she walked over to the kitchen table and sat with a sigh. Wasn't this exactly what she had been worrying about a week ago at Riley's house? She wanted to feel like this. She wanted to be *wanted* like this.

She just didn't think she wanted it with Ben.

And what was so wrong with Ben?

*Um, the whole crush on Savannah thing*, she reminded herself. But then instantly, she pushed that aside. He had a point last night, and so did Anna. Darcy knew she was flirty with some of her guy friends, and it had nothing to do with being attracted to them.

Right now, she needed to come to grips with why she was being so closed-minded about Ben.

He was sexy, attractive, considerate—he had saved her from being stranded in an airport in a storm—and when she wasn't arguing with him and actually let herself relax and have a conversation with him, she found he was funny and someone she enjoyed talking to.

Looking around, she took in her surroundings and sighed. There was the whole he looked a little like a lumberjack and lived like a mountain man thing, but was that so bad? Probably not. She wasn't looking for forever with him. Maybe she was looking for a hot and heavy fling.

And boy, did she want to get flung.

For hours at a time.

And after discovering how Ben kissed and how she responded to those kisses, Darcy had no doubt that getting *flung* by him would be incredibly satisfying.

So how did she get them to that place? How did she approach him when he came inside after shoveling and let him know she would be agreeable to…flinging?

"Ugh," she murmured as the timer on the oven went off. Rising, she walked over to her baking station and started rolling the dough into little balls to place on the baking sheets. "I need to come up with a better metaphor than that."

Rather than obsess on euphemisms, she simply let herself get into the groove of getting the cookies formed and onto their sheets. It was mindless work and the perfect distraction at the moment. Once she had everything ready to go, she began placing things into the oven and setting timers and starting her cleanup.

This was good.

This was what she needed.

Part of the problem was that she'd stayed up late reading sexy snowed-in stories. It was feeding her imagination.

At least partly.

Ben being sexy as all get-out was feeding the rest.

And she was just going to have to wait and see what she could come up with where Ben was concerned.

# Chapter 5

THE DAMN SNOW JUST KEPT FALLING.

Every muscle in Ben's body ached, and he knew the only thing he was going to accomplish by staying outside was getting a case of hypothermia. With a sigh of disgust, he walked into the house. As much as he wanted to get at least a small path to the workshop, Mother Nature was refusing to cooperate, and he couldn't fight anymore.

Plus, he was too damn distracted to put the effort he needed into the task.

Darcy.

As soon as he closed the door behind him, it was like she was everywhere. The hum of the washing machine, the smell of freshly baked cookies... Even if he didn't know she was there, he would *know* she was there. It was a very domestic scene and one that should freak him out, and yet it didn't.

It comforted.

It soothed.

And dammit, he instantly had images of her waiting for him upstairs in nothing but an apron and maybe some lace and high heels and...

Where the hell did *that* come from?

"I'm losing my damn mind," he muttered as he slowly peeled off his snow-covered coat and gloves. His hands were mildly numb, his jeans were soaked, and it was almost painful to sit on the bench to pull off his boots.

"Hey, I was… *Oh my God!* Are you okay?" Darcy cried as she stepped into the mud room. She instantly dropped to her knees in front of him and swatted his hands away from his boots. "Let me do that."

Ben was too tired to argue. If anything, he suddenly felt more fatigued than he had a minute ago. Leaning against the wall, he let her remove his boots, and then she did the same for his socks.

"You are soaked to the skin! What were you thinking?"

"I was trying…I needed to…" Hell, even speaking felt like it required a herculean effort.

Slowly, she pulled him to his feet. "Come on. Use the shower here, and get warmed up. I'll go upstairs and get you dry clothes and make you something hot to drink. Just please go and get under the hot water or something." She led him into the bathroom and had the shower turned on before he could respond. Steam began to fill the room.

"Do you need any help?" she asked, but he heard the hesitation in her voice. A few minutes ago, his answer would have been an enthusiastic "Hell yes," but right now, all he could do was shake his head. "I'll be right back," she said and then fled from the room, closing the door behind her.

It took him longer than he would have liked, but he stripped and stepped under the shower spray. It stung like a son of a bitch, but it didn't take long for him to adjust and simply relax. Damn. What had he been thinking? He'd purposely stayed out there longer than he knew he should have, and he could have hurt himself because of it.

And for what? Because he was hiding from a beautiful woman?

Yeah. That made sense.

He lathered up and rinsed off and simply gave himself the chance to enjoy the water before he shut it off. It
was amazing how much better he felt. Reaching out, he
found two towels stacked on the vanity, grabbed one of
them, and began to dry off. Darcy knocked softly on the
door, and for a moment, Ben froze.

"Ben? Are you okay?"

"I'm good," he replied, his voice a little gruff.

"I…I have some dry clothes for you. I'll leave them
outside the door."

Actually, he had been hoping she'd come into the room,
but he supposed it wasn't the best time for that. "Thanks."

He waited a few minutes before stepping out of the
shower and getting the clothes. When he opened the
door, he had no idea where she was, and he didn't linger
to find out. He grabbed the clothes and got dressed.
When he stepped out of the bathroom, he headed for
the stairs. But then he stopped when he heard a noise in
his office.

Stepping into the doorway, he froze.

It was clean and organized and…

And that's when he spotted Darcy sitting on the floor
in the corner, sorting through a pile of paperwork.

"What the hell are you doing?"

She looked up at him as if he were crazy. "What does
it look like? I'm organizing your office."

Ben stepped into the room and began to look around
frantically. "Darcy, you can't…you shouldn't…dammit!"
He raked a hand through his damp hair in frustration.

"You have no idea what I do or how I want it done. How the hell am I supposed to find anything now?"

Rising with a sigh, she walked over to his desk. "First of all, this is my thing."

"No," he interrupted. "It's not. This is my office. My business. My stuff."

She looked over her shoulder at him and rolled her eyes. "I didn't mean it like that, doofus. What I meant is organizing office stuff is my thing. I've done it for my dad and his business and helped my brother Aidan with his business too." She shrugged. "It comes naturally to me."

Walking over to stand beside her, Ben rested a hip on the desk and tried to control the rage he felt. "Darcy, you had no right to come in here and touch anything. I had it under control. Somewhat. I mean, I know it needed to be organized, but everything was in a place where I knew where it was."

The look she gave him showed she knew he was lying. "Really? And you feel like your system was working for you?"

Now he had to try to save face, so he crossed his arms over his chest and nodded. "Yup."

"Okay, then," she began, and he knew instantly she was prepared for this response from him. "So tell me this—were you aware that you have not one, not two, but three checks for large amounts of money sitting on your desk that you have yet to deposit?"

"Three?"

"One of them is dated over a month ago," she said, picking it up and waving it at him. "This check is for almost ten grand. Are you telling me you are *so* financially secure you can afford to have this much money sitting here collecting dust?"

"Well, no. But—"

"And this one is for eight, and the third is for about five. So you're looking at over twenty grand sitting on your desk because you couldn't take the time to do your paperwork or go to the bank."

"It isn't any of your business," he snapped.

"And then there's the phone."

He sort of stopped and stared at her for a minute. "The phone?"

She nodded. "It rings. A lot."

He groaned, almost growled. "Please tell me you didn't answer the phone."

"Of course I did. It wouldn't stop, and it was getting annoying."

Straightening to his full height, he towered over her in hopes of intimidating her.

It didn't work.

"Oh please. I have five brothers who are all as big as you. Save the effort," she quipped. "Anyway, you had three calls from people looking to have you do work for them—new homes, unique pieces, blah, blah, blah. I told them you were booked well into next year, and if they were interested to email you their specs, and when you had a free moment, you'd look at them."

"Darcy—"

"But the phone was not the best way to reach you," she went on. "They all thanked me and mentioned they had each left several messages for you that you haven't returned."

"I listened to the messages."

"When?" she asked with a knowing grin.

What was the point in all this, he wondered. "So now they're all going to email me?"

She nodded.

"I won't get to the emails any faster than the phone messages," he told her, feeling he had trumped her in some way.

"Sure you will. You can check email on your phone. Set a reminder on it for each day at a certain time, and see what's new in your inbox. I can help you with that if you don't know how. It will only take a few minutes, and you can start getting caught up so you don't get so behind again."

"I'm not behind—"

"You are so totally behind that it's not even funny," she said and then laughed for emphasis. "Besides the checks, I saw several of the invoices for work you're currently doing. They had notes on them—I'm assuming from you—and they're not closed out." She picked up several papers from his desk and held them up to show him. "And from the dates on them, they are close to being due. I haven't seen any updates on either paper or your computer or—"

"You went on my computer?" he yelled and then had to step away from her because he was ready to throttle her. "Do you have any concept of boundaries?"

"Of course I do," she said mildly and began stacking up the papers she had showed him and putting them in neat piles. "The system you use isn't very complicated, and if you want my opinion—"

"I don't."

"—you need a better program for keeping track of all

this stuff. Something where you can incorporate not only your specs and design and notes but also the financials. I think I can find one that will work for you and won't be hard for you to use. Are you good with computer stuff?"

Was she serious? Didn't she see how he was using a Word document for everything? Of course he wasn't good with computer stuff. He didn't *want* to be good with computer stuff. Hell, the last thing in the world he wanted to do was computer stuff.

"By your lack of response and the scowl on your face, I have my answer," she observed. "So I'll make a note to find something very basic."

"Darcy, I don't want you finding a program for me. I don't want you cleaning the office for me. I don't want to *change* the way I do things. And finally, I don't want anyone touching my stuff. You have the book to work on. That's it. The rest of this is off-limits. Do you understand?" Ben was almost breathless by the time he got all that out, and he let out a ragged sigh and went back to leaning against the desk. And instantly regretted his outburst.

The room did look a hell of a lot better than it had hours ago.

He had forgotten about those checks.

And really, this was one big mess that he no longer had to deal with.

So why was he so upset, again?

When he dared to look over at Darcy, he expected to see defiance. Or outrage. Or anger.

He didn't expect to see hurt or those big, beautiful eyes filled with tears.

*Shit.*

He instantly straightened and went to go to her, but Darcy quickly swiped at her eyes and turned away.

"You know what? You're right. I'm sorry. This was all very presumptuous of me. I...I was bored, and I thought you wouldn't mind me coming in here and doing this. I could tell you were overwhelmed with all of it, and I just wanted to help. I'm sorry."

"Darcy. No. I—"

"It's okay. Really. I...I need to go and make a call. I'll see you at dinner," she said as she brushed past him and walked out of the room.

Ben's immediate reaction was to let her go, give them each time to cool down before he apologized.

"Screw that," he murmured and went after her.

She must have run up the stairs, because he didn't catch her on the flight up to the main floor, and by the time he was at the foot of the stairs to the second floor, he heard her bedroom door close. He took the stairs two at a time, and at her door, he didn't even knock.

Maybe it was rude, or maybe it was his turn to be presumptuous, but he didn't care. Darcy Shaughnessy had been turning his life upside down for the better part of a week, and he was tired of it.

Tired of the constant roller coaster of emotion.

Tired of second-guessing himself.

And so damn tired of simply fighting with her. And himself.

She gasped when the door flew open, and she turned to face him. But she said nothing. Good. He didn't want her to talk. Didn't want to hear what she was thinking right now. He wanted to say what he had to say and then deal with the fallout.

"I was wrong," he said, his voice strong and firm. "What you did down there was…it was exactly what I needed and didn't want to admit I needed. I don't like asking for help. I don't like *needing* help," he corrected. "Every day, I tell myself I can do it all, and every day, I know I'm lying."

One lone tear trailed down her cheek, and it nearly brought Ben to his knees. But he stayed where he was, because touching her right now would certainly be too much of a temptation.

"I don't know what it is about you that makes me react the way I do. I'm normally a little more civilized. I know you might not believe that, and the history you have of me would certainly be in opposition to that statement, but… I may not be the most eloquent man or the most polished, but for crying out loud, I never argue with someone the way I do with you." He paused. "You make me crazy, and I have no idea why."

They were silent for a moment, and Ben hoped she would say something. Respond in some way so he had a clue about where he stood.

Finally, she did. She wiped a hand across her cheek, and her voice was so small, so quiet, he almost didn't hear her. "It's me," she said. "It seems to be the way most people react to me." She shrugged and looked at the floor. "I don't know why. I don't know why I bring that side out in people, and I wish I didn't. I didn't mean to upset you. I thought I was doing something good. Something nice. I thought I was helping."

She was gutting him, and she didn't even know it, he thought.

Unable to help himself, he moved closer. And kept

moving until he was able to wrap her in his arms and simply hold her close. He felt her shuddery sigh as she relaxed against him, and God, if she didn't feel good. He kissed the top of her head and simply enjoyed the feel of her in his embrace.

He looked around the room, unable to believe the transformation it underwent in less than twenty-four hours. She had stuff on every surface—jewelry, lotions, scarves. On the nightstand was a stack of paperback books and a tablet. But most of all, the room smelled of her perfume. Of her.

At that moment, he could have easily tilted her head and kissed her senseless. It was what he wanted more than anything. He wanted the woman he had tasted earlier, the woman who had both melted and ignited in his arms. It would be so easy to do, and there was a bed not even five feet away.

But instead, he decided that it wasn't the right time.

"What kind of cookies did you bake?" he asked softly.

Darcy lifted her head from his chest. "What?"

"The whole house smells like freshly baked cookies. Tell me what you made," he said with a lopsided grin.

"Well, I made chocolate chip, peanut butter, and chocolate spice, and then I baked a cake."

His smile grew. "What kind of cake?"

"It's a good one—devil's food. You had about three boxes of it, so I figured you must like it."

"It's my favorite." He paused and studied her face. "Which icing did you use?"

"I went for the overkill," she said with a hint of sass. "The milk chocolate. You had many, many, many cans of it."

"Sometimes I eat it right out of the can."

"A man after my own heart," she teased, and then it didn't feel quite so much like teasing. The atmosphere in the room changed in a heartbeat.

There wasn't a doubt in his mind that if he leaned in and kissed her, he'd get the exact response he most wanted from her.

And he still opted to be the gentleman.

"Let's go and have a slice," he said as he took her hand in his and led her from the room.

---

The instant Ben's hand wrapped around hers, Darcy's decision was made.

There would be cake.

Later.

They walked slowly to the kitchen, and as she made her way over to the island to go through the motions of serving them each up a slice, Ben didn't let go of her hand. Finally, she looked at him, one hand on the plate, the other in his, and one brow arched. "I'm going to need that," she said with a sexy grin.

Never before had the slide of a finger across her palm felt so erotic.

Lethal.

The man was positively lethal.

She took the lid off the cake plate and revealed her chocolate masterpiece. It seriously looked good and, well, maybe a little taste right now wouldn't be the *worst* thing in the world they could do.

Just as she was about to turn to grab plates and forks, she saw Ben move. One arm snaked out as he swiped a finger across the top of the cake, effectively grabbing a large dollop of icing. Darcy's eyes immediately met his, even as her heart simply kicked hard in her chest.

Ben's gaze—more heated than she'd ever seen it— told her exactly what he wanted from her, and right now, Darcy was more than willing to give it.

Leaning forward, she let her tongue trace the line of his finger before she took a taste of the sweet confection he was offering. It was a little bit of sensory overload—the saltiness of his skin, the sweetness of the chocolate, the heat of it all—and it left her breathless. When she looked up at Ben's face, his eyes were closed, and she could feel him vibrating with a low moan of pleasure.

She knew exactly how he felt, because she was feeling it too.

When he opened his eyes, he gently pulled his hand away from her and finished the rest of the icing that was on his finger, and then it was Darcy's turn to moan.

"Next time I taste that," he said thickly, "it will be to lick it off you."

And that was all she could take.

Later, it would be hard to say who made the first move, and honestly, she didn't care. All she knew was that Ben's arms were around her, his mouth was on hers, and everything suddenly felt right with the universe. He lifted her, and Darcy wrapped her legs around him. Without a word, he immediately began to walk toward his bedroom, and all she could think was *yes*. With her hands anchored in his hair and her legs locked around his waist, every move kept them close.

The friction was delicious.

As if in the distance, she heard the bedroom door close, and for a second, she could almost see him kicking it shut. At the side of the bed, he didn't so much as lay her down as he simply followed her to the mattress. One minute, they were upright, and the next, they weren't. Ben stretched on top of her; the full-body contact was even better than she could have ever imagined. He was so big and hard and strong, and yet he was so careful not to crush her.

But then he moved, and Darcy had no choice but to open her eyes. He was sitting up, straddling her, as he unbuttoned the flannel shirt he was wearing. Her hands twitched to help him or to rip the shirt open herself, but his gaze held her pinned in place. He peeled it away and revealed a thermal shirt under it, and she almost couldn't help but laugh at her frustration at all the layers he was wearing. As if reading her mind, he began to chuckle too.

"Had I known this was happening when I got dressed, I would have skipped a layer."

"Good to know," she replied breathlessly and silently cheered that she had far less to remove when they got started.

As soon as the thermal was gone, Darcy reached up to touch him. She wanted to sit up and kiss his chest, which was perfectly sculpted, but his position on her prevented that. So she squirmed enough to make him shift, and once she could move, she immediately began raining kisses on his heated skin. Ben fisted her hair in his hand and gave her a minute before he gently tugged her head away.

"One of us is still overdressed," he growled.

It was on the tip of her tongue to say they both were. He had only taken his shirt off. She wanted—needed—more skin-to-skin contact. Without even thinking, Darcy reached down and tugged her sweater up and over her head and flung it across the room. Ben's nostrils flared, and for a moment, she regretted not letting him be the one to remove it.

His hand left her hair and immediately came around to cup her breast.

"I pictured you in lace earlier," he said as he watched his hand move over her curves.

"Really?"

He nodded. "When I came in from shoveling and the whole house smelled of your baking, I imagined you in an apron and lace and stilettos."

She smiled up at him mischievously. "That's a pretty specific image."

He nodded again. "And if there were any way to make it happen right now, I'd take you out to the kitchen and do it."

The wheels in her mind were already spinning.

"No stilettos," she replied with a pout. "But every-thing else…"

Ben seemed to be considering it but then shook his head as he gently pushed her onto her back and stretched out over her. "Later," he said as he lowered his head to her breast. "Much, much later."

---

Darcy was sprawled on her stomach beside him as Ben traced lazy circles on her back. All he could think of was how soft her skin was.

And how she had completely rocked his world and turned it upside down.

Her eyes were closed, and he had a sneaking suspicion she was asleep, but he didn't want to say or do anything to break the mood or the silence. And honestly, he needed a moment to wrap his brain around everything that had happened.

It wasn't as if he was a virgin or a prude, but sex for him was more of a...well, it was a good and pleasurable act. End of story. What he'd experienced with Darcy was all of that and...damn. He didn't even have something to compare it to.

Under his touch, she slowly stretched and made a low humming sound.

And just like that, he was turned on again.

Darcy turned her head and looked at him with a sleepy smile.

He was in serious trouble.

"Hey," she said softly.

"Hey, yourself." Without thinking, Ben simply shifted them until she rolled over and was tucked in at his side. There was so much he wanted to say and yet not say. The silence was comfortable, and honestly, he was already letting his hands roam up and down her back and her arms, and the softness of her skin was enough to entrance him.

With a small kiss on his chest, she looked up at him. "So..."

Clearly, she was a talker. But rather than respond, Ben arched a brow at her and waited.

She settled against him. "I guess you liked the cake, huh?"

That was the last thing he expected her to say, and he lost it—completely laughed out loud. When he felt her body shaking with laughter beside him, he decided Darcy Shaughnessy brought something to his life he hadn't realized he'd been missing.

Excitement.

Laughter.

Joy.

"Technically," he began after a moment, "I never got to taste it."

"There was the icing," she corrected. "And you did mention how you tend to eat more of that than anything."

"It's really good icing."

Shaking her head, she made a tsking sound. "Clearly, you've never had real icing."

Ben lifted his head and looked at her. "Are you telling me there is something *better* out there than icing in a can? Because I'm finding it hard to believe. That's been my dirty little secret for years."

In a move he didn't see coming, she chuckled and then shifted to straddle him until they were chest to chest. "*That's* your dirty little secret?" She shook her head. "We're going to have to work on that."

Now it was his turn to shake his head. "Uh-uh. That's the extent of keeping secrets for me." His tone went serious, more so than he had intended. "I don't do secrets. My life is an open book. I enjoy my privacy, but what you see is what you get with me. No lies. No pretense." He paused. "No games."

The playful expression was gone as she considered him.

"I wanted you from the first moment I saw you," he said, carefully watching her reaction. "It bothered the hell out of me when your attitude toward me changed, but it didn't stop the want."

"So this was to prove—"

"No," he immediately interrupted with an edge to his voice. "This wasn't about proving anything. This happened because I find you fascinating and beautiful and sexy as hell. This happened because you're all I've been able to think about." One hand anchored in her tousled hair and gripped it lightly. "And it's going to happen again, because I love the way you feel in my arms and when you're completely wrapped around me."

He pulled her head down and kissed her with a ferocity he didn't recognize in himself. And when they broke apart, panting, Ben positioned her so her forehead rested against his.

"And I love the sounds you make," he stated. "And I want to hear them again."

Darcy's gasp was soft, her eyes wide. Ben could tell she was trying to come up with something to say, but he didn't want that. He didn't want her coming up with something she thought she should say—he wanted her honesty. The kind of thing that would simply slip out unfiltered.

So rather than wait, he kissed her again. Rolled her beneath him.

And did his best to keep her from thinking of anything other than him for the next several hours.

———

"And you're sure you're fine? I mean, I know it's got to be weird and all."

Darcy looked across the room to where Ben was sitting and reading later that night and had to stop herself from sighing happily. He was in a pair of faded jeans and nothing else, and there was a roaring fire beside him, and all she could think was *yum*.

"Uh, Darce? You there?"

Oh. Right. Riley was on the phone.

"I'm fine. And this is way better than being stranded at the airport," she said lightly. "I've done some reading, I've baked—"

"I feel guilty," he said miserably.

Just then, Ben looked up and smiled at her—a sexy smile—and she could feel herself blushing. "Well, you shouldn't."

"What's going on with you?" he demanded.

"What do you mean?"

"That was the perfect opening for you to throw a guilt trip at me. You never miss an opportunity to do that. If you have to, speak in code. If you're in danger, say something about…wildflowers. If you're hurt, say something about salmon. Or…or if you need me to send in an emergency helicopter, say something about… about…*shit*! Say something!"

"Are you having a stroke?" Darcy asked mildly. "Because you sound like you're stroking out."

Riley muttered a curse. "Look, I'll admit sending you to Washington seemed like fun, but I had no idea you'd get stuck there. I've met Ben, and I like him, and I'm sure you're fine, but…I don't know. You seem distracted."

He had no idea.

"I'm fine. The snow is still coming down, and honestly, I gave up trying to watch the forecast. It will end when it will end, and then I'll deal with finding a flight home." She shrugged even though she knew he couldn't see her. "And I'm willing to wait a few days, because I know there are going to be thousands of people trying to do the same thing. Dad knows I'm safe, and Aidan doesn't need me at the office, so I can let the masses deal with the craziness first."

"So you're going to go home and not come back to us?"

"By the time I can leave here, it would almost be pointless to add an extra leg to the trip. We'll catch up at Christmas, right?"

"Absolutely," he said, and Darcy could almost hear the smile in his voice. "Savannah and I tossed around the idea of not going home for Christmas, but how could we miss it? Aislynn should spend it with all of her cousins, and I think it's going to be amazing to have everyone together under one roof."

"And crowded," she joked.

"Well, we won't all be sleeping under one roof. Aidan and Quinn have houses close to Dad's, so we can spread out at night. But think of Christmas morning with all of the kids!"

She couldn't help but laugh. "It's going to be wild, that's for sure. Dad's so excited about it, and he's been in such a better mood since he and Martha got back together. Longest three months of my life."

"I know. I was talking to him earlier, and you're right. He sounds good. Content. Not that he was ever not, but I know their breakup was a little hard on him."

"It was. And as much as we all reminded him that, you know, he hadn't dated anyone in over thirty years and not all couples stay together forever, I could tell he missed her. She's so good for him, and I hope they do stay together forever. He deserves to be happy again."

"It's still a little weird," Riley said cautiously. "I
know you don't understand it, but—"

"I get it. I do. But the fact remains that Dad is entitled
to a life of his own where he's just Ian Shaughnessy and
not everyone's dad. You all moved on and had relationships, and you don't think it was hard on him?"

"It's not the same, Darce."

"Maybe not exactly, but he had to get used to his
children becoming adults and starting lives of their own.
We need to respect him and allow him to have a life of
his own. And if that life involves someone other than
Mom, then we need to let that happen."

"Wow. When did you become the voice of reason?"
Riley mused. "I think the mountain air is getting to you."

"I have my moments," she replied and smiled when
Ben winked at her. "So, um…yeah, everything's good.
I'm fine and I'll let you know when the weather breaks
and I'm heading home, okay?"

"Behave yourself. Don't give Ben any grief. Please,"
he teased.

It would have been very easy to get into a debate on
her giving people grief, but Darcy was done talking to
her brother. What she wanted most was to be off the
phone so she could crawl into Ben's lap and make love
in front of the fire.

"No worries," she said distractedly. "Give Aislynn a
kiss for me, and I'll talk to you soon."

And with that, she hung up. But she didn't move right
away. Instead, she let herself relax in the oversized chair
and look her fill.

Ben's admission earlier about wanting her from the first
moment he saw her was a heady thing. No one had ever

admitted to wanting her like that, and Darcy had to admit she liked it. And now that she had a moment, she also had to admit there were a lot of things she liked about Ben.

A. Lot.

How could she have misjudged him so badly?

Maybe misjudged wasn't the right word, but when she moved beyond those initial concerns about him and Savannah—which she knew would always lurk in the recesses of her mind, no matter what—at the core of it all, Ben was an incredible man.

And an incredible lover.

It didn't take long for Darcy to realize she'd merely been with immature men, practically boys, up until now. The skill and attention Ben put into making love to her? Her skin was still hot and tingly from it. Sex with a man who knew what he was doing was fan-freaking-tastic.

"What are you smiling about?" Ben asked from across the room.

Why keep it to herself? "Thinking about you."

His smile grew as he put his book aside and studied her. "Anything in particular about me?"

"A whole lot of particulars," she replied, rising from her chair. All she was wearing was his flannel shirt, and even though it was big enough to hit her midthigh and be a dress, she still felt sexy in it as she slinked across the room toward him. Playing the seductress was never something she excelled at, but watching Ben's eyes heat up the closer she got? Um, yeah. She could totally get on board with doing more of this.

Ben shifted on the sofa so Darcy could place her knees on either side of him, and as she rested her hands on his bare shoulders and moved in close, she hummed with pleasure. One of his arms banded around her waist to hold her to him.

"You're looking pleased with yourself," he said as his gaze zeroed in on her lips.

"I was enjoying the way you were looking at me."

He gave a low chuckle as he reached up and unbuttoned the top button of her shirt. "And I was enjoying watching you," he replied, toying with the next button. "Plus, you look good in my shirt."

That made her smile. "I have to admit, this is the first time I've worn flannel, and so far, I'm enjoying it."

Ben laughed again. "Sweetheart, I have a whole closet of it, and I think you should wear nothing but this until the snow clears."

"I thought you mentioned something about an apron and some lace?" she couldn't help but tease.

"Hmm, I don't know. I think watching you walk around in my shirt pretty much pushed all those other images aside."

She tilted her head to the side with a dramatic sigh. "Damn. And I was thinking of making dinner like that."

"I'll make you a deal. Tonight we can do flannel, and tomorrow, we'll reconsider our options."

A throaty laugh was her immediate response. "Oh, we will, will we?"

The hand that was still in her hair tightened slightly, and Ben's smile turned a little bit predatory. "Definitely."

Right then and there, she would have agreed to anything just to hear that deep growl in his voice and to keep that look on his face. Squirming slightly in his lap, Darcy let out a low moan of her own before agreeing with him. "Okay."

The word was barely out of her mouth when Ben captured her lips with his. God, she loved how he did that—swooped in with no warning and devoured. So damn good. She kissed him with equal need, heat, and hunger. Tongues dueled and tangled. Hands scraped and scratched and soothed. Over and over until Ben lifted her and maneuvered them until Darcy was on her back on the sofa.

She almost wept with gratitude when his body covered hers.

Legs wrapped around his waist as he yanked the flannel open—sending buttons flying in every direction. Darcy cried out as his mouth left hers to latch onto her breast.

So good.

Her head turned to the side as she panted his name, and when she opened her eyes, all she could see was the snow falling. In the darkness with only one light on out on the deck, it was a complete whiteout.

And all she could think was how if she had her way, it would go on snowing forever.

---

After lunch the next day, Darcy was in Ben's office. He had finally cleared a path to the workshop—after they had worked together to make it happen—and Ben was working on one of his sculptures. Not that she minded. Right now, the silence and the time alone felt like a good thing.

She was tired and sore in the most delicious of ways, and she respected the fact that he needed to work. After they'd made love on the sofa the previous day, Ben had made dinner for her and then taken her back to bed.

And she seriously loved his bed.

Besides the incredible amount of detail in that particular piece of furniture, which still amazed her, his bed was beyond comfortable. She'd slept like a baby. When Ben had let her sleep. Just thinking about all the times they'd woken each other up in the night had her feeling all warm and tingly.

A feeling that was almost a constant where he was concerned.

Filing away the last stack of paperwork, Darcy looked around with a sense of accomplishment. The office looked amazing. And organized. Before Ben had gone out to the workshop, she had asked him if she could finish what she'd started the day before. He apologized profusely for the way he had reacted, and looking back, she completely understood why he had said the things he'd said. She had overstepped the boundaries, and even though her heart was in the right place, it didn't mean that others would take it the same way.

Lesson learned.

With all the surface areas cleared along with the floor, Darcy made quick work of dusting and vacuuming. Once that was complete, she sat at the desk and went online to research computer programs to help Ben out, something she had gotten his permission for as well.

An hour later, her eyes were starting to cross from staring at the computer screen for so long. Standing up, she stretched and decided to go upstairs and grab something to drink. The view out the back windows when she got up there showed that it was snowing again. There had been about two hours after breakfast where it had finally stopped, and there was well over two feet of snow already on the ground.

Maybe the thought of more snow should have bothered her, but it didn't. If anything, it had the complete opposite effect on her. It made her happy. The longer it snowed—the more accumulation there was—the longer she could stay in this amazing little cocoon she and Ben had created. Of course, there was a very real possibility Ben wasn't feeling quite the same way, but she had a sneaking suspicion he did.

He was intense. In everything he did, and even though she could see it and knew how he sometimes fought it, it made him the man he was. He was interesting and funny and talented and... She sighed.

He was a perfectly flawed man.

That description made her smile, because she knew he wouldn't appreciate the title, but it was true. He wasn't perfect—no one was—but the man he was *was* perfect in his own way because of those flaws.

"Yikes," she murmured as she put the kettle on to boil. "I am making no sense whatsoever."

She moved around the kitchen and grabbed a mug and a tea bag and then went to look out the window as she waited for the water to boil. Her eyes immediately went to the workshop. Should she bring Ben something to drink? Eat? Would he get upset if she disturbed him while he was working? These were things she needed to know. The last thing she wanted to do was upset him, and she knew he was used to being here alone without any disruptions.

But she missed him. Wanted to see him and talk to him.

Behind her, the kettle came to a boil. With a small

sigh, she made her tea and then sat at the kitchen table and contemplated her options. She was curious about Ben's work. Sure, she'd seen pictures, and looking around his house, she saw what he was capable of, but the thought of being in the workshop and seeing him work and watching him create made her feel a little giddy.

"Okay, stop obsessing and just go," she muttered. It didn't take long to make a travel mug of coffee for Ben and transfer her tea to one as well. Then she grabbed a small container and put a variety of cookies in it. "Who doesn't enjoy a good coffee break, right?"

Practically skipping down the stairs, excitement bubbled up in her. She slipped her boots on and then her coat and stepped outside. It was freezing cold. A shiver racked her body, and she made quick work of following the path to the workshop.

She knocked lightly before opening the door and peeking inside. Ben was standing on the far side of the room staring at the sculpture in front of him. Quietly, she came into the room and closed the door behind her, but she didn't go to him. If anything, she wanted to wait and see if he noticed her and if he would welcome her.

While she waited, Darcy scanned the room. There was a huge variety of tools; some were large machines like saws and sanders, and there was an entire wall of hand tools. The smell of sawdust was a little overwhelming but not unpleasant. On a table, she spotted a sculpture of an eagle. Its wings were spread, and it stood easily three feet tall and equally wide. The details were so true, so spectacular, that she wanted to reach out and touch it, even as she was afraid it would fly away. "Holy crap," she whispered.

"Was that a good holy crap or a bad one?" Ben said from across the room.

Looking over at him, Darcy couldn't help but smile. "Holy crap good," she replied. "That eagle is…it's breathtaking, Ben." She wanted to go to him but was still afraid to move around in his space.

Without a word, he gave a nod and then looked at the sculpture in front of him—a ten-point deer bust. She was a little confused—most people who hung those in their homes were hunters. Why would someone want a wood sculpture of a deer rather than one they had killed?

"Come here," he commanded softly.

Swallowing, Darcy carefully made her way across the room. There was sawdust on the floor, and she was afraid to get too close to the power tools. When she was at his side, she handed him the mug of coffee.

"Thank you," he said before leaning in and kissing her distractedly, his eyes almost never leaving the deer. "What do you think of this?"

Shit. The last thing she wanted to do was critique his work, even if it was amazing.

"I brought you some cookies too," she said instead. "You know, in case you were hungry and ready for a break."

Ben took the tin from her hands and placed it on the workbench beside him.

"Darcy—"

"I know you missed several days of work and might not stop what you're doing to get something to eat or drink. I didn't want to bother you though. Kind of agonized over whether I should come out here. But then I thought I could drop off the coffee and cookies and go and leave you be and—"

"Darcy—"

"I've got a stew going in the Dutch oven. It's starting to smell really good in there. Maybe I'll bake some biscuits or something," she said and then chanced a look at him. "That will work, right?"

Ben sighed and took a sip of his coffee, and she couldn't tell if he was annoyed or amused with her ramblings.

"Maybe I'll see if you have the makings for some bread. I can make bread bowls! Ooh, those are great with stew. I should have thought of that sooner. Bread can take a while and—"

"So you're not going to answer my question," he stated, effectively interrupting her.

Her shoulders sagged with defeat. "I don't know. Maybe."

"Why?" he asked. There was no accusation or condemnation in his tone; he seemed genuinely curious.

She shrugged.

Putting his mug down, Ben faced her, tucked a finger under her chin, and gently forced her to look at him. "What do you think of this deer?"

She looked at him for a moment and then at the bust. "Can I ask you something first?"

He nodded.

"Why would someone want a bust of a deer made of wood? Don't hunters usually want these things to be the actual ones they've killed?"

He nodded again. "Normally? Yes. This particular client is married to a woman who refuses to allow it. She does not want dead animals hanging in the house.

Personally, I don't blame her. So they've compromised. He can have a trophy room, but the trophies need to be sculpted. I've done several pieces for them already. He doesn't hunt anymore, but he liked the idea of adding exotic animals to the collection just for the beauty of them. I thought it would be ridiculous, but when I saw the room put together with the first few busts, I got the vision and understood what he was doing."

"That sounds kind of cool."

"I have pictures I could show you."

Her eyes lit up. "I would love that!"

"After you answer the question."

Well, damn.

Stepping away from his touch, she faced the sculpture. He wanted her opinion? He wanted to know what she thought? Then so be it. She studied it and moved from side to side to take it all in and then turned to him.

"It's scary."

Ben's brows furrowed. "Scary?"

She nodded. "I look at this, and like the eagle, it seems real. I mean, I can tell it's wood, but the amount of detail you've put into it just makes it feel like it's a living thing. I almost feel like I can count the hairs on it or that I can see it breathing. It's incredible." She looked at him and smiled. "I've seen pictures of your work, but none did them justice. There is no way anyone could appreciate the amount of work you put into your pieces unless they see them in person."

Silence.

*Uh-oh.*

Reaching out, she touched the deer. "I never appreciated the texture of wood. Back up at the house, I find myself walking around and touching all the furniture because it feels so amazing. Right now, as I'm touching this piece? I don't feel wood. I feel an animal's coat. I mean, how do you do that? How does a person learn to create something that is so lifelike?" Her smile faded slightly. "That's such a gift. I have met a lot of talented people—talented artists—but this, Ben? This is just…" She paused. "Seriously, I have no words. I'm in awe of what you can do and—"

She didn't get to say another word, because Ben hauled her to him and silenced her with a kiss.

He took the cup of tea from her hands without breaking contact with her and put it next to his coffee. The second her hands were free, she raked them up into his hair. On and on and on, he kissed her until she almost couldn't breathe. When he finally lifted his head, she was dazed.

"Wow."

He nodded. "Yeah."

"Not that I'm complaining, but what was that for?"

Resting his forehead against hers, he took a minute to catch his breath. "For years, I've listened to people talk about my work. I've listened to the praise and the critiques, and most of the time, I let it all roll off me. Mainly because their opinions didn't matter. But standing here watching you and listening to you? I wanted to know what you thought, and I was even a little nervous that you wouldn't like it."

"Are you serious? How could I not like it?" she asked incredulously. "Look at this!"

He chuckled softly and then shrugged. "It felt good to hear such honesty from someone I respect."

A lump formed in her throat that almost choked her. He respected her? That was…it was…

"No one's ever said that to me before," she admitted softly, and she hated the slight tremble in her voice. "People let me talk or ask for my opinion, but most of the time, it doesn't seem to matter."

Caressing her cheek, he said, "It matters to me."

His admission felt better to her than it probably should—it made her heart skip a beat, and her entire being felt lighter. "Thank you."

Darcy was more than happy to stay like that—close— for as long as Ben wanted to hold her. In the past, she tended to fall hard and fast for the wrong guy. But this felt different.

It felt deeper. Serious. And more mature. Ben wasn't a frat boy; he was a man.

And what a man.

That almost had her sighing giddily, but she didn't want to ruin the moment. Which was still going on, and they were both still quiet.

"So," she said softly.

"So," he repeated.

"I should probably let you get to work. Or at least have your coffee break."

Lifting his head, Ben gave her a mischievous smile. "I have a better idea."

She knew that look.

She *loved* that look.

"I'm listening."

A delicious little shiver went along her spine as Ben's hands cupped her bottom and lifted her. He placed her on the workbench and stepped between her legs. She didn't think a workshop could be sexy, and yet some-how, he managed to make that work too.

"The smell of sawdust turn you on?" she teased.

"*You* turn me on."

Yeah, she was pretty much a goner.

"Is this like the apron and lace and stilettos fantasy?"

He shook his head. "No."

Studying him, Darcy hoped he would explain a little bit more.

"It's better," he growled before leaning in and kissing her. It was deep and wet and over way too fast when he lifted his head. "I've had a hard time getting things done on the sculpture today because I kept picturing you here. Everywhere I looked, I could see you."

When he said things like that, Darcy had no idea what to do, what to say. All she knew was she was cursing the fact that they were still dressed.

"I know it's dirty in here, and there's sawdust all over the place, but..." His gaze met hers—hot and intense. "Let me. Just let me, Darcy."

Far be it from her to argue.

—⁓—

Three days. Darcy had been in his home for three days, and neither of them seemed to be in any rush for her to leave. Ben's first thought was that he should be a little more alarmed by that, but really, he wasn't. He liked having her there. He liked having someone to talk to when he was done working for the day and to share meals with.

He liked how she was already putting her stamp around his home—from the baked goods all over the kitchen, to her romance novels on the nightstand and coffee table, to her clothes scattered on his bedroom floor.

And he'd be a complete liar if he said he wasn't enjoying the hell out of the sex.

Slowly, his hand moved across the wood to do some fine sanding on the deer bust as a smile crossed his face. He'd gotten less sleep these last few nights than he'd had in a long time, and yet he'd never felt more energized. The sculpture was almost finished, and he had already completed some rough sketches for his next project.

And the one after that.

Something about the time he and Darcy were spending together had unleashed a new wave of creativity in him. A couple of weeks ago, he had been feeling sluggish and ready for a break, but now Ben had a vision of the work he wanted to do, and he was excited to get it started.

His phone beeped with his daily alarm to check his emails. As promised, Darcy had set it up for him—twice a day rather than once—and he found it very helpful. And he had made sure he told her that too. And thanked her. She had beamed under his praise, and he had to admit, making her smile was one of his new favorite things, and it made him feel lighter as well.

Taking a step back from the piece, he studied it. This had come naturally to him—taking a block of wood and turning it into something. Sculpting and breathing life into a piece was what made Ben tick. And for so long, it was all he'd allowed himself to do. With the loss of his parents almost six years ago, the responsibility of being the head of the family and taking care of his two younger brothers fell on his shoulders, and he took it

seriously. He worked when he didn't want to. He perse-
vered when he wanted to give up. And mostly, he made
sure he filled his time with enough work that he didn't
have time to grieve or think about all they had lost.

Ben had gotten so used to having this single-minded
focus on survival that what he was feeling right now
felt strange and more than a little out of character for
him. The survival instinct—that need to keep working to ensure financial security for himself with extra
padding for his brothers—was still strong. That hadn't
changed. What was changing was how he also desired
a life outside of work. Outside of his home. All day, he
had been thinking about places he wanted to show Darcy
but couldn't because the roads weren't fully cleared yet.
If he lived closer to the city, they'd be fine. But this far
out, most of the roads weren't suitable for driving.

He wanted to take her to dinner. Maybe a movie. He
wanted to take her to the first gallery he had ever dis-
played his work at. Or to meet his high school art teacher
who still kept some of Ben's work in his classroom.

Yeah. Ben wanted all those things and more.

But he couldn't have them.

Though neither of them talked about it, they knew
her time here was temporary. And honestly, Ben didn't
want to think about when she'd have to leave. Turning,
he looked out the window and sighed. The snow had
stopped early yesterday morning. The temperatures
were still well below freezing, and he knew the roads
weren't safe, but eventually, that was going to change.
Darcy had a life in North Carolina. On the other side of
the country. Far away from him.

They had talked about it last night over dinner—her

life. Her family. From what he could tell, her family
meant the world to her. And other than Riley and
Savannah, most of them lived in the same small coastal
area. She had gravitated to her hometown after college
and had been working toward finding a career that had
to do with the business end of the arts. She knew what
she wanted to do, and she liked living near her family,
but those two things weren't working out for her. She
knew if she really pursued her career in the art field,
she'd need to move. And while she was open to it, she
also seemed to have issues with it—like she'd been willing to work at other odd jobs strictly because of logistics. Not that he understood that. Ben had always known
what he wanted to do and never wavered from it. It was
mildly fascinating to listen to her talk about all the jobs
she'd had over the last several years.

All of them involved organizing and administration.
She was damn good at it. Every time he walked into
his office, he was amazed. Today, she was working on
setting up his new software. They hadn't had any mail
delivery in days, and she had been able to do everything
she needed to do online. It didn't matter to him at all.
She was welcome to do all the computer crap. He was
much happier in his workshop. And his next assistant—
temporary or otherwise—would benefit from all of
Darcy's hard work.

Just the thought of someone else in his home, in his
office, bothered him. He'd done it before—normally
under protest and out of necessity—but now, after
having Darcy here, it was even more unappealing.

"Better get used to it." He sighed. No matter how
much he didn't want to think about it, the snow would

eventually melt. The temperatures were going to warm up, and the roads were going to clear.

And Darcy was going to go home.

To her life, her family.

And in time, maybe she'd forget about him.

But Ben didn't want that, couldn't allow it. This time they had together may be short, but he wanted Darcy to remember him. Looking around the shop, he remembered how they had talked about his work and how she described it. Other than his grandfather, no one else had ever grasped what he did. Not even his clients. They all wanted what they wanted and didn't really care about how he made it happen. If anything, it made Ben want to create something specifically for Darcy—because he knew she'd appreciate it and understand all the thought and sweat and labor that went into it.

Standing, he went to look through his wood supply as thoughts for a design swirled through his head.

She might have to leave him, but he wanted her to take part of him with her.

# Chapter 6

"I'M A LITTLE CONCERNED THAT YOU'RE SO CHILL about this. Wasn't it you texting and calling me and freaking out a week ago?"

Darcy sighed as she got comfortable on the couch. "I was wrong," she said simply. "I jumped to conclusions, I guess. Ben's a good guy, and if you saw his home, you'd realize there are worse places to be stranded. The view out his back door is amazing."

Anna Shaughnessy chuckled. "Isn't it all covered in white right now?"

That made Darcy laugh too. "It is, but it doesn't diminish the beauty. There's a lake, and the way the snow looks covering the trees... I'm telling you, it's like something off of a Christmas card. I didn't think places like this actually existed."

"So when are you coming home?"

She totally wasn't ready to leave yet.

Not by a long shot.

"Ben's house is out in the boonies. We haven't seen a plow come through yet. I'm not going to look at flights until I know the roads are cleared. But I promise that as soon as I have a seat, I'll let you know. How's your mom? Your dad? Everyone good?"

"Everyone's fine. Bobby's coming to visit next weekend. Your brother's thrilled," she deadpanned.

"I can imagine. Is he staying with you?"

"Uh-huh. He said he wanted to have some quality time with Kaitlyn, but I have a feeling he's really coming to make sure Quinn is being a good dad."

"Oh, for crying out loud." She laughed. "Still? I thought the two of them buried the hatchet? You and Quinn have been together for years now. Isn't it time for them to stop with the animosity?"

"You would think, but they've been this way for too long. Quinn's already planning on us having a date night and leaving Bobby here to babysit."

"Yikes."

"Then I slapped him upside the head for thinking using our daughter as punishment was okay."

"Not cool. Not cool."

"Exactly." Anna sighed. "But back to you. I take it you and Ben are getting along now?"

Squirming on the couch, Darcy cleared her throat. "Um, I think so. I mean yes. Yes. We are." She shrugged. "I mean, he came and got me in a blizzard and…and he's letting me stay here, and he's crazy talented. You should see the furniture he's made. It's insane! And you know—"

"Oh my God, you slept with him!" Anna cried excitedly. "Right? Am I right? Oh, I am so totally right!"

"If my brother is anywhere within a ten-mile radius of you right now, I'm going to kill you," Darcy hissed.

"Relax," Anna said mildly. "As if I'd say something like that out loud if Quinn was here. Please. You think I want *that* grief?"

All Darcy could do was groan.

"Sooo," Anna prompted. "Come on. You have to give details."

"I am so not giving details. Ever. As a matter of fact, right now, I would welcome a tree crashing through the roof and effectively ending this call."

"Nice try, but details," Anna persisted with a giggle.

"Come on. No. Just no." Shaking her head vigorously, she wished there was a way to get her sister-in-law off the phone.

Anna went quiet for a moment before saying, "Fine. I'll let this go for now. But when you return, we're having lunch—alone. I'm not inviting my mom or Zoe or anyone. And you are going to tell me everything." She let out a girly squeal. "And I've seen pictures of Ben. He's a hottie."

"Oh my God, you did *not* just say that!"

Anna let out a slightly devious laugh.

"You're killing me." Darcy sighed wearily. "Seriously killing me."

"It's what big sisters do," Anna replied happily.

And that one simple statement made Darcy relax. Anna was now her sister because she was married to Quinn, but they had been sisters long before that.

"So, whatcha doing right now? Thinking about the sexy sculptor?" Anna giggled.

"You are so lame." Darcy sighed again. "Lame, lame, lame."

"That's me," Anna said. "I have to go. I need to get your niece down for her nap. Stay safe and be careful," Anna said seriously. "I know this is like a little break from reality. For the both of you. I don't want you to get hurt."

Darcy nodded and then realized she'd have to speak. "I'm fine. I promise. And, Anna?"

"Yeah?"

"I love you."

"Love you too, Darce. Call me when you know when you'll be home."

"I will."

Putting her phone aside, Darcy sat back and let out a long breath.

She looked at the clock on the wall and saw it was almost dinnertime. Whatever it was that Ben was working on, he had been like a man possessed for the last twenty-four hours. She'd barely seen him.

And she missed him, dammit.

She'd eaten dinner alone last night—not a big deal. A sandwich was all she'd made, and then she'd eaten it in the office while she worked some more on the book stuff. It was finished, and they'd emailed the files to the publisher, but she was a stickler for details and just wanted to review the work they'd done. When it was pushing eleven and Ben hadn't come in, Darcy had decided she was going to call it a day and go to bed. Without him there with her, she hadn't felt right about getting into his bed, so she went up to the guest room.

Somewhere around two a.m., Ben had crawled in beside her and woken her up with light kisses and caresses before making love to her. It had been slow and sweet and so intimate that it had brought tears to her eyes.

Never before had she been so thankful for the darkness.

When she had woken up this morning, he was gone. He'd come in for lunch, but she could tell he was distracted—grabbing a sandwich and giving her a steamy kiss before leaving again.

Maybe it was time to start looking at going home.

The last thing Darcy wanted was to be in the way. It wasn't a good feeling, and it was something she'd battled her entire life. With such a big age difference between her and her brothers, Darcy always felt like she was in the way.

Right now, she and Ben were having fun, but he had a job and a career and commitments. There was no way she could expect him to entertain her all day or put his life on hold any more than he already had. So maybe it would be best if she didn't wait for him to ask her to leave. Maybe it would be better for both of them if she sort of left gracefully, before things got awkward.

God, she would hate if Ben turned to her and asked her to leave. Or told her they were over. Jumping to her feet, she shook her head and willed the tears that were burning her eyes not to fall. No. She didn't want to think of him saying that to her.

Even though she knew it was inevitable.

"Great. Now I'm depressed," she murmured. She walked into the kitchen and grabbed a handful of cookies before pouring herself some milk. Taking a bite of one, she grimaced. In her concocting stage, she had made a bourbon maple bacon cookie. Because bacon. Unfortunately, she had used way too much bourbon and realized after that how much she disliked the taste of the drink.

"Ugh, why did we keep these?" she said as she walked over and dropped the cookie in the trash and then went back and did the same with the remainder of the batch. She guzzled the milk as she made her way to Ben's office to try to get the taste out of her mouth.

At the computer, she began searching flight options.

There had been a plow down the road earlier in the day, but the temperatures were in the single digits, so everything was still pretty frozen and slick. As she scanned her options, she made a mental note to look for flights that left in, say, two days. And midday so the sun would be out the entire time Ben was driving. Or maybe she should consider having a car service pick her up or an Uber.

Did they have Uber up here in the mountains?

She'd have to Google that too.

"What are you doing?"

Turning in her seat, Darcy found Ben standing in the doorway. "I didn't hear you come in," she said calmly, even though her heart was ready to beat right out of her chest.

Slowly, Ben advanced into the room. He sat on the edge of the desk, blocking her view of the computer. "What's going on?"

This was not the way she wanted to do this. At all. "Um, I was seeing what the flights were looking like. The roads have been cleared—somewhat—and I know you're busy with work and…I don't know…I need to look into getting home. The book stuff is done, and your office is organized and…" She shrugged. "Everyone's freaking out that I'm still here."

"Everyone?" he asked levelly, arching a brow at her.

"Pretty much. I've talked to Riley and Savannah, my dad, Anna, and that's not including texts from them plus Aubrey and Brooke." She shrugged again. "I mean, it's nice to be missed and all, but I do need to get home." Darcy couldn't even look at him as she spoke.

"I see."

Then he didn't move or say anything else. It got to the

point where it was awkward, and as much as she tried not to, Darcy couldn't help but squirm in her seat. With nothing left to do, she finally looked up at him, and her heart kicked hard in her chest. The intensity with which Ben was looking at her was overwhelming. Swallowing hard, she cleared her throat. "So, um…"

Ben stood, reached for her hand, and yanked her to her feet. Even when he was aggressive with her, he was always gentle. This time? Not so much. She gasped as her chest hit his, and her eyes flew up to meet his gaze.

"What's. Going. On?" Ben enunciated each word slowly, his eyes never leaving hers.

"I…I told you…"

"I don't think so."

Now she felt a little defensive. Why was he giving her so much grief? He should be happy she was getting out of his way so he could work without worrying about entertaining her.

"Rather than arguing it out in your head," he said in a low voice, "why don't you just say it to me?"

Darcy's eyes narrowed, and she tried to pull away from him, but Ben was having none of it. He banded an arm around her waist and held her close.

"Fine. It's obvious that you're busy. You've got work to do, and you don't have to keep normal hours or any-thing. And honestly? I'm bored. I have nothing to do now that all the work stuff is done. I've baked enough cakes and cookies and bread for a dozen people, and now…" She shrugged. "I have nothing left to do. You're not my babysitter, and I don't expect you to drop every-thing to entertain me. The roads are clear, and flights are starting to get back to normal, so…"

"So?"

*Why? Just why?*

"Look, what is your deal?" she demanded, lightly stomping her foot.

Ben looked mildly amused at her question. "My deal?"

"Yes. Your deal. We both know I have to go home eventually. I don't know why this is such an issue to you. All I'm doing is—"

"Do you want to leave?" he interrupted.

"What?"

"You heard me."

"Ben—"

"Answer the question, Darcy. Do you *want* to leave?"

"I have a job and—"

"Not one you want," he reminded her.

"And my family needs—"

"To mind their own business. They all have lives of their own and should respect you enough to let you live yours."

Wow. He totally had a point there, and at any other time, she'd love that, but right now, it was confusing her.

"You're working and—"

"I'm going to ask you this one more time," Ben stated firmly. "Do you—"

"No! Okay? No, I don't want to go! But you're busy, and I don't want to be in the way."

He released her but then immediately took her by the hand and led her from the room. He led her to the back door and then handed her her coat.

"Ben…"

"Just follow me."

So she did. Out to the workshop, and damn, it was

cold. How did people live like this? The temperatures
could get pretty low in North Carolina, but not like this.
This almost wasn't livable. It was like being in Antarctica
or at the North Pole, for crying out loud. She almost wept
with relief when they stepped into the workshop.

The first thing she noticed was that the deer bust was
gone. After a minute, she saw it in the corner and that Ben
had added some colored stain to it. If anything, it looked
even more amazing. She was about to comment on it
when Ben pulled her along to the far corner of the shop.

Sitting on a large swath of red silk was a small, intri-
cately carved box.

Darcy looked at Ben questioningly.

"I was inspired the other day," he said gruffly. "I was
thinking about how you, more than anyone I've ever
met, really understand my work. You look at it, and you
don't just see something that's visually appealing. You
look at it and understand all that goes into making that
piece of art happen—my process, the hours of planning
and carving and working." He paused and squeezed her
hand. "I thought about that deer bust and how my client
will see it, and he'll love it and he'll gush, but he has
no idea the hours I put into it. The cuts, the blisters, the
sweat, the hours of sleep I lost. He won't even think
about those things."

"But I would," she said softly, understanding slowly
dawning on her.

Ben nodded. "You would." Turning, he let go of her
hand and reached for the box. "I wanted to create something for you. Something you could have and use and…
and know I did it for you. Only you."

Tears instantly filled her eyes as she finally turned

and looked at the box. It was small—maybe six inches
square—but the details were amazing. Out of the corner
of her eye, she saw Ben nod, so she reached out and
took it from his hand. The wood was as smooth as the
silk it had been resting on. And carved into the top was
a winter scene, similar to what she saw out his back door
from the deck. There was a lake and trees, and he'd used
paint and stain to give hints of the snow on the ground
and the reflection of it on the water.

Around the sides were probably a hundred different
snowflakes. She ran her finger over each and every one
of them, simply in awe of how this man had taken the
time to create something so incredible, and yet it hadn't
taken him that long. She looked up at him. "How did
you do this? You only started—"

His smile was slow and sweet. "Like I said, I was
inspired. I started it after you left that first night. At the
time, I didn't realize why I felt the need to create something so delicate. But then yesterday, I thought of you,
and this image came to mind. When that happens, I can
work fairly quickly. Not that I was rushing it, but once
I started, I couldn't stop. I forced myself to come inside
last night. If I had been here alone, I probably would
have stayed up all night working on it."

She sighed. "And that's what I'm trying to avoid,
Ben. I don't want to interfere with your process. I mean
look at this!" She held the box up to him. "I can't even
believe that someone—*you*—made this with your bare
hands. It doesn't seem possible. And because of me, you
*did* rush and you *did* stop."

Taking the box from her hands, he put it back on
the silk. "I wanted to stop. I *needed* to stop. I need to

remember to take care of myself. And for the record, I hated that you went to sleep in the guest room last night. I thought we were past that."

She gave him a bashful smile. "It didn't seem right to be in your room without you."

"I want you in my room. In my bed. The thought of finding you there waiting for me was the only thing spurring me home last night."

Everything in her melted at his words and the huskiness of his tone.

"I don't want to go," she whispered.

His hands—those wonderfully large, work-roughened hands—came up and cupped her face. "Good."

At that moment, Darcy thought for sure Ben would kiss her, the kind of wild and uninhibited kiss that always turned her a little inside out. But he didn't. Instead, he seemed to be studying her face, with his eyes as well as his hands.

"You're so beautiful," he murmured.

Darcy felt herself blush. She'd never seen herself that way. Ever. Her initial reaction was to tell him he was crazy, but she didn't. Something was happening here. Everything suddenly felt different and yet incredibly familiar. She whispered his name but didn't know what else to say.

Ben took a step back, reached for the box, and handed it back to her. "Open it."

Intrigued, she did as he asked and gasped softly. The inside was lined with the red silk he had on the table. There was some sort of padding beneath it to cushion what he'd placed there.

A Christmas ornament. A wooden snowflake that matched the style of the ones on the outside of the box.

"Oh, Ben," she said with awe as she placed the box on the table and picked up the ornament. "It's beautiful." In actuality, it was stunningly fragile. So much so that Darcy was almost afraid to handle it at all. "I love it."

That seemed to please him more than anything. "My original idea was to do a jewelry box. But as I was working on it, I had an idea about the ornament and thought it would fit nicely inside and could stand as a gift box. Of course, you could use it for whatever you want," he added quickly.

"This snowflake is so delicate that I think this box is the safest place for it." She smiled up at him. "And I want you to know, I sort of have a bit of an obsession with Christmas, as you've probably figured out, but particularly Christmas ornaments."

His eyes widened slightly. "Seriously?"

She nodded. "I do. I've been collecting them for years."

Now it was his turn to smile. "What kind do you collect?"

"All kinds. When I travel, I always find a shop that sells ornaments. So I have a decent collection of ornaments from my travels. And I love snowmen, so whenever I see a cute snowman ornament, I buy it."

"How big is the family Christmas tree?" he asked with a small laugh.

"Oh, I haven't put any of them on the family tree. My dad is a stickler about the ornaments on that one. I have a little artificial tree that I set up in my bedroom and hang all my ornaments on." She shrugged. "It's only about three feet tall, but it's getting full."

He nodded.

"Anyway, the family Christmas tree is overflowing

already with personalized ornaments of six kids and six grandkids. Plus, I'm a little protective of my collection," she added sassily. "And I'm going to be particularly protective of my newest addition." Standing on her tiptoes, she kissed him on the cheek.

"I'm glad you like it," he said gruffly.

Gently, Darcy put the ornament in the box and put the lid on. How was it possible that Ben could know her so well? They'd never talked about her love of Christmas ornaments.

But it wasn't just the ornament. It was everything. There was a bond forming between them that ran deep, and yet she felt as if they'd just begun to scratch the surface. The thought of leaving him—even to go home to her family whom she loved more than anything—felt wrong. There was still so much here. How could she just let that go?

Tears stung her eyes. That was another thing that was becoming overwhelming to her—her emotions. She normally only seemed to have two—happy or pissed off. But Ben had her feeling myriad emotions that she had no idea how to handle. Maybe he wanted to get some more work done here in the workshop, and she could have some time at the house to get herself together. But when she allowed herself to turn and look at him, she couldn't hold back what was on her mind at that exact moment.

"I need you."

That slow and sexy smile returned. Taking her hand in his, he replied, "I'm yours."

———

For four more days, life was idyllic. There had been another small round of snow, but it had only ensured that

Darcy couldn't leave just yet. Ben couldn't remember a
time when he'd felt so free. Even before his parents'
death, he had been serious and more closed off than the
rest of his family. After his parents had died, he knew
he had gotten worse. His brothers reminded him of it
often enough, but it wasn't something he'd ever thought
he could change.

And then Darcy Shaughnessy had walked into his life.

Taking a sip of his coffee, he looked over to where
she stood at the kitchen island stirring some batter.
There were enough sweets and baked goods in the house
to last him through the winter, and yet she kept baking.
She had gone through his basic baking ingredients and
had moved on to getting creative.

The results weren't always good.

Just yesterday, she had come up with three new recipes, and they had waited until after dinner to try them
and decide if they were keepers. She had been so excited
about the experiment, telling him she had done some
research on the use of different spices in cookies and
that her first foray into using them included some spicy
ones—chili powder, jalapeños, and garlic. Even now,
he had to suppress a shudder at the garlic ones, but the
other two had been fairly decent.

Either way, it made her happy, so Ben was happy.
And as long as they could stay in this little cocoon
they'd created, he knew he would stay that way.

He wondered what she planned on baking today.
Right now, he smelled bacon, and he hoped it had
something to do with lunch and not cookies. After the
bourbon cookie disaster the other night, he hoped she'd
moved on from that combination. Then he chuckled,

because he knew that no matter what, he'd be a good sport and try them and then distract her from making any more for a while.

The idea definitely had merit.

Unfortunately, all good things usually come to an end. It came in the form of a phone call from his brother Jack.

Darcy looked at him as his cell phone rang and clearly saw his frown. "You okay?"

Nodding, Ben stood. "I have to take this. Excuse me." He waited until he was in his office before he answered. "Hey, Jack. What's up?"

"Hey! I was calling to see how you were doing. I caught the news of your snowstorm."

Ben shared with him all the stats about the storm. "Plows are finally coming around, but the temps aren't budging, so everything's still pretty much frozen."

"Were you prepared for it? All stocked up?"

"What do you think?" Ben teased.

Jack laughed. "I know, I know. You're always prepared. Nothing takes you by surprise."

*If he only knew*, Ben thought. "So what about you? How are you doing? How's the job going?"

"If all goes as planned, I'll make junior partner by Christmas," Jack replied proudly. "And I'll be the youngest one in the firm's history."

"That's awesome, Jack! Congratulations!"

"Yeah, well, I know it's not a glamorous job—it's just accounting—but I'm pretty psyched about the whole thing."

"You should be. I'm proud of you."

"Thanks, Ben. Really. I wouldn't even be here if it wasn't for you."

Ben hated when they had this conversation. He didn't want his brother's gratitude. Helping him finish school was something his parents would have wanted. And he didn't want to keep rehashing it.

"Nonsense. You got yourself there with hard work and good grades," Ben said dismissively. "Have you heard from Henry lately?"

"I talked to him last night. We talked about having Christmas here in Boston this year. Donna and I want to host it, since it's our first one together, and Henry's on board. He has a week off, and he's going to spend it here with us. We were hoping you'd do the same."

*Shit.*

He sighed wearily as he shifted in his chair. "Jack, we've been over this."

"Yeah, yeah, yeah. I know. But it's enough, Ben. Seriously. We all understood in the beginning, but enough time has gone by, and…man, don't make me say it."

Ben raked a hand through his hair. "Say what?"

"They would hate this. They'd be so disappointed in you," Jack said, but there wasn't an ounce of sympathy in his voice. "You can't spend your whole damn life on that mountain. You work all the time. You don't go out, you don't socialize. Hell, when was the last time you even got laid?"

"Look, Christmas isn't important to me, Jack. And you know what? It's not a crime. And for your information, as soon as I'm done with the two commissions I'm working on, I plan on taking a lengthy vacation and doing some traveling."

"Great! Travel your ass here to Boston."

Damn. He'd stepped right into that one. "Gladly. Just not for Christmas. I promise to come in January or maybe February."

"Come on," Jack said with disgust. "You're going to pull the same crap you do every year. You say you'll come, but then something comes up—a client, a project, a storm. Dude, I've been living here for almost three years, and you haven't come to see me once."

"Don't even," Ben snapped. "We saw each other three months ago, so don't be so dramatic."

"I'd like you to see *my* home. I'd like you to meet *my* friends. It's not that much to ask."

"I can't help that my work sometimes gets in the way!"

"Maybe we'll hop on a plane and come to you for Christmas, and you can host," Jack said sarcastically. "Then what would you do?"

"I imagine I'd have to sit here and look at your disappointed faces, because there won't be a tree or a big Christmas goose or whatever the hell it is you make."

"Come on, Ben." Jack sighed. "Why?"

"Listen, I have to go. Thanks for checking on me, and I'll give you a call next week." He hated being pushed into a corner.

"Fine," Jack said after a long pause. "We'll talk next week."

They said their goodbyes, and Ben had to fight the urge to throw his phone out of frustration. How many times were they going to beat this subject to death? Why couldn't his brothers accept that he wasn't going to join in the holiday festivities? He shouldn't have to keep explaining himself time and time again.

And it pissed him off to no end that his brothers were

able to move on. Didn't they miss their parents? Didn't their loss mean anything to them? Why was he the only one still grieving?

Above him, he could hear Darcy's footsteps, and he sighed.

Her constant chatter about the wonders of Christmas were starting to get to him too. Not that she was changing his mind or anything, but he knew it was only a matter of time before he exploded on her—like he'd just done to his brother—about all the reasons why Christmas sucked. No doubt he'd yell, she'd yell, and then she'd look at him with disappointment and possibly disgust. But what was he supposed to do? There was no way he could pretend to give a damn about the holiday when he didn't. There was no Christmas joy anymore. All that was left was a gaping hole in his life where his parents used to be. How could he ever celebrate that without feeling guilty?

Yes, he had made the snowflake ornament, but at the time, it felt more like a winter decoration and not a Christmas one. It wasn't a big deal. It didn't mean anything.

And then he knew he was lying. The truth was, he had a whole collection of ornaments that he'd carved over the years since his parents died. Why? Because it was something he used to do for his mother. She loved them so much, and it was a gift he gave her every year.

And he still did.

He just packed them away and never took them out.

It was crazy, and for the life of him, he had no idea why he kept making them, but he did.

And someday he'd donate them to a hospital or a charity and move on.

His phone beeped with his check email alarm. Since he was sitting at his desk, he decided to check them on the computer instead. The phone was great, but the screen was small and a bit annoying. The twenty-three-inch computer screen made it much easier to navigate around and do his thing.

An email from Henry.

Go figure.

The subject line read "Christmas in Boston," and the entire body of the email was a list of reasons why Ben needed to be there and the importance of family and supporting Jack and Donna as they start their lives together, blah, blah, blah. And it ended with *Stop being such a fucking grinch!*

Nice.

It would have been easy to blast off a reply telling his youngest brother to go to hell and leave him alone, but he knew that wasn't how he felt.

Just how he felt at the moment.

"And I'll leave this for another day," he murmured and closed the message. There were a few spam messages that he deleted and one from his editor confirming her receipt of the book files. He muttered a curse as the phone rang again.

Thinking it was one of his brothers, he answered with a curt, "What!"

"Wow! Not quite the greeting I was expecting," Savannah said with a chuckle. "How are you doing? Is Darcy making you crazy? Is that why you sound so snappish?"

Ben let out a ragged sigh as he raked a hand through his hair. "Nah. She's not so bad. And she has some serious organizational skills. I let her loose on my office. Well, actually, she let herself loose on my office. I'm benefitting from the results."

Savannah laughed. "Yeah, she has some serious skill in that department. But why would she organize your office?"

"She was bored, the office was a disaster, and I was out in the workshop," he said and had to stop himself from thinking about everything that transpired after that.

"Oh, well, good for you," she said finally.

"So, what's up?"

"Your editor called to thank me for helping you finish the book."

He cursed. "Sorry, I forgot to tell her that you weren't the one doing it. I just saw an email and was about to get back to her."

"You should. Still, you must be relieved to have it done and off your plate."

For the next ten minutes, Ben talked about all he and Darcy had accomplished on the project. "It was kind of amazing how just getting the stuff organized and having basic conversation about the pieces helped me."

"Like I said, she has some serious skill in that area, and I'm so glad she was able to help."

"Thanks for sending her my way." He couldn't help but smile as he thought of all the ways he was thankful.

"I'm glad it all worked out."

"I am too," he agreed. "And hopefully I won't have to think about it again for a while."

"For a couple of months, I would think," she commented. "Where's Darcy at? Has she booked her flight home yet?"

"Um, I don't think so."

Savannah was silent for a moment. "Well, that's odd."

Ben cleared his throat and shifted in his seat. "Really?" he croaked. "Um, why?"

"Well, flights should be back to normal. So what's the delay?" Gone was the lightness of a moment ago, and maybe it was Ben's imagination, but he got the hint of an accusation there.

So he did what he'd been doing for the last few minutes. He lied.

"It's kind of my fault."

"Oh. Really?"

"Uh, yeah. The plows don't get up here right away, so the roads only got cleared yesterday. And then the temperatures have been brutal, so it's still pretty slick. I don't mind driving in the snow up and down the mountain, but ice is another story. So I'm waiting for the roads to be safer. And I'm in the middle of finishing a sculpture, and you know how much I hate to be interrupted while I'm working."

Silence.

"So, um, yeah. My fault. If you'd like, I'll talk to her about it tonight and get her flight booked, and then I'll call you and let you know. Or I'll let her call you and tell you. Or I can email it to you so you have her itinerary. You know, whatever you want."

"Ben?"

"Huh?"

"You're rambling. You never ramble. What's going on?" She paused. "Oh my God!"

*Oh no.*

"Oh my God!" she repeated.

*Shit*. She'd figured it out. How the hell was he supposed to explain himself or ever face Savannah—or
Riley—again?

"You threw her out, didn't you?" Savannah said,
interrupting his thoughts. "She totally made you crazy
with her chatter and changing your office around, and
you kicked her out! Dammit, Ben! I trusted you!" She
let out a growl of frustration. "Riley is going to freak
out." Then she cursed. "So where is she? Is she at the
hotel where she stayed when she first flew in? Dammit,
I know I have the number around here somewhere."

He wished he could go along with her theory, but
he couldn't.

"I didn't throw her out, Savannah. I wouldn't do that."

"Then I'm confused."

*Join the club.*

How the hell was he supposed to explain himself—
them—to Savannah?

"Ben?"

"The truth is," he began slowly, "I don't know…I
kind of like hanging out with her." He paused. "We have
a lot in common."

Silence.

"I spend so much time working and being alone that
it's been nice having someone to talk to," he went on.
"And Darcy didn't have anything to rush home to, so I
guess there wasn't any urgency for her to leave."

"Oh, well, okay," Savannah replied. "I guess I can
see that."

*Crisis averted.*

"Can I ask you a favor?" she said hesitantly.

"Anything."

"Talk to her about her career and her future. Maybe talking with someone who isn't family will make her feel better. It might be good to talk to someone who has his shit together and isn't related to her. She won't look at you as trying to control her or tell her what to do. Maybe you can, you know, guide her. Like you did for your brothers."

"I don't think—"

"No! It's perfect. Trust me. She's always felt that her brothers were overprotective and that they don't take her seriously. And most of her friends are, well, they're young and not focused, and they're all struggling with finding their way like she is. So someone like you, who's accomplished so much and helped his siblings in a non-controlling way, would be the perfect choice. Please. Please say you'll do it."

"Savannah, you have no idea what you're asking."

"Yes, I do. I trust you, Ben. You're one of the good guys," Savannah said confidently. "Sometimes the people who help the most are the ones with the least connection. Does that make sense?"

"I guess, but—"

"She's already there with you, and you know if she isn't agreeable to anything you say, she'll be leaving in a couple of days. C'mon, Ben. Do this for me."

Sighing, Ben sank lower in his chair.

"Only for you, Savannah," he said. "You're the only one I'd do this for."

"You're full of it. Deep down, I think you're a softie. You prefer to look like a hard-ass to the rest of the world. But I know the real you. You should embrace the real you more often."

"Yeah, yeah, yeah."

"I have to go. Aislynn's on the move, and when it gets quiet for too long, I panic. Go and share your wisdom with my girl."

"I will." But there wasn't much power behind his words.

"Ben, promise me you're going to talk to her."

"Okay, okay."

"Say it. Say you promise me," she prompted.

"I promise, Savannah," he said softly.

"Thank you."

"Sure. No problem."

He hung up, placed the phone on the desk, and heard a sound behind him.

Turning, he saw Darcy standing in the doorway, looking more than a little devastated.

It took all of three seconds for him to realize what she must have heard and how it must have sounded to her.

"Darcy, I—"

She swallowed hard. "I…I'm sorry. I wanted to see if you had something in mind for lunch. I was thinking of making some soup." She looked away, as if she couldn't stand to look at him. "But, um, you can let me know when you're done. Sorry."

As soon as she turned to walk away, Ben jumped up. "Darcy, wait." But she was already running up the stairs. He took them two at a time and caught her at the top. "Wait," he said more emphatically as he reached out and grasped her arms.

"What?" she snapped, her eyes full of defiance.

Hell, he wasn't even sure what to say. He was about ninety-nine percent certain she was upset because he was talking to Savannah, but what if he was wrong? Did he want to bring that topic up again?

"What's going on?" he asked instead.

Rolling her eyes, Darcy yanked out of his grasp and gave a mirthless laugh. "Seriously? That's what you're asking me?"

Ben raked a hand through his hair and cursed the fact that women needed to come with instruction manuals.

"Look, can we skip the whole dancing around part of this and you tell me what I did that has pissed you off?"

She crossed her arms as she did her best to level him with a glare. "Who said I'm pissed off? I asked you about lunch." She shrugged. "And I apologized for interrupting you. Why don't you tell me what has *you* all riled up?"

Best. Opening. Ever.

Taking a step toward her, he almost smiled when her cocky expression faltered a bit. Good. "I'm riled up because I had to take a phone call from my brother and deal with shit that I don't want to deal with. I had to listen to the guilt trip about why I should be embracing Christmas, and I don't want to. It's bullshit. I hate the holiday. The whole damn thing. And I wish he'd leave me alone about it. And when I thought I was done, I got an email from my other brother, who sent me a list of all the reasons I need to spend Christmas with them and ended it by calling me a grinch. That one I ignored, but it annoyed me." He took another step toward her as she moved away.

"Then I got an email from my editor about the book. I guess they were tired of waiting to hear from me, because they reached out to Savannah. I had originally told them she would be the one helping me and never notified them it would be you. So she called to let me know they had called to thank her. I took a few minutes to talk to your sister-in-law, who thought I must have thrown you out because you weren't on your way home yet!" When she started to comment, he stopped her. "And just when I was done with that, when I was looking forward to coming up here and seeing you—*you!*— you show up and look at me like I killed your dog or something." He paused. "So is that enough for me to be riled up about, or do you have something to add to it?"

"I made bacon chocolate chip cookies," she said weakly, and he knew she was trying to change the subject. "I found a small bag of chocolate chips in the back of the pantry."

Unable to help himself, he muttered a curse as he stepped away from her. Raking a hand through his hair, he didn't know whether to keep yelling or kiss her.

At least she had the good sense to look mildly ashamed. Her arms dropped to her sides as she grabbed onto one of the kitchen chairs. "Why do you hate Christmas?" she asked softly. She was staring at the floor as she asked, and her whole body had gone from confident and defiant to meek.

It almost made Ben feel bad.

Reaching out, he took her by the hand, led her into the living room, and sat them both on the couch. Darcy rebelled and tried to move away from him, but Ben held firm and kept her close to his side, sliding his arm around her.

"I love my brothers. I really do." He knew he wasn't directly answering her question, but at the same time, she needed to know the history behind it.

"But?"

"But they lead very different lives than I do. Jack's an accountant, and Henry's an IT guy. They wear suits to work and make conference calls and have 401(k) plans. I don't particularly understand what they do or how they deal with the nine-to-five thing, but it's what they love, and I don't argue it with them. They, however, feel the need to argue with me over how I live."

"Really? Isn't what you do the reason they could finish school? And therefore have the careers they love?"

Ben couldn't help but chuckle. Leave it to Darcy to put it so bluntly.

"Pretty much. And it's not like they begrudge what I do. They've always been very supportive of my career. It's how I live that they have an issue with."

"Why do people do that?" she asked. "What gives anyone the right to tell anyone else how to live?"

"Speaking from experience?"

Looking up at him, she gave him a small smile. "Maybe."

Ben went on to tell her what he and Jack had talked about. "I guess I can understand his frustration, but our parents died two weeks before Christmas. I can't...I can't fathom celebrating a holiday that is a direct reminder of losing the two most important people in our lives," he said with a detachment that he didn't quite feel. When he'd talked to his brother about this, Ben had been able to talk about it as if he was just stating random facts. But sitting here with Darcy and talking about it? His heart was beating wildly, and he felt sick to his stomach.

"How is it right for us to celebrate?" he asked harshly, letting his emotions take over. "What gives us the right to go on and be happy and...and exchange gifts when they'll never get to do that again? Maybe my brothers can justify it, but I can't. My mother used to love Christmas. She loved to decorate and bake and…" He paused. "I can't do it. I *won't* do it."

This time when she made to move away from him, he let her.

"So you haven't celebrated Christmas since?"

He nodded again.

"Wow."

He waited for her to expand on that, but she didn't.

"That's it? That's all you have to say?" he asked when he couldn't take the silence anymore.

Her shoulders relaxed a bit, and she twisted around so she could face him head-on. "Everyone handles grief in their own way, Ben. It's not for anyone to tell you—or for you to tell your brothers—how they should do it."

Well, damn. That kind of made sense.

"My mom died when I was a baby."

His heart ached for her. Reaching out, he took one of her hands in his and held it.

"I was too young to remember her," she went on quietly. "My whole life, people have shown me pictures and told me stories about her, but it's hard to feel a connection to her. I wish I did, but I don't." She paused. "My brothers are still struggling with losing her, even after all these years, and they each handle it in different ways. Sometimes I listen to them talk about things they did as a family before I came along, and it makes me feel awkward and alone. Like there was this whole other family that I never got to be a part of. There are times when it really makes me angry, and other times, it's like I feel nothing."

"Darcy, I don't even know what to say."

She shrugged again. "There's nothing you can say.

You didn't know," she said mildly. "Every year on her birthday, the anniversary of her death, holidays, we make this family trip to the cemetery. I put flowers down, but it's weird to me. I know that I love her. I mean, she's my mom. But at the same time, how can I love someone I didn't know? Does that make sense?"

"I honestly don't know."

She sighed. "She loved Christmas—everyone who ever met my mom will tell you that—so I know I get that from her. And my love of baking. So there's a bunch of stuff that we have in common, and people compare us, but it's like being compared to a distant relative I've never met. I get asked if I miss her, and what am I supposed to say? Of course, I miss her. I wish she hadn't died and left me. I wish I had known her and had her here to guide me and watch me grow up. I love my dad and my brothers, but they don't *get* me. I like to think that my mom would have."

Then he pulled her in close again and held her. He felt her tears through his shirt and wished there was something he could do or say to take away her pain.

"People look at me and think I don't grieve," she said, her voice going quiet again. "I don't cry in front of them. I don't get sad when I talk about her. At least not most of the time. But that doesn't mean I don't feel the loss of her." She sniffled and curled up closer to him. "Basically what I'm saying is, don't be so hard on your brothers. Just because they're not grieving the same way as you doesn't mean they're not grieving at all."

Placing a kiss on the top of her head, he sighed. "Thank you."

"For what?"

"For putting that in a way I could honestly understand. For so long, I was angry with them and thought I was right to feel that way. You proved to me that my way of thinking isn't the only way. So thank you."

"You're welcome."

"Are we okay?" he asked carefully.

She sighed again. "I guess we're both guilty of jumping to conclusions, huh?"

He chuckled and kissed her again. "Clearly, we are much too much alike."

"No such thing," she said with a small laugh of her own.

Ben reached down, tucked a finger under her chin, and guided her face up to his. "It's a good thing, right?"

She nodded. "A very good thing."

But there was a bit of hesitation, a wariness in her eyes that told him there was still something more to deal with.

"It makes me sad that you don't think you deserve to celebrate Christmas," she said softly, her hand caressing his temple. "I don't think it's what your parents would want for you."

Closing his eyes, Ben took a minute to compose his thoughts, because his first instinct was to lash out again. When he opened his eyes and looked at her, he could only state the truth. "It may not be, but it's what I want for myself. What I *need* for myself."

Sadness. Her entire face was one of sadness, and as much as he wanted to take that away, to see her smile and hear her laugh, he knew he couldn't do it this time. This was who he was, and if he was able to accept it about himself, then she would need to as well.

Maybe the timing was off. Maybe he should wait, but she was so close and so warm and pliant in his arms that Ben couldn't wait any longer to taste her, to kiss her properly. He was lowering his head when he heard a phone ring in a tone he hadn't heard before. Darcy instantly moved out of his embrace and stood.

"That's my dad's ringtone," she said as she scurried across the room to get her phone. "Hey, Dad!"

Ben sat and felt mildly frustrated. Not that he begrudged her talking to her family, but he had been looking forward to kissing her and then taking her to bed. Technically, they'd had a fight, and he was completely on board for some makeup sex.

He watched as Darcy paced in the kitchen as she talked. It wasn't like he was eavesdropping, but she wasn't particularly quiet either.

"Are you kidding?" she cried happily. "When?" She paused. "That is amazing! Oh my God!"

If he had to guess, he'd say it was good news she was getting, but in a family the size of hers, Ben would be hard-pressed to figure out what the news would be and who it was about.

Darcy squealed happily, and he watched as she did a little shimmy where she was standing. "This is amazing! No, no, no, I'm on it. I'll see what I can find, and I promise to let you know as soon as I can." She paused. "No, no, I'll be sure to call and let them know right away." Another pause. "I will, I will. Thanks, Dad!"

He didn't need to hear the other end of the conversation to know what was coming.

She had to leave.

Soon.

This, what they had, was ending. And a lot sooner than he'd thought.

"I love you too," she said. "I'll call you as soon as I have a flight. Bye!" Hanging up the phone, she put it on the kitchen table and then skipped back into the living room with a huge smile on her face.

Ben wanted to speak, to say something, but he couldn't seem to make himself do it.

"So that was my dad," she said with a big smile, bouncing onto the couch.

"Everything all right?" he asked, hating how tight his throat felt.

"Everything is great. But I have to head home." She sighed and crawled into his lap. "As much as I want to stay and was hoping for more time, I can't."

All Ben could do was nod. Darcy curled around him, hugging him close. He inhaled deeply, loving the way she smelled and knowing he was going to miss her more than he'd ever thought possible.

She kissed his neck, his jaw, and finally reached up and cupped his face as she claimed his lips. The kiss went from soft and sweet to hot and urgent. Ben didn't want to hear that she was leaving or what her plans were. He didn't care that her family wanted her home. He wanted to brand her as his—claim her—and make her want to stay.

His arms banded around her as she straddled him. His hands raked into her hair and gripped it tight as she began to grind against him.

It didn't matter what they had been talking about. Right now, all that mattered was that he keep touching her, kissing her, having her. He was about to carry her to the bedroom when she broke the kiss and rested her forehead against his.

"Damn, Ben," she said breathlessly.

He knew exactly how she felt.

"I could sit here and kiss you all day," she admitted, "but I can't. I need to find a flight home."

"You're not planning on leaving today, are you?" he forced himself to ask.

She shook her head. "No. But probably tomorrow." Lifting her head, she looked at him, and Ben saw the play of emotion there, the conflict. "You have no idea how much I want to stay here with you—at least for a little longer—but I have to go."

His curiosity got the better of him. "So what's going on?"

"I got a job interview!" she said with a big grin. "Apparently, I typed one wrong number for my cell phone in the online application, and they couldn't reach me, so they called my home number. And yes, we're totally those people who still have a landline. My dad hasn't moved completely into this century yet. They've been trying to reach me for over a week. That must mean they're really interested in hiring me!"

He smiled, or at least he tried to smile as he continued to listen to her.

"It's with the media relations department with a large gallery in Charlotte," she went on. "From everything I got from the ad, it could be a good fit for me. A really good fit—not too far from home, in a big city."

Ben could see that she was excited, and he wanted to be happy for her—he really did—but...

"It's amazing, right? Oh my gosh, I can't believe I typed the wrong number. I mean, I'm usually such a detail-oriented person, and to go and make a stupid mistake like that is crazy. Thank God I had a secondary phone number on the application, or I would have totally missed this opportunity."

"That's…that's great," he forced himself to say, still feeling a little bitter that a job opportunity had to happen *now* and mess up his plans.

"And now I feel like a complete doofus because of the whole phone number thing, and I've kept them waiting for a week already, so I need to go call them and find a flight." She climbed off his lap and noticed his reaction—or lack of reaction. "I need to be there. This could be the job I've been waiting for."

"I know."

She stood and sighed. "I'm sorry. I…I don't know what else I'm supposed to do. I can't be in two places at once."

"I know that too."

"You can come with me!" she said excitedly. "Seriously, just come home with me. You can meet everyone and—"

"Darcy," he quickly interrupted as he stood as well. "I can't go home with you."

Her expression fell. "Why not?"

Closing the distance between them, he took both of her hands in his and squeezed them. "For starters, I need to finish the work I have out in the shop. Then there's some new orders I need to start working on. And on top of that, I don't think your family would appreciate you bringing me home and dealing with me sleeping with you. Probably not the best first impression to make."

Frowning, she studied him for a moment. "Damn you for being practical."

He chuckled. "I can't help it. And believe me, sometimes I don't like it either."

This time when she sighed, it had a sad sound to it. "I'm not ready for this to end."

Thank God she said it, because it was all he could hear in his own head. "I'm not ready for that either."

"So where does that leave us?"

Refusing to think or to keep up this depressing conversation, Ben moved swiftly and bent to pick her up and throw her over his shoulder.

Darcy squealed excitedly. "Ben! What in the world are you doing?" Then she giggled as he started to walk toward the bedroom. "C'mon! Put me down! Stop!" She was laughing the entire time, so he knew she wasn't serious.

"We'll find you a flight. Later." He strode into the bedroom and kicked the door closed. "Right now, I want us to forget about everything else—our families, our jobs, our obligations, you leaving—all of it." He maneuvered her until she bounced on the bed, then he crawled over her and covered her body with his.

"Ben." It was more of a sigh than a complaint.

Immediately, he began kissing her—the sweet spot on her neck that he knew she loved, then downward. His hands snaked up under her sweater, but she was faster than him, whipping it off and away in the blink of an eye.

Her hands raked through his hair, scratching his scalp. "This doesn't change anything," she said, breathing heavily.

"I know. But for now, let's pretend that the rest of the world doesn't exist. That it's just you and me." His mouth latched onto her nipple through the lace of her bra, and Darcy's back arched off the bed. She purred with delight.

"Yes."

It was the last thing she said for a very long time.

# Chapter 7

TWO WEEKS LATER, DARCY WAS OUT SHOPPING WITH her sisters-in-law—something they tried to do at least once a month. Everyone around her was chatting and making plans for the holidays. It was good. It was fun. She had her Starbucks and was looking at cute clothes. That was a good thing, right? She was enjoying herself.

*Sort of*, she thought with a sigh.

The elbow to her ribs nearly had Darcy jumping out of her skin and spilling her drink. She turned and glared at Anna. "What the hell?"

"That is, like, the tenth time you've sighed in the last five minutes. We're supposed to be having fun here."

"I am having fun."

"No, you're a total buzzkill right now. I was elected the one who had to come and talk to you about it," Anna said quietly.

"Great."

"Have you talked to him since you got back?"

It was pointless to pretend that she didn't know who Anna was talking about. Nodding, she said, "We talk or text or Skype every day."

"So what's the problem?"

Darcy looked at her with disbelief. "Seriously? You have to ask?"

"Okay, fine. You're on opposite coasts. I get it. But... that's not a forever thing, right? He can come and see you, and you can go back and see him. Have you made plans for that?"

"No. Well…sort of. Or at least, I've been trying. He's had pieces to finish, then I was waiting to hear on the job at the gallery. Thanksgiving's coming up, and then there's Christmas and…" She sighed. "Realistically, it would be after New Year's before we could work something out. It's so damn far away."

"It is, I know, but if you're really serious, you'll find a way to make it work."

It was the same thing she and Ben had been talking about—along with a lot of dirty talk and phone sex—but it didn't make Darcy feel any better. If anything, she felt worse. If it were up to her, she'd hop on a plane this weekend to see him. Or she'd have him fly here to spend Thanksgiving with her. Actually, the more she thought about it, she had mentioned both of those scenarios to him, and he'd made excuses for each of them.

And some of the other ones she brought up.

She sighed again, and Anna smacked her in the arm. Hard. "Ow! Dammit, Anna!"

"Stop doing that, then! Seriously, if you want to pout or sigh or listen to sad songs while you doodle Ben's name in hearts, then do it when you get home. Right now, you need to put on your game face, smile, and pick out a dress, because we all decided that we're going to buy dresses for New Year's while we're here. So get moving!"

"We did? When? We're barely into November, for crying out loud. And I don't remember—"

"You were too busy moping and sighing over in the lingerie department," Anna stated, and then they both started to laugh. After a minute, Anna wrapped her arm around Darcy's shoulders and hugged her close. "C'mon, let's go get our sequins on."

"Oh, good lord. Sequins?"

"Nothing says New Year's Eve like a sparkly party dress," Anna said as she took Darcy's hand and led her to the dress department.

Thirty minutes later, Darcy studied her reflection and thought she didn't look half-bad. The jade-green dress was strapless with minimal beading, and it came to right above her knees. It hugged her curves, and as she did a turn in the 360-degree mirror, she had to admit that she had found her sparkly party dress. When she stepped out of the dressing room, her sisters-in-law—with the exception of Savannah—were all stepping out in their dresses as well.

"Doing this whole girly-girl thing normally annoys the crap out of me," Anna said as she admired her reflection, "but now I'm kind of looking forward to it."

Darcy nodded and smiled as her other three sisters-in-law—Zoe, Aubrey, and Brooke—joined them. "I know this is going to come out wrong," she said as she looked at Zoe, who was trying on a dress in the same color as hers, "but I hate you."

"What? Me? Why?" Zoe asked with wide-eyed bewilderment.

"You have a killer figure, and that color green looks amazing with your red hair," Darcy said with mock disdain. "Therefore, I have to hate you."

"Oh, stop," Zoe said with a laugh. "You've got more curves than any of us, and your boobs haven't had to deal with the trauma of having a child. You're braless and look amazing. I've got some sort of wonder contraption on under this dress to hold the girls up."

"Ditto," Aubrey said.

Darcy looked over as Anna raised her hand too. "Not that I'm complaining. This contraption makes me look better than I ever did."

Brooke adjusted the top of her dress and frowned. "Why strapless?" she murmured. "My whole life, I never had cleavage like this, and it just feels weird to be so on display. I need to find something else. Besides, I think Owen would freak out if I wore something like this in public."

They all laughed, and Darcy couldn't help but feel a little bit better. It was good to laugh. Then she looked down at her own breasts and remembered how much Ben had loved them—the way he'd touched them, kissed them, and… She sighed.

"I swear if you make that sound again," Zoe began and then turned to Anna. "I thought you were going to talk to her?"

"I did!" Anna cried. She turned to Darcy. "Now what? What could you *possibly* be thinking as we're standing here talking about boobs and bras that has you all mopey again?"

Darcy looked at each of them and tried to come up with a reasonable explanation. There was no way she was going to talk about how much she missed Ben's touch right now in the middle of a department store fitting room.

"I…it was…I mean…"

"Oh God," Brooke said. "It's Ben. You're thinking about Ben again, aren't you?"

"Um, I don't know," she murmured. "Maybe."

"For crying out loud," Zoe cried with exasperation. "If I buy you a plane ticket, will you just go back to Washington already?"

"Yes," Aubrey said before Darcy could come up with anything of her own to say. "I'd be willing to chip in for that."

"Hey!" Darcy cried. "I haven't been that bad!"

"No, no, she's right," Anna said sarcastically. "We can all remember what it's like when you're crushing on a guy."

"Oh, and she's *totally* crushing on him," Zoe said with a hint of an evil grin.

"Big time," Aubrey agreed, and Darcy had to wonder why she'd thought having sisters would be better than brothers. At least her brothers scared easily and never wanted to talk about her crushing on any guys.

"She's a little distracted," Anna said casually, "and needs to go and call him before we all take turns smacking her." They all laughed. "Now go. We'll do a little more shopping and meet up with you in the food court." Then she sighed dramatically. "The sacrifices we're willing to make for you."

"Oh, knock it off," Darcy said, having heard enough. "You are all just happy to be out of the house and away from the kids and loving the fact that my brothers are having to play babysitter for the afternoon."

"That's right," Aubrey said with a big grin. "Girls' day out!"

"Woo-hoo!" Brooke cheered.

"It is a beautiful thing," Zoe agreed. "I find that Aidan is much more agreeable to just about anything I ask for after a day of being alone with his daughter." She laughed. "He won't even complain about how much I'm about to spend on this dress."

Darcy couldn't help but laugh at that. It was interesting and comical to learn about this other side of her brothers. And if anything, it made her love them that much more, which made her sigh, and Anna, Zoe, Aubrey, and Brooke all turned to her immediately with cries of "Go!," "Just call him!," and her favorite, "For the love of it!"

"Okay, okay, I'm going," she said with a small laugh. "I just have to slip out of this dress and get changed. Geez."

And as she turned to walk away, she heard Aubrey mutter, "Damn her and her perky boobs." They all burst out laughing.

Darcy couldn't help but laugh along with them and then remembered that *this* was why she'd wanted sisters.

Ben stared into the refrigerator and tried to will something to come out and make itself. He was tired and hungry and more than a little cranky because he was missing Darcy. She'd only been in his home for a short time, and all of a sudden, it was like he hated everything about living alone. All the things he used to enjoy about it—the peace, the quiet, the freedom to do what he wanted when he wanted—held little to no appeal.

As if reading his mind, his phone rang, and he saw Darcy's face on the screen—a sexy picture he'd taken before she went back to North Carolina. Smiling, he reached for it and answered.

"Hey, beautiful."

"Hey, yourself," she said softly. "Whatcha doing?"

"Missing you," he said honestly.

"I miss you too."

"Where are you right now?" he asked, his own voice going soft.

"I'm at the mall with everyone—the girls. It's our monthly shopping trip."

"Monthly shopping trip? Really? That's a thing?"

She laughed. "It really is. Once a month, we leave all the kids with my brothers and hit the mall."

"For anything in particular or just to wander around?"

"Normally, it's just to wander around. Today, we all found dresses for New Year's Eve."

"It's November."

"That's what I said!" she exclaimed with another soft laugh. "But I found one, and it's fabulous, and I also found some amazing lingerie."

"You're killing me," he said as disappointment washed over him. He wished she was alone. Ben never would have thought himself the kind of man who got off on phone sex or that sort of thing, but something about this woman made him feel a bit wild and reckless like that. "Tell me about the dress. And do it slowly and in that sexy voice I love."

She laughed. "Stop! I'm in the middle of the mall." She paused. "But I will say this. It's a jade-green strapless dress that has some sparkly beading on the top. And if I do say so myself, I look good in it."

"You look good in everything," he said automatically, but he meant it.

"Mmm, I wish I was home right now," she purred.

"I wish you were here."

"That would definitely be better," she said with a soft sigh. "So I was thinking…"

"Uh-oh."

"C'mon. I'm serious," she said and then waited a moment. "Have you finished those pieces you were working on last week?"

"I did. The clients are coming to pick them up—one tomorrow, the other on Friday."

"Okay, good." She cleared her throat before going on. "So the book is done, you finished the two pieces you were working on, so really, your schedule is kind of open. You could come here to North Carolina and maybe spend Thanksgiving with me."

"And your family."

Another sigh, this one not so soft. "We're kind of a package deal." The laugh that followed was more out of nerves than humor, he knew.

"Darce, if I won't spend the holidays with my brothers…"

"Christmas. You said it was just Christmas. This is Thanksgiving. Completely different," she argued. "You could come here and stay with me."

"I'm sure your father will love that."

Her laugh was lighter this time. "Okay, maybe he won't *love* it, but between the holiday and a house full of grandchildren, he'll be distracted. The whole family will be in town, so even with all that, there are plenty of options for places for you to stay. My brother Aidan has an apartment over his garage that everyone has used at one time or another. We could take our turn there."

The thought of seeing her now rather than waiting

until after New Year's had Ben ready to go and pack his bag right now. "I don't know."

"Promise me you'll at least think about it."

"I will. I promise," he said and realized she was definitely sounding a bit more tense than she was when she first called. "So what are you wearing now?" he asked silkily.

She burst out laughing at that. "You're such a perv!"

He missed seeing her laugh and smile. Missed the soft feel of her skin and hearing her sigh his name. But more than anything, he just missed her.

And although he wouldn't admit to it right now, come hell or high water, he was going to see her.

Soon.

---

"Is this naughty? Because it feels naughty."

"Do you want it to be naughty?"

Darcy stopped what she was doing and considered the question. "You know, I kind of think I do."

"Then I guess this is naughty. Hand me that pillow."

They had been working for the last hour to get the apartment cleaned and stocked up with food. Zoe had a habit of cooking a few extra meals for whoever was going to be staying there and making sure the pantry was well-stocked. And even though Darcy knew this, she had brought over several grocery bags of her own filled with goodies.

"I wish I had been a fly on the wall when you told your father what you were doing," Zoe said with a smirk.

"Ugh…I wish I had been a fly on the wall instead of the one to tell him. It was beyond awkward."

"You told Martha you were going over to talk to him, right? I figured she would have paved the way for you."

"Oh, she did. That's the only explanation I can think of for why he took it so well," Darcy said, fluffing the last pillow.

Zoe straightened and looked at her quizzically. "You just said it was awkward."

"It was."

"Okay, I'm confused then. How can he take it so well and have it be awkward at the same time?"

"That's what was so awkward. I mean, beyond having to say 'Um, Dad, I'm going to stay with my boyfriend at Aidan and Zoe's for the week because, you know, I already slept with him after knowing him for less than a week, and I'd really like to have crazy-monkey sex with him again.'"

"Oh God! You didn't say that, did you?" Zoe asked with a horrified look on her face.

"Of course not! But it was implied."

Zoe nodded in agreement. "Okay, that I can understand." She looked around the bedroom and seemed pleased. "So what did he say exactly?"

"He sort of looked down at his mug of coffee and gave a curt little nod and said, 'Okay. Just make sure you're here on Thanksgiving.' It was…weird."

"I guess it could have been worse."

"Oh, I'm not done."

"Uh-oh."

"You mean your husband didn't tell you that he was there when all this happened?"

"What? No!"

"So was Hugh."

"No!"

"And Quinn."

"Oh God."

"And you know what? Even Bobby Hannigan was there."

"Wait, what? Why was Bobby there? I didn't know he was in town."

Darcy nodded. "He's here for Thanksgiving—took the whole week off—and apparently, he's staying with Quinn and Anna, and when he heard what was going on, as my honorary *sixth* brother, he thought he should be there."

"That's just crazy."

"Tell me about it. The only one missing besides Riley was Owen. And if anyone could guarantee that he wouldn't die of embarrassment, I'm sure he would have been invited too."

"He's gotten way better about his freak-out factor since he met Brooke. She's really been a good influence on him. I think—"

"Can we please stay focused on me?" Darcy shouted with frustration.

"Sorry. So what did they say?" she asked hesitantly. "And how did they even know you were going to have that talk with Ian?"

Darcy leveled her with a look. "Really?"

"Damn. You're going to have to talk to Martha about the way this family works. I can't believe she called in your brothers."

"That's not what I meant. She told Dad that I wanted to talk to him about a man, and he called in the cavalry."

"No!" Zoe cried and then started to laugh. "You've got

to be kidding me. And I am so going to kill Aidan when I get back to the house for not telling me any of this."

"Make it slow and painful, please."

They walked out to the living room, and Zoe collapsed on the sofa. "So what happened? What did you say? What did they say? Is it even safe for Ben to be coming here?"

"Ironically, they were a little more upset with Riley than Ben," Darcy said with a grin as she sat down.

"How? Why?" Pausing, Zoe let out a long sigh. "Why is nothing simple with this family?"

"They were all pissed that Riley sent me to Washington and then didn't do more to get me home."

Zoe rolled her eyes. "You explained the snowstorm? How you gave up your seat so that mother and baby could get home?"

Darcy nodded. "Didn't matter. Ultimately, they fixated on Riley, and personally, I'm relieved."

"Sure, it took the focus off you and Ben doing it."

Laughing out loud, Darcy had to admit that she loved how blunt Zoe was. "Hell yeah, it did. Thank goodness. Do you have any idea how awkward it's going to be for Ben as it is?" She shook her head. "He's already skittish about coming here. So if they can keep their anger and frustration focused on Riley for a little bit longer, I would greatly appreciate it."

"Is Riley aware of this? I have to think that he's been blindsided by all this. Did Savannah even know about you and Ben?"

Shaking her head, Darcy looked away. "No. I, um, I really haven't talked to her since I got home, and with her and Ben being friends, it just felt a little awkward to be talking to her about him." She walked to the kitchen and pulled open the refrigerator door. "What's in the casserole dishes?"

Zoe came up behind her. "There's a chicken pot pie, a lasagna, and a shepherd's pie. I also made potato salad for you, and there are some cold cuts for sandwiches." Then she looked at Darcy and gave her a sassy grin. "You could stay locked up in here for about three to four days and not run out of food."

"Wow! You certainly think of everything. Thanks!"

"Yeah, yeah, yeah. But I would appreciate it if you did come up for air and at least let me meet the man who has turned this family upside down before they've even met him."

"Oh, stop. This isn't anything new. My brothers have been freaking out about my dating life since I was born."

"Personally, I think it's sweet," Zoe said, closing the refrigerator door.

"That's because you're not the one under the microscope."

With a shrug, Zoe grabbed her jacket and walked to the door. "What time are you picking Ben up?"

"I need to be at the airport by three." She looked at the clock on the wall. "It will take me at least an hour to get there, so I need to freshen up and head out soon."

"You've already got your stuff here, right?"

Nodding, Darcy suddenly felt her heart start to race. "I can't believe in a few hours, he's going to be here."

Zoe simply leaned against the door and grinned.

"I'm nervous! Am I supposed to be nervous? Is that normal?"

Then Zoe walked over and hugged Darcy. "Yes, it's normal, and it's a good thing. Enjoy it."

When Zoe turned and opened the door, Darcy quickly called out to her, "Thanks. For everything."

"Anytime, Darce." Then she let out a happy sigh as she looked around the apartment one more time. "This place? It's been good for all of us. I know it's going to be good for you and Ben, too." And with a wink and a wave, she was gone.

---

The weather was almost balmy, and as Ben walked out of the airport terminal, he immediately regretted dressing so warmly.

Glancing at Darcy's text, he noted that she would be pulling up in front of the baggage claim doors any minute. She was driving a black Nissan SUV, she'd said, so he kept his eyes peeled for it.

Anticipation. It had him by the throat.

This wasn't supposed to happen. None of it. This wasn't how he'd imagined his life. He had accepted the cruelty of his fate—losing his parents and living an isolated existence. It wasn't what he wanted, but he'd come to terms with it. He'd even learned to handle the fame he'd acquired from his sculpting. Being in the spotlight wasn't comfortable for him, but Ben was learning to deal with that as well.

But meeting Darcy Shaughnessy?

He shook his head.

Nothing had prepared him for that.

If anyone had told him three months ago that he'd be flying across the country to be with a woman, he would have laughed at them. And if anyone said he'd be doing it so he could be with her and her family for Thanksgiving? He would have told them they were out of their damn minds. Deep down, he still wasn't sure this was a good idea.

But he had to see her. He was slowly going insane with missing her.

For the life of him, he didn't understand what was happening to him. They'd really only been around each other for less than two weeks. In the grand scheme of things, that was nothing. True, for most of that time, they were together twenty-four hours a day, but still. They'd never gone on a proper date—hell, they'd never even left his house—and yet he felt they knew each other better than most couples who'd been together for years.

He missed their late-night conversations in bed where they were naked and tangled up together and just talking about their lives.

He missed watching her dance around the kitchen as she prepared a meal.

He missed her crazy, concocted spiced cookies.

He just missed her.

So much so that he was ready to start walking to go and find her and her damn black SUV.

In the blink of an eye, there she was. The vehicle came to a stop right in front of him, and everything in him instantly relaxed. She stepped out, came around the hood of the car, and launched herself right into his arms.

And damn if she didn't belong there.

He kissed her as his hands cupped her ass and held her close, and if it wasn't for a car beeping behind them, he would have kept on kissing her. When he lifted his head, they were both breathless.

"Please tell me you live close," he growled as he lowered her feet to the ground.

"Not close enough," she said breathlessly as they worked quickly to stow his luggage. "It's about an hour. How was your flight?"

Small talk totally wasn't his thing, but since they had a bit of a drive ahead of them, he went with it. He told her about his flight from Seattle to Charlotte, and then from Charlotte to here. He told her about the difference in the weather and grumbled about how much he hated traveling.

She looked over at him with a grin. "I promise to make it worth it."

"Really?" he asked silkily.

She nodded.

"Although this trip was kind of a necessity."

She glanced at him out of the corner of her eye. "Really?"

He nodded. "I could have said that we would simply wait until after the holidays, but I couldn't. I couldn't wait to see you, Darcy."

Her cheeks turned the loveliest shade of red, and he reached out and caressed her there. God, how he loved the way her skin felt. Like silk.

He couldn't wait to get her into bed.

"I felt the same way," she replied softly. "It didn't feel like this day would ever get here."

Ben chuckled. "I know. I thought I needed more time to get things done, but I ended up getting through it all really fast, and then I had nothing else to do but sit around and wait."

"You could have come sooner. I would have totally been on board for that."

He laughed again. "What about work? What has your brother had to say about all this?"

If he wasn't mistaken, she groaned.

"That good, huh?"

"Okay, so here's the thing. This job with Aidan? It's temporary. I know it. He knows it, and he doesn't even really need me. He's helping me out until I find something that I want to do. And I appreciate it. I do. So taking the time off this week? It's not a big deal. Except it is."

Frowning, Ben twisted slightly in his seat to look at her. "You lost me."

She sighed louder this time. Clearly, she was frustrated, but he also knew that sometimes she needed to talk things out—out loud—to help her get a little perspective.

"I'm twenty-five years old, and I have no career. I'm trying, I really am. I didn't get the job at the gallery, and everyone's like 'How hard can it be to find a job?' And you know what? It's very hard! I hate it! Everyone thinks I'm being difficult, but I'm trying to get my shit together, and for the most part, I think I am. But this job thing? For some reason, I just can't seem to find something that clicks."

"That's not a bad thing," he tried to reason.

"Yes, it is. Don't you see?"

Honestly? He didn't.

"I am tired of being…this! I'm tired of living at home. I want to move out, get a place of my own, and that's hard to do when you don't have a job."

"But you have a job."

The growl that came out of her bordered on scary.

"Please don't be obtuse," she argued. "I need to find a *real* job. One with a future. One that I actually enjoy."

"Not everyone loves their job, Darcy."

The look she gave him pretty much confirmed that that was the wrong thing to say.

This was not the way he wanted to start their week together.

"Just hear me out," he said as she opened her mouth to speak again. "I love what I do."

"Not helping, Ben," she huffed.

"Can you just listen and not comment for, like, two minutes?" Then he didn't wait for her response. "Growing up, this was a hobby—sculpting, carving, making things out of the trees my grandfather cut down. I never thought it was going to be my career. I did pieces for friends and an occasional commission piece on referral, and I was making enough to get by. Then my folks died." He shrugged. "And that's when I knew I needed to get serious. I knew if I really pushed myself, I could help my brothers with school. And for a long time, I didn't love it. Even though it was something I loved doing, I didn't have any joy in it, because of the pressure and expectations I put on myself."

"You don't get it."

"I do. I swear I do," he said. "But maybe you're putting too much pressure on yourself. The job you get doesn't have to be the one that you're going to have forever, and that's okay. Not everyone knows what they want to do. Sometimes, you have to try a couple of different jobs or positions before you find the one that sticks. I lucked out. I know that and—"

"It's not just you. It's my whole family. Aidan always liked to build, and now he has his own construction company. Hugh has a head for business, and now he has a chain of luxury resorts. Quinn loved cars, and when he stopped racing, he started his chain of repair shops and restoration. Riley is, well, you know. And Owen…" She stopped and let out a soft laugh. "Damn, we all made fun of him for how much he used to obsess about the stars, and now he's a well-known and respected astrophysicist." She sighed. "And then there's me."

"What are you passionate about?" he asked softly and then smiled when she gave him a sexy grin. "Focus, woman. We still have about forty minutes until we get to your place, according to your timeline."

"Okay. What am I passionate about?" She shrugged. "Art, business, the combination of the two, but I can't seem to find a position that fits."

"I don't think that's true. You've worked at several places that you enjoyed."

"But it's all been temp work."

"Right."

"I love baking," she began. "But that's something I do to relieve stress or because I'm bored or…hell, is there ever a wrong time to have extra cake or cookies in the house?"

He laughed softly and waited for her to continue.

"It's not something I want to do as my job," she went on. "I can run an office like a drill sergeant. I love doing the administrative stuff, setting up systems, and getting things organized."

"It sounds like there would be thousands of jobs in that category."

"Oh, there are," Darcy agreed. "However, once things are set up, I get bored and want to move on. It's pretty boring dealing with the day-to-day crap. I like a challenge, and in an office, once things are in place and everyone knows what they're doing, it's…ugh. I hate it."

"I can understand that."

"Although…"

She huffed softly as if she was deciding whether she was going to share this next bit of information with him, so Ben waited and swore he wouldn't push. If she wanted to tell him, great. If not? Well, he'd have to deal with it and find a way to change the subject.

"Owen's wife, Brooke, is an artist."

"O-kay."

"I was fascinated by what she does. It's…it's amazing. She paints, she draws, she… It's all just incredible."

He nodded, because he wasn't sure what he could add to that.

"Anyway, while she and Owen were dating, I got to know her, and she would talk to me about the classes she taught at the community college and about how much she really wanted to work in a gallery and maybe someday show her work in one."

*Been there. Done that*, he thought. Didn't see what the big deal was.

"Anyway, she and Owen broke up briefly, and when they got back together and moved closer to home, she and I started spending even more time together. She loved talking about her paintings, and we would take day trips to galleries in the surrounding areas—we went as far as Virginia to the north and Georgia to the south.

So we didn't get to see any, you know, real galleries like the ones you'd find in New York City."

Ben was sure there was a point to this story, but for the life of him, he couldn't see where she was going.

"We would go into these places, and Brooke, she was always so passionate when we talked about her work, but when we talked to anyone at the galleries, she sort of clammed up and lacked confidence. By the third time she'd done it, I'd had enough. So I spoke up. And I always went prepared by having examples of her work on my phone."

"So you acted as, what, her representative?"

A smile crossed Darcy's face as she nodded. "One minute, I was kind of singing her praises, and the next…I don't know…I just kind of turned into this person who commanded attention and talked about all the reasons why Brooke's work should be on display."

"And?" Ben had to admit, he was curious as hell to see if she'd made it happen.

"And Brooke's paintings are now on display and for sale in about a dozen different places. There's a gallery near Wilmington where she's on display, and one in Virginia Beach, and one in Myrtle Beach. And then I got her into several boutiques and shops on the Outer Banks," she said, clearly pleased with herself.

"That's impressive," he said, unable to hide his grin. "Very impressive."

She shrugged. "I thought so."

"So maybe that's your thing. Maybe you should be doing that."

Immediately, Darcy shook her head. "It was easy to do that with Brooke. She's my sister-in-law. I didn't have to go out searching for her—she was right there. I don't have any idea how to find clients to take on so I could do this full-time. And besides that, I didn't charge Brooke anything. She's family, and I was happy to do it."

The wheels in Ben's mind began to turn, but he wasn't going to get into it with her right now. "Tell me about where we're staying. You've been a little vague about it other than saying it's an apartment above your brother's garage."

"It's nicer than it sounds," she said. "One bedroom—"

"What size bed?" he asked as he began to tease lazy circles on the palm of her hand.

"King."

"Good." While his fingers teased her skin, he saw her cheeks begin to flush, and her breath began to quicken. "Is there anything we have to do tonight or tomorrow?"

"Um…"

"Do we need to food shop or anything like that?"

She shook her head.

"That's good," he said, his voice a little gruff as he leaned closer to her. "Because once we get to the apartment and get inside, I don't want to have to do anything except strip you down and take you to bed and keep you there."

"Oh." It was a breathy sigh.

"Is that okay with you?" Leaning in even closer, Ben used his tongue to trace the shell of her ear.

"Keep that up, and I'm pulling the car over and we won't make it to the apartment."

He instantly straightened and looked at the clock. "Thirty minutes," he said and then grinned. "But if you get us there sooner, I promise to make it worth your while."

And with her foot pressed down a little harder on the gas, she got them there in twenty-three.

# Chapter 8

IT *HAD* BEEN HER PLAN TO STOP AND EAT DINNER ON their way home, but once Ben started talking in that deep, gruff voice that she loved and started caressing her hand—which he knew got her excited—Darcy couldn't seem to get them home fast enough.

She knew she parked her SUV in her designated spot on the driveway.

She knew they got out, grabbed Ben's suitcase, and walked calmly up the stairs to the apartment.

But once they were inside and the door was closed? It was chaos.

Ben dropped the suitcase next to the door and reached for her. Or maybe she reached for him; she couldn't be sure. And really? It didn't matter. All that mattered was that she was here with him and his hands were roaming over her body with an urgency that was driving her crazy.

Skin. She wanted his hands on her bare skin, and he wasn't getting there fast enough. But no matter how hard she tried, no matter how much she squirmed and tried to grasp the bottom of her sweater, Ben stopped her. He had even gone so far as to grasp her hands and hold them firmly behind her back.

It was a turn-on.

"I know what you want," he whispered huskily against her lips. "And I promise we'll get to that, but for right now, I want to kiss you."

"Can't you kiss me in the bedroom?" she asked, gently nipping at his bottom lip.

"Sweetheart, I plan to kiss you everywhere."

*Oh. My.*

"And then I'm going to touch you everywhere too," he went on. "And when I'm done, I'm going to start all over again."

"Ben," she sighed.

"What is it, princess? What do you want?"

Oh God. Didn't he know? Couldn't he tell? "You," she said, more than a little frustrated that they were still even talking. "I want you."

"You have me."

Leaning in, she kissed him softly, then with a little more urgency. Ben was instantly on board, and when he released her hands, she let them roam up his arms, over his shoulders, and down his broad back. Letting them drift lower, she squeezed his incredible ass and couldn't help but smile against his lips as he groaned. She swiped her tongue across his bottom lip to soothe where she'd nipped at it, and then reached up and cupped his face before going deeper.

The truth was that she loved kissing Ben. Loved being kissed by him. But it wasn't enough. Darcy wanted it all. And she wanted it all with him right now.

Then she lifted her head, grabbed his hand, and led him to the bedroom.

He was smart enough not to argue.

———

Darcy Shaughnessy was lethal, and she was going to be the death of him.

But what a way to go.

The room was dark, and she was curled up against his side. Ben realized that for the first time in weeks, he felt relaxed and at ease and content.

It only seemed to happen when she was with him.

*You're falling hard and fast*, he thought. And it was true. He was. He had. And there wasn't a damn thing he could do about it. What about Darcy called to him so strongly, he couldn't say. All he knew was that from the moment he laid eyes on her, it was as though everything made sense. She was his.

The real problem was trying to figure out what to do about it.

They were going to have this week together—uninterrupted for the most part—so they could talk about it. Them. Where they saw this relationship going. And if he were honest, Ben would admit he wanted to get that discussion out of the way before he had to meet her family.

Her brothers.

He personally had no idea what it was like to have a sister, but he did know from all the things Darcy had shared with him that her brothers were extremely over-protective of her. So he was fairly certain that unless his intentions were clear, there were going to be a lot of awkward interactions between him and her five brothers at Thanksgiving.

"I can hear you thinking from here," Darcy said softly beside him as she stretched. "You okay?"

Here was his opening. "I was thinking about Thanksgiving."

She raised her head. "Seriously? I blacked out after

that third time, and you have enough brain cells to think about Thanksgiving? Big fan of turkey?"

Laughing softly, Ben pulled her in close and kissed the top of her head. "I wasn't specifically thinking about it," he said carefully. "My thoughts just sort of ended up there."

"And where did they start?" she asked, amusement lacing her voice.

"With you."

Even in the dark, he knew she was smiling. Darcy shifted beside him, placed a kiss on his chest, and hugged him. "I like the sound of that."

"I was thinking about how much better I feel when you're with me," he began. "And I miss you when we're not together."

"I miss you too." Another kiss.

Maybe he wasn't too clear. "Darcy, what I mean is, I know we haven't known each other for long, but you mean a lot to me."

She stilled beside him.

"This isn't about sex," he quickly added. "This is about you. And me. And I see a future for us."

She snuggled in close, burying her face against his bare chest, and he felt her tremble.

For a moment, he held her, and then he tucked a finger under her chin and tilted her head so he could see her face. "I didn't mean to freak you out."

She let out a soft sigh. "I tend to jump into things without thinking. I've told you that already."

Ben nodded.

"Most of the time, it gets me in trouble. Something bad happens, or in the case of relationships, I usually find out I'm the only one seeing a future that isn't there." She looked up at him, her dark eyes bright with unshed tears. "You're the first man to tell me you saw a future with me. Ever."

Well, damn. That was a kick in the gut to him, mainly because he heard the pain in her voice. What man could *not* want a future with her? Didn't they realize how incredible she was? How special?

"That was their mistake," he said softly. "Their loss is my gain. Because when I look at you, Darcy, from the very first time I looked at you, I knew."

Her eyes went wide as she looked at him.

"When I'm with you, I feel like a better person. You make me hopeful. Like I don't have to live my life alone, tucked away in my workshop, cut off from everything and everybody."

"You shouldn't be so isolated," she said softly. "It's not good for you."

He shrugged.

"Now I have motivation to find balance. I'm not saying I've got it all figured out, but I think maybe together, we can."

Darcy lifted her head and stared at him. "I don't want to be the reason you have to turn your life upside down. I wouldn't be able to handle that."

Turning toward her, he cupped her face in his hands. "Listen to me. The only person responsible for turning my life upside down is me. I should never have let myself get to this point. You are my motivation, but I'm the reason why I need to change. Not you. Do you understand that?"

She stared at him in disbelief. "But you said you were doing this because of me."

"You're the reward for doing it," he said softly. "And I'm so thankful to you—*for* you—that it makes me kind of excited to do this. To make the changes." Leaning in, he kissed her softly on the lips.

Darcy smiled and said, "I've been thinking about a future with you, too. But I'm afraid to jump in too soon."

He shook his head. "I'm here with you because I want to be. I'm thinking about a future with you because I want one. And I want one with you because I love you."

She gasped, and her eyes were as big as saucers.

With a lopsided grin, he went on. "I'm in love with you, Darcy Shaughnessy. It's fast and it's crazy and it's wonderful and exciting. Just like you."

She squeezed his hand. "The first time we kissed, I just…knew. And I tried telling myself that I was being impetuous and crazy, but deep down, I knew I wasn't. I knew this was different."

His heart began to beat erratically.

With a steadying breath, she smiled at him. "I love you too."

Pulling her close, he rolled onto his back until Darcy was on top of him, and she rested her forehead against his.

"This is good," he said softly.

She nodded.

Ben's hands traveled up her spine and to her nape as he angled his head and kissed her.

Deeply.

Thoroughly.

He poured everything he felt into that kiss, and as she melted against him, he could feel all she felt for him. It was heady and wonderful and so damn good.

Two days later, Darcy was busy making lunch while Ben was showering when her phone rang. Without looking at the screen to see who it was, she simply answered, "Hello?"

"Would you like to explain to me why I have a band of angry Shaughnessys ready to strangle my husband?"

Oh. Shit.

"Oh…hey, Savannah," Darcy said casually. "What's up?"

"What's up? I don't think our phone has been quiet for days. *Days!* It's like all your brothers—*and* Bobby Hannigan—have set up a schedule where they take turns calling here to yell at and lecture Riley. And me!" She sighed loudly. "I kept waiting for you to call. The only reason I'm calling you is because I got tired of waiting. Dammit, Darce, why didn't you tell me what was going on with you and Ben? This all could have been handled a lot better if Riley and I had been prepared. We both felt ambushed, and that's not cool."

With her own sigh, Darcy sat at the kitchen table. "At first, I thought we were fooling around and that it was sort of like a naughty weekend kind of thing. But then…"

"Then it was more."

"Exactly."

"I don't get it," Savannah went on. "How did this happen? Or do I not want to know?"

They were going to have to talk about this eventually. Looking over her shoulder toward the bathroom, Darcy silently prayed Ben was going to take his time in the shower.

"I'll admit it—I was attracted to him the minute I saw him. That first night, he was nice, and I thought he was incredibly good-looking, and I was enjoying the whole thing. His house was gorgeous, the view was great, and…I don't know, it was all fun."

"But…"

"But then he said some things that kind of freaked me out."

"What did he say?"

"It wasn't just what he said, but kind of how he was saying it."

"Which was?"

Ugh. This was beyond awkward. "He was just…he said…it was like…"

"Use your words, Darce," Savannah prompted.

"He was gushing over you. Like seriously gushing. And not in a respect for your work kind of way, but in an all about *you* kind of way."

Silence.

"It annoyed me, and I felt like…I don't know…like he was into you, and I was—"

"You were what? A friend was saying nice stuff about me, and you were what?"

"Jealous, okay? Looking back, I know that I was jealous." She sighed loudly. "And I don't even know why *that* was my immediate reaction, but there it is. Happy?"

"Seriously?" Savannah cried. "Are you freaking kidding me? You thought Ben had a thing for me? That is insane!"

With a huff, Darcy got up and began to pace. "I know I was wrong. I can see that now. But at the time, it just made me…it made me really not want to like him—not as a person, and certainly not as anything more. If he would be interested in a married woman—"

"Oh God."

"Look, at the time, I was seriously pissed off," Darcy admitted. "Then I figured I'd talk to you about it. But there was never the right time, and then the storm moved in, and that became the priority. When Ben showed up at the airport, I was livid. The last thing I wanted was to be stuck with a guy who had a thing for my sister-in-law and who was such an incredible pain in the ass to work with!"

"Darcy, for crying out loud."

"I didn't tell him that. At first."

"You didn't—"

"Eventually I did. Mainly because he confronted me on my attitude toward him. And the worst of it was, no matter how mad I was and how disgusted I was with him, I was still attracted to him. And that made me feel even worse."

"You should have called me."

"Ben said the same thing. But I was too embarrassed."

"Darcy, there never was nor will there ever be anything romantic between Ben and me. I love your brother. He's it for me. Ben is someone I interviewed who became a good friend. That's it."

"I know that now, but..." She shrugged. "You can't blame me for feeling insecure. I mean, look at you."

"Me?" Savannah exclaimed. "What about me?"

"You're beautiful. And confident and...and what guy wouldn't want you?"

"The list is endless," she deadpanned. "But that's not the point. The point is that Ben is into *you*. And believe me, I'm going to have some words with him too for not calling and telling me what was going on. Seriously, the two of you ruined my week."

"Sorry about that."

"Not good enough," Savannah replied lightly. "There will be some major babysitting duty in the future for you. Like during-the-terrible-twos-when-Aislynn's-hopped-up-on-sugar babysitting. And you're going to have to talk to Riley. He's pacing behind me right now, waiting his turn."

"Oh, come on. I said I was sorry!"

"Right. Because that's enough to make one of your brothers be quiet. You know better than that."

"Any chance he could wait until tomorrow?"

"Any chance you could sprout some wings and fly to the moon?"

"Point taken," Darcy said with a sigh. "Fine. Put him on the phone."

They said their goodbyes, and then she heard Savannah whispering to Riley to behave.

This was *not* going to go well.

"Give me one good reason why I shouldn't be on a plane right now to kick Ben's ass," Riley said as he got on the phone.

"Because you're not that guy," Darcy responded dryly. "Be real. You're not someone who goes around kicking people's asses. You wouldn't risk messing up your face. Or your hands. And you're not the violent type, so cut that out."

He let out a low growl of frustration.

"What the hell, Darcy? I've got everyone calling me, telling me how irresponsible I am, and for what?

Because you went and screwed around with Ben? And really? Ben? Of all the guys in the world, why him?"

"What's wrong with Ben?"

"He's a nice enough guy, but he's a friend. I don't want to think about you doing, you know, with anyone! I especially don't want to think about you doing that with someone we know. And now whenever I see Ben, that's what I'm going to be thinking, and I'm going to want to kick his ass!"

"Yeah, but you're not going to, so let that go," she teased. "Look, I'm sorry everyone ganged up on you. I had no idea that was going to happen, and for what it's worth, I did defend you. But you know how they are. They were looking for someone to blame because they all think I'm a kid." She paused. "I'm not, you know. I'm an adult. I'm a grown woman. I date and—like it or not—I have sex."

"Oh God," he said with a groan. "Just stop."

"No! This is why we're in this predicament! None of you want to accept the fact that I've grown up. You all scared away the guys I liked while I was in high school, and even some while I was in college. I stopped bringing guys home because of it. Hell, even Owen tried to scare away the guy I was with in Vegas."

Riley chuckled. "And I'm still sorry I missed that. I would have loved to see Owen standing up to someone like that."

"Yeah, yeah, yeah. Good for him," Darcy said sarcastically. "But the fact is, there was going to come a time when you were all going to have to *stop* with the intimidation and the freaking out. Eventually, I was going to fall in love and want to get married. Have kids.

You can't keep me locked away and treat me like I'm a child forever."

He sighed. "Look, I get that. I even agree with you. And while it freaks me out to think about you and Ben," he said with a hint of disgust, "what I'm pissed about is how everyone is blaming me for this."

"Just because you're open-minded doesn't mean the rest of them are. It was a ridiculous scene, and believe me, if I could have convinced them to calm down and think like logical people, I would have. If Anna or Zoe or Aubrey had been there, this could have gone in a completely different direction. But all the testosterone in that room didn't equal any brain cells."

"So what am I supposed to do?"

"They're all going to meet Ben tomorrow at Thanksgiving dinner, so until then, stop answering your phone," she said with a small laugh. "After all this time, what else could they possibly have to say?"

"Sometimes it's a one-word text," he said miserably. "And they're normally pretty crude and colorful."

"That's Quinn."

That made Riley laugh. "Look, are you sure about this? About Ben? Is this…is this serious, or are you two messing around?"

"Messing around? Seriously?"

"You know what I mean," he said wearily. "Work with me here."

Darcy looked over her shoulder one more time and noticed that the shower wasn't running anymore. Any minute, Ben would be walking out. Hopefully in nothing more than a towel.

"Look," she said, her voice going a bit quieter. "This

isn't just messing around. I'm crazy about him. I'm in love with him, and the feeling is mutual. It's not easy, because he's all the way on the other side of the damn country, but this is new to us both. So I don't have all the answers. All I know is that we're looking for them."

Riley sighed. "Wow. I...I don't even know what to say to that. That was remarkably—"

"Mature? Logical? Not at all like the comments of a child?" she mocked.

"Fine. Point taken."

"Good. Share that with your brothers when you talk to them."

"You know, you could talk to them and take the heat off me. I mean, why wait until Thanksgiving?"

"It's one more day, Riley."

"Yeah, but you're staying at Aidan's. Let him meet Ben and talk to him. Once he gives his seal of approval, the rest of them will back off."

"Because I'm not ready to share yet. You already know Ben. You should be giving the seal of approval and making them listen."

"God, you're such a brat," he said with a huff.

"Aww, such sweet words. You should put them in a song."

Laughing, Riley took a minute before saying anything else. "Fine. I'll keep doing damage control, but tell Ben he better dazzle the hell out of them on Thursday."

"Don't worry. He will."

"Good. Do you want to talk to Savannah again?"

She was about to answer when she heard a sound behind her. Turning, she saw Ben standing in the doorway to the bedroom in nothing but a towel.

*Yes.*

He grinned at her and crooked a finger to call her to him.

*Hell yes.*

"Uh, no. That's okay. We'll all talk on Thursday. So give Aislynn a kiss for me. Love you! Bye!"

Maybe Riley said goodbye, maybe he didn't. Either way, Darcy finished the call and turned off the phone as she stood. Slowly, she walked toward Ben.

"Everything all right?" he asked.

She nodded.

"That sounded a little intense."

"Riley and Savannah found out about us. From my brothers."

"I guess I should be expecting a call from her, huh?"

"Probably." By now, they were toe-to-toe. "Hopefully not today."

Nodding, Ben reached out and wrapped an arm around her waist. "I should probably follow your lead and turn off my phone."

A slow smile crossed her face. "That's up to you." Standing on her tiptoes, she gave him a light kiss on the lips. "I can't believe I'm going to say this, but go and put some pants on so we can have lunch. I'm starving."

Ben threw back his head and laughed. "Oh, thank God! I didn't want you to think there was something wrong with me for wanting food more than sex right now."

Laughing, she stepped out of his arms and went toward the kitchen. "They're both good choices, but yeah. Lunch is the priority right now. I'm making some grilled ham and cheese sandwiches and soup, if that's okay with you."

"Absolutely. Give me five minutes to get dressed, and I'll join you."

Darcy went back to work, and sure enough, five minutes later, Ben was beside her. When they sat to eat, they both sighed in unison at the first bite. That made her smile — how in sync they were with one another.

"I followed your recipe," she said with a grin. "I haven't mastered it yet, but I think I'm off to a good start."

He nodded in agreement. After a few bites, Ben put his sandwich down and wiped his hands before looking at her. "So I was thinking…"

"Uh-oh. You sound serious. Am I going to like this?"

Ben couldn't help but chuckle. "I hope so, because I really do."

"You? You really like something?" she teased. "Color me surprised, Mister Grumpy. Okay, lay it on me. Whatcha got?"

"I have an opportunity to go to New York next week to meet with my editor, Laura. She wants to get together and have me meet with a couple of gallery owners and talk about plans for next year when the book comes out." He shrugged. "I'll have some dinners to go to and a couple of meetings to go over schedules and whatnot, but I thought you might want to come with me."

"You're sure about this? You really want me with you? This is a big thing for you — for your career. I don't want to be in the way."

"You know, you throw that phrase around a lot, and I know that I personally keep telling you that you're never in the way. So let that go," he chided softly. "I want you there with me, Darcy. I think it might be nice to have a week away together."

"We're away now."

He laughed softly as he shook his head. "Sweetheart, we're hiding out here in your brother's apartment until we have to face your family. I'm talking about being away and staying at a five-star hotel, going out to dinner, a Broadway show, sightseeing." He took one of her hands in his and caressed it. "I've yet to take you out on a proper date. I kind of like the idea of taking you out to a nice restaurant, then touring a gallery, and then maybe a carriage ride through Central Park."

"That does sound good."

"Plus, I think this could be something that's interesting to the both of us because of your interest in working in the art world. Maybe you can talk to some people, make connections…"

"In New York? But that would mean…I mean…I guess I could, and…"

New York had always been on her radar as a place to work—it was one of the best places for art galleries and museums. But now that she and Ben were together, did she really want to consider job hunting there? It wouldn't bring her any closer to him and, if anything, it would put even more demands on her time.

Ben must have sensed the same thing, because he immediately changed the subject. "So are we making anything to bring to your father's tomorrow? A pie? A side dish?"

"I'm supposed to bake some stuff tonight, but nothing major. Martha wants to do the dinner on her own this year. We're all a little nervous about it."

"Really? Why?"

She shrugged. "It's always been just us. We have

our own traditions, and it was weird enough when my brothers started getting married and their wives wanted to contribute to the meal."

"I don't understand."

"The Shaughnessys are big on routines and traditions. When something works, we stick with it. So when someone suggests using fresh cranberries instead of the jellied kind, we freak out a bit."

"Ah, I get that. There were things my parents always made on Thanksgiving—we had a set menu that we never wavered from. It was all the basics, but since they died, whenever I've eaten at someone else's house on the holiday and the menu is different, it feels weird."

She laughed. "Then we can be weirded out together, because I have a feeling tomorrow is going to be different for all of us."

"And we agreed to this why?"

She smiled and reached for her glass of soda. "Because it's family," she said simply. "And you're supposed to be with family during the holidays." Then she realized what she said. "Sorry. That was wrong for me to say."

"Why?"

"Because you're here with my family and not with yours. I'm sure your brothers would have liked to spend the time with you too."

He shrugged and picked up his sandwich again. "It's not like that for us. I think they would like it, but I'm okay with the way things are."

"Ben, you need to make time for your brothers. They're the only family you have. If we're going to be up in New York, you should invite them to come and see you. I bet they would love it and get a kick out of some of the events that are being held in your honor."

He rolled his eyes and took another bite of his lunch. "I doubt it. They don't get excited over my work, and I don't get excited over theirs."

"Well, that's just sad. We're always celebrating and supporting each other's jobs in our family."

"Can we drop this for now?" he asked.

The rest of the meal was spent in silence, and after they were done eating, Darcy excused herself to go and take a shower. Ben said he'd clean up the kitchen, and she didn't even bother to argue or offer to help. She needed the time away from him for a few minutes to let everything they had talked about sink in.

The idea of going away with him for a week was exciting, and she loved that it had been his idea. Using the trip to scope out jobs had some potential. After all, she kept talking about being serious about this career choice. How could she pass up the opportunity? His family? That was going to be an issue for sure.

"Too much to think about," she murmured.

Turning on the shower, Darcy waited for the water to heat up and then stepped under the spray. And for a few minutes, she allowed herself the luxury of not thinking about anything at all.

---

He knew she was disappointed in the way their conversation had turned, but he couldn't help it. There were going to be things that they were going to have to agree to disagree about. And no matter how much he loved her and wanted to make her happy, he didn't like the idea of being pushed, especially not where his family was concerned. And he certainly didn't want to argue about it when there were so many other things they could be doing.

A few minutes later, Ben heard the water in the bathroom turn off. He smiled and strode purposefully toward the bathroom.

To Darcy.

She opened the door as he was approaching. Her skin was dewy and rosy from the hot water, she didn't have on a stitch of makeup, and she was wrapped in a towel that barely covered her.

She was perfection.

Her dark eyes went wide as he reached for her, taking the towel from her body. With a soft gasp, she stood perfectly still as if waiting for what he was going to do next.

Words. Dozens, hundreds of words buzzed in his head that he wanted to say to her, but for the life of him, he couldn't voice them. Instead, he lowered his head and kissed her. It wasn't gentle. It wasn't seductive. It was a kiss that took and claimed and demanded.

And she instantly wrapped herself around him.

God, he loved that about her.

Without breaking the kiss, Ben picked her up and carried her to the bedroom and thought of nothing else but the woman in his arms and pleasing her until he had nothing left to give.

# Chapter 9

IT WAS EASY TO IGNORE THE DEAFENING SILENCE AND the intimidating glares.

Well, easy for her.

Darcy breezed through the living room with the pies she had baked and gave everyone a wave and a smile on her way to the kitchen. And while it may have seemed mean to leave Ben standing in the middle of the angry mob, they had discussed it on their way over, and he had asked for the opportunity to talk to her family without her hovering.

So as she put the pies down on the kitchen counter, she peeked out into the living room and held her breath.

This was her.

Not hovering.

She almost laughed as her brothers all seemed to sit at the same time, their wives beside them. *Traitors*. Although it was probably for the best that her sisters-in-law stayed in there. Less of a chance of things getting out of hand.

"So what kind of pies did you decide on?" Martha asked.

"Oh, um, I did two pumpkin and two apple. The basics," she said distractedly. Martha placed her hand on her shoulder, and she turned toward her.

"They're going to behave. Trust me."

"How can you be so sure?"

"Because your father had a long talk with everyone before you arrived. And by the way, showing up thirty minutes late was brilliant," Martha said with a wink. She turned and went toward the oven. "At first, everyone thought you were being fashionably late, but I figured you wanted to make sure everyone was here and settled in before you arrived."

That wasn't totally the plan, but Darcy was glad that was how others were seeing it.

"So how bad was it? Was there yelling?"

Martha bent over to baste the turkey before answering. Closing the oven door, she smoothed her hands over her apron. "No. I think everyone got that out of their system the other day."

"Whew."

"However, they're still going to grill that poor young man, so I hope he's prepared."

Darcy nodded and craned her neck to look into the living room. "He is. This is all so…stupid."

"Don't look at it like that." Martha grabbed her hand, gently pulled her toward the kitchen table, and motioned for her to sit down. "I think it's incredibly sweet."

"Sweet?" she cried, and then her hand instantly covered her mouth. *Inside voice*, she chided herself. "How can you say that?"

With Darcy's hand still in hers, Martha gave her a patient smile. "They are concerned about you. They want you to find a man who is worthy of you."

"Um, no. They are trying to control me and my life because they all think they know what's best. Ben is—"

"Ben is wonderful, and they're not going to find fault with him," Martha interrupted, and when Darcy looked at her quizzically, she added, "We talked to Riley and Savannah. Based on what they said to your father, I can't imagine anyone in there having an issue with Ben."

"Oh, well then, why are they doing this, again? Why couldn't we come in and sit like normal people?"

"They're curious. You haven't brought a boy home in ages."

That made Darcy laugh. "Ben's not a boy."

"No, he's not. He's a fine-looking man."

"Martha!" Darcy cried and then started to giggle.

"What? I know I'm old enough to be his mother—his *young* mother," she added. "I can still appreciate an attractive man."

"I cannot believe we're having this conversation." Darcy felt herself blushing and wanted to crawl under the table and hide.

"Oh, stop. I think all your brothers are very attractive, and don't even get me started on Bobby Hannigan! He grew up to be a very sexy man too."

"Oh my God! Please don't ever say that again!" Darcy giggled.

"What? You can't tell me that seeing that man in uniform isn't reason enough to speed down Main Street. You have no idea how many of the girls who work for me have said the same thing. There was a city-wide moment of silence when Bobby moved away."

Darcy shook her head. "Bobby's cute, but he's not all that. And please don't let him hear you talking about him like that or you'll inflate his already over-inflated ego."

"Oh, I don't think he's like that."

"They're all like that," Darcy countered. "Trust me. I saw it with my brothers."

They shared a smile, and right then and there, Darcy felt a bond. Like they were sharing an important moment.

Looking at the clock on the wall, Martha turned to Darcy. "I think we gave them a solid ten minutes. Let's go join them and save Ben from any more grilling."

Darcy considered that for a minute and replied, "Nah. Let's give them another five. It's what he planned on."

Martha's smile grew. "How about you and I find a place for these pies and then get the potatoes started?"

It felt good to be working together on preparing the meal, she thought. "That sounds great!"

---

As far as interrogations went, the Shaughnessys could probably work with the FBI or the CIA. There was a minute or two where Ben seriously started to sweat.

Over the past ten minutes, he'd been asked everything from where he was born to how much he made per year and where he saw his career in five years.

"Darcy lives here, near her family," Aidan, Darcy's oldest brother, was saying. "And you're all the way in Washington state. Don't you think that's a little too long-distance for a relationship?"

He did. But he had no doubt they'd find a workable solution for them both. His genuine hope was that she'd come to Washington to live with him.

"Darcy's not sure where she wants to be right now or where her career might take her," Ben said casually. "Geography isn't currently on our side, but it's not so great of an obstacle that we're going to let it define our relationship."

Aidan didn't look quite so convinced. "She has a job here."

Ben nodded. "One that she knows isn't permanent and that you offered to her as a way to fill her time until she found something that she wants to do. I think she's on her way to figuring that out, but that's her story to tell and not mine."

"And yet you went and brought it up," Hugh, the resort owner, commented.

Man, these guys were tough. It was like Ben couldn't catch a break. He would have thought for sure they would have been impressed with him not pressuring Darcy to move closer to him, and somehow, they weren't.

"It was pertinent information," he countered. "This whole Q and A thing we have going on right now deals specifically with the two of us."

"More so with you," Hugh replied.

Ben shrugged. "That may well be, but ultimately, it's about me and Darcy." He sighed and straightened in his chair, looking at each of them as he scanned the room. "Look, I never had a sister. I have two brothers. But I can respect how you're all looking out for Darcy. I'm not some irresponsible guy. I'm a grown man with a good career, I own my own home, and I have a healthy savings account and retirement account. I helped put both of my brothers through college after our parents died, but more than any of that, I love your sister."

You could have heard a pin drop.

He looked at them all levelly again. "I am in love with your sister. Her happiness means the world to me. You all don't have to like me. I'm fine with that, because right now, I'm not feeling too kindly toward some of you," he said honestly. "But what we all have in common is that we love Darcy."

And then suddenly, there she was beside him. Sitting and taking one of his hands in hers and kissing him on the cheek. Then she looked at her family as she relaxed against him and began to speak.

"Okay, the interview portion of our Thanksgiving is now officially over. For the rest of the day, if you'd like to talk to Ben, you'll have to talk to me too. And I think you should all think hard before you do, because while Ben was gracious enough to sit here and answer all your ridiculous questions, I'm not going to be quite so accommodating. So choose your words wisely."

And although her tone was firm, her smile never faltered, and he was beyond impressed with his girl. Unable to help himself, he placed a kiss on her temple and faced the family again.

If there had been a cue, he missed it, but everyone stood and started talking to one another at once. He was taken aback by the abrupt change, but Darcy turned to him and explained.

"Sometimes they need to be reminded of their manners," she said softly. "And for what it's worth, you were brilliant."

"I don't know about that. I almost wish I had brought another shirt with me. I'm pretty sure I sweated through this one."

She laughed as she stood and tugged him to his feet.

Hugh and Aubrey walked over first. "I have a question," Aubrey said with a sassy grin.

"If it's about bank accounts or history of heart disease in his family, you're out of luck," Darcy teased, and they all laughed.

"No, but I'm almost sorry I didn't think of that

sooner!" Aubrey said with another quick laugh. "I was kind of wondering if you do things like tree houses. Custom tree houses."

*Interesting*, Ben thought. "You know, I've read a lot about them, and I know there are companies out there who do them, but no one's ever approached me about one before. I think that could be fascinating to try."

"Well, if you ever want to do a test run, we would be more than happy to serve as the guinea pigs. Our little boy Connor would love one."

"He's five," Hugh added.

Ben considered them both for a moment. "Tell you what, why don't the two of you work on making up a list of things you'd like to see in a tree house, and after Christmas, I'll try to sketch it. That's probably the soonest I could get to it."

"That sounds perfect. And it wouldn't be a huge rush," Aubrey commented. "If anything, maybe something for next Christmas?"

Ben nodded. "If I can figure out how to do it, I'll make it happen." Then he paused. "Oh, and if you could send me some pictures of your yard and the tree you want it in or the spot in the yard you want it—if you decide to go with a clubhouse sort of thing—that would be great."

"I know I'd feel better with a clubhouse on the ground," Aubrey said as she looked at Hugh.

He immediately shook his head. "A boy should have a tree house. Hell, he loves to climb everything now. Think how excited he'd be to have his own fort up in a tree!"

Aubrey didn't look too convinced, but Ben didn't have time to hear any more of their discussion, because as soon as they stepped away, Quinn and Anna walked over.

"Hi, I'm Anna. I figured you got hit with a lot of names when you first came in, so I wanted to reintroduce myself and my husband, Quinn." She turned and frowned at Quinn. "And I wanted to talk to you about your work."

He was noticing a pattern here.

"I own a pub in town, and I want to make some changes. It's been there forever and is due for a face-lift. I always wanted a custom bar. Do you do anything like that?"

Before Ben could answer, Darcy started bragging about the furniture he had in his house. She and Anna stepped to the side, and that's when Quinn moved in.

Great.

For a minute, it was like a standoff, and Ben felt that if he blinked first, this was the brother who would pounce all over him. So he waited.

"So," Quinn began after a moment, "you're seriously in love with my sister?"

Standing a little straighter, Ben nodded. "I am."

"You realize how this will end for you if you hurt her, right?"

Another nod. "I do."

Quinn studied him before giving a curt nod. "Do you know anything about this bar Anna mentioned?"

And that was pretty much how the rest of the day went.

—◆◆◆—

The next day, Ben glanced at the kitchen clock and tried not to be annoyed.

Eight hours.

Darcy had been gone—shopping!—for eight hours!

He tried not to let it bother him. After all, this was some kind of family tradition. But he'd been hoping they'd spend that time together.

Throwing out the remnants of his lunch, he decided to see what was on the TV to kill some time. Just as he got comfortable and found a home improvement show to watch, he heard the front door open. He instantly got to his feet and went to meet her at the door.

And was tackled to the ground.

"*Oof*," he grunted as his back hit the floor. Darcy was straddling him and laughing as she kissed his face. Ben's hands immediately went to her ass to hold her still, but he soon found himself laughing with her. After a minute, he moved his hands to put some space between them. "Quite the greeting."

Her smile was dazzling. "Did you miss me?"

"Hell yeah," he replied, smiling back at her. "But maybe next time we can skip the surprise throwdown. I'm not as young as I used to be."

That started her laughing again. "Sorry," she said as she moved off of him and climbed to her feet. "I just felt like I was never going to get home, and once I was through the door, I just couldn't wait to touch you."

Ben stood up and stretched before hauling her into his arms and kissing her properly. When they broke apart, he noticed that the front door was still open, and there were about a dozen packages strewn around the floor. "I take it you were successful?"

"Oh yeah," she said, stepping away and making her way around to pick up the bags and shut the door. "I still have a few more things to get, but overall, it was a good trip." She stripped off her coat and kicked off her sneakers.

"I'm curious," he said, sitting back down on the couch. "How is it possible to shop for eight hours?"

Giggling, she sat down beside him and put her head on his shoulder. "We didn't shop the entire time. There was drive time, coffee breaks, and then lunch."

"Oh, well, that makes it much better. So seven hours of shopping?"

Darcy playfully swatted at his arm. Then she sighed against him, snuggling close. "I'm sorry I was gone so long."

He kissed the top of her head. "Quite all right. I can't buck tradition. Plus, I've heard how this is the best day to do Christmas shopping, so who am I to say no?"

"That's very kind of you," she teased.

He sighed dramatically. "It was very lonely here, but I guess it's okay, since I'm sure I'm going to benefit from some of that shopping."

Beside him, he felt Darcy go still.

Pulling back, he looked at her. "Seriously? There are a ton of bags there and nothing in them is for me?" He did his best to look appalled. "And here I was, all by myself, eating a sad peanut butter sandwich and imagining you buying something for me. You know, since I got left behind today."

Rolling her eyes, Darcy sat up and straddled his lap. "Okay, okay, okay." She sighed. "And there is no way you had a sad peanut butter sandwich for lunch. There isn't any peanut butter here. All the food is top-notch, so don't even try to play that card." He knew she was trying to sound firm, but her lips were twitching.

"Okay, fine. It wasn't a sad sandwich. But it was still me here all by myself. Missing you."

"Poor baby," she cooed as she leaned down and kissed him slowly, leisurely, on the lips. "Lucky for you that I have no plans for the rest of the day, so I'm all yours."

He definitely liked the sound of that.

She pulled back and smiled at him. "I told everyone to leave us alone until dinner tomorrow night. So not only am I all yours for the rest of the day but a good portion of tomorrow, too."

He liked the sound of that even more.

"I've had an awful lot of time to think about what I'd do if I had you all to myself again," he said, trying to be serious.

"You have, huh? Can I guess what you were thinking?"

Unable to help himself, he laughed. "Sure. Go ahead."

Wiggling in his lap, she looked like she was giving this a lot of thought. "You were thinking that you'd like to...play a board game."

He shook his head. "Nope. Try again."

"Hmm, you want us to...go sightseeing."

Ben's eyes went a little wide. "Sightseeing? Why?"

Darcy gave him a curious look. "This is your first time to North Carolina, and all you've seen is my brother's apartment and my dad's house. Not very exciting."

"I don't know about that. This apartment has provided plenty of excitement," he said, waggling his eyebrows at her. "However, I think I'll pass on the sightseeing," he began and immediately noticed the disappointment on her face. "But I'd love to take you out to dinner later."

Her smile was back, and it grew as she crawled off his lap and walked over to her pile of shopping bags. She picked up a small one before walking over and taking him by the hand.

"Where are we going?" he asked coyly.

"I've also been thinking about what I'd do if I had you all to myself," she said with a sassy wink. She shook the small shopping bag at him. "And part of it involves modeling the lingerie in this bag."

And as he let her lead him to the bed, he couldn't help but marvel at how much they thought alike.

---

"This is the part I hate."

"Me too."

"Can't you...I mean, is there any way—"

"Darce, I have to go home. I've got things that I have to do and take care of before we go to New York. And besides, it's only a week."

She sighed and kept her eyes on the road. "It's still going to feel like forever."

"I know," he said quietly.

They drove on toward the airport in silence. It wasn't as if this was a surprise—they'd known Ben had to leave on Sunday, and Darcy swore she was going to be okay with it.

But she wasn't.

They hadn't talked about their geographical challenges. There hadn't been a good time to bring it up. After she had dragged him to bed on Friday, they'd spent the afternoon consumed with each other. Then Ben had surprised her by insisting that they go someplace romantic for dinner. She had planned on casual, but it was nice to dress up a bit and experience a real date with him.

And what a date it was!

Dinner, dancing, a romantic — albeit chilly — walk on the beach under the moonlight. They'd ordered dessert to go, and back at the apartment, they had spent hours sitting on the couch talking about everything and nothing at all while feeding each other cake.

Looking back, Darcy realized that might have been the perfect opportunity to bring up where they saw themselves going from here, but hindsight and all…

"You're quiet," he said, turning to look at her.

She shrugged. "Just thinking."

He nodded. "I've come to discover that when you stay quiet for too long, it's not always a good thing." He chuckled, and she knew he was trying to lighten the mood, but she wasn't feeling it.

"So, um, what else do you need to do before you go? You know, to get ready?"

"I've got calls to make on some upcoming commissions and some general stuff around the house. Nothing major."

"You could do that all from here, you know," she said carefully. "You have access to your emails, so you have the contact information for your clients. We can buy you more clothes if you need them for New York. You could totally stay and—"

Ben reached over and took one of her hands in his. "We talked about this. Believe me, no one hates all this traveling more than me, but it's the way it is for right now. It's only a week, and then we'll have all that time together. It will be like a vacation for us both."

She sighed. "I know."

"What are you looking forward to seeing the most while we're in the city?" he asked.

"You."

He laughed softly. "Oh, come on. I've never been to New York City before. I know there are a ton of things I want to see and do while we're there."

"I'm hoping I'm one of them," she teased.

"You're at the top of the list," he said with a wink and a smile. "But seriously, what is something that you really want to do while we're there?"

"I think I would love to see a real Broadway show and just walk around and look at all the Christmas displays." The thought of it was starting to get her excited. "Maybe a carriage ride in Central Park or shopping at Macy's at Herald Square?"

"Such a girl," he said, but he was still grinning.

"That's right. Sugar and spice and everything nice."

That had him laughing again. "That is you and a whole lot more, Darcy."

"You think so, huh?"

He nodded. "Absolutely. You've got the sugar part down pat."

"You mean because I bake?" she teased.

His eyes went dark and serious, and if there were time, she'd pull over and crawl right into his lap. She loved that look and where it normally led.

Shaking his head, he said, "No, because you taste so sweet." He let his words sink in. "And trust me, I've tasted every inch of you."

She swallowed hard and forced herself to keep her eyes on the road.

"And as for the spice?" he went on. "I can't even begin to describe what that side of you does for me."

Her pulse rate kicked up a notch.

"And everything nice?" she prompted.

"Baby, you are so much more than that. Nice is too mild of a word for what you are. You're everything that is good and sweet and kind in this world."

She had to do something to break the tension or they'd crash. Giving him a sassy look, she said, "You didn't think that about me when we first started working together."

A bark of laughter was his first response, and it did exactly what she needed it to do—it broke the tension. "And you didn't think that of me, either." He paused and studied her face. "I've never been so glad to be wrong in my entire life."

"Me too," she agreed.

They drove for several minutes in silence, and when Darcy saw the first sign for the airport, she had to fight the urge to turn the car around.

But she didn't turn around.

And they didn't talk anymore.

The silence was oddly comforting.

And when she pulled up in front of the terminal, Darcy did her best not to cry. Ben pulled her in close and kissed her until she was breathless.

"It's going to be good, right?"

She nodded.

"We're going to make it a good week," he said firmly. "And before we know it, we'll be together in New York and having the world's greatest time, right?"

She nodded.

"Okay, then," he said, pulling away. "C'mon. Let's get this over with."

Within minutes, he had his suitcase on the curb and was holding her again.

Tucking a finger under her chin, he forced her to look at him. "One week. We can do this."

"I know."

"And it will all be worth it."

Rather than argue, she nodded again. "I know."

"I can't wait to experience the Big Apple with you as my tour guide, Darcy Shaughnessy. I have a feeling it's going to be amazing."

She couldn't help but smile. It wasn't often that Ben was so enthusiastic about anything, so the fact that he was trying so hard for her meant a lot.

"Yes, it is. I know it."

# Chapter 10

TEN DAYS LATER, BEN WAS SERIOUSLY LOSING HIS SHIT.

The crowds. The noise. The constant everything. This was not a situation he was comfortable in, and no matter how much everyone kept telling him to smile and relax, he couldn't. It was impossible.

"You're doing it again," Darcy murmured beside him.

He didn't need to ask what she meant. He knew. "How much longer do we have to be here?"

"Ben, we got here seven minutes ago. Relax. All these people are here to see you." She looked around the room and smiled. "Laura said it's twice the number of people they were anticipating, and it's all for you!"

"I think the open bar has something to do with it." It was supposed to be a small cocktail party with his publisher and a couple of "industry" people. Looking around the room, he could tell it was much more than that.

"Oh, stop."

A weary sigh was his only response. He was tired, he was hungry, and he hated being on display. What he wanted was to be back in his workshop with country music playing in the background and his tools in his hands. Was that too much to ask?

"Ben! Darcy! There you are!" His editor, Laura, was weaving her way through the crowd toward them. "I have some exciting news."

"Ooo! Yeah!" Darcy said giddily, practically

bouncing on her toes, and it was all Ben could do to hold in a groan. He had a feeling the news wasn't going to be exciting to him.

"You see that gentleman over there in the gray suit?" Laura asked. "He's with HGTV. He's very interested in talking to you about doing a series with them. It wouldn't be like a typical show. It would be more like six episodes at a shot where you walk the viewers through some special projects, and we do that two or three times a year. Preferably around the holidays. I don't have all the specifics but—"

"No," Ben said firmly.

Both Laura and Darcy turned and looked at him, but he wasn't going to be swayed.

"I'm not interested. Tell him no."

"But, Ben—" Laura began, and Darcy whispered something to her until she nodded and excused herself.

Doing his best to stay calm, he stood perfectly still as Darcy came to stand in front of him.

"Ben, you at least need to talk to the man."

He shook his head. "Why? I already know I'm not interested. What makes you think I'm going to want a television crew and cameras watching me work?" He stopped and raked a hand through his hair in frustration. His suit was suffocating him, his skin itched, and his feet were killing him. How much more was he supposed to take?

"We can negotiate a deal that's not so intrusive," Darcy countered. "Remember Mark Sawyer who we talked to last night, with the woodworking magazine? We were discussing photo essays and how—"

"When did you do that? I never talked to him about any photo essay."

"It was while you were talking with Laura and your rep. Anyway, we were talking and—"

"Darcy, stop," Ben said. "Just stop."

The look she gave him was patient, but he could see the tension building in her posture. Didn't she get it? This wasn't his thing. It was *never* going to be his thing. He had met every demand they had thrown at him, and he'd smiled and waved and played nice, but now he was done.

"You're passing up some amazing opportunities. If you would talk to them, you'd see that. I know you wanted to take some time off, and you will. We'll negotiate it into your contracts, and when it's all said and done, you'll be able to take even more time off. It's a win-win."

"No, it's not," he said through clenched teeth. "And what is this 'we'll negotiate' stuff? Last I checked, this was my career we were talking about."

All signs of his relaxed and patient girl were gone, and in her place was the intimidating one he had first brought home with him.

*Bring it*, he thought to himself.

"Yeah, it is your career, but you're refusing to participate in it right now. But you know what? I can. I can stand here and talk to anyone in this room and make them see how amazing you are, and I can even get them to agree to whatever crazy-ass terms you want. Why? Because I have confidence in you, and I can make them work for it."

"Oh, so now it's you with the talent and not me?" he countered incredulously. "Like I need someone to *sell* me because my work doesn't speak for itself?"

"Ben, that's not what I'm saying." She sighed. "Stop twisting my words. Can we please—"

"You know what? No. We can't. I've had about all I can take here tonight. You can stay and schmooze and kiss people's asses and do your best to tell them I'm the greatest thing since sliced bread. But it won't matter, because no matter what deal you come up with, no matter what deal you try to pitch, I'm not going along with it. I want to go to my workshop and sculpt. I don't want to be on TV, I don't want to be in a magazine, and believe me, had I known that this was what I'd have to deal with, I certainly would have never agreed to do the book."

When he turned to walk away, she reached out and grabbed his arm. "You can't leave! All these people are here for you!"

He cocked a brow at her. "Are you sure? Because for a few minutes, it seemed like you thought they were here for you."

She huffed with annoyance. "Stop doing that! That's not what I said."

People were starting to stare, and she quickly pulled him over to the side of the room. "Please stay. There are some people that it's very important for you to see."

"You don't get it, do you?" he snapped. "None of this is important to me. Do you want to know what is? You. You're important to me. My art, my home? They're important to me. Standing here drinking with strangers isn't!"

"If I'm so important to you, then do this for me," she pleaded, and that almost got to him. It almost made him change his mind.

"I guess that's the difference between the two of us. I would never ask you to change who you are or put you in a position where you were uncomfortable for my sake," he said, his voice deadly calm.

Her lips moved like she was going to talk, but nothing came out.

"Surprise!"

Ben turned and found both of his brothers standing there with giant smiles on their faces.

What. The. Hell.

It didn't take a genius to figure out who had done this. Who had overstepped her bounds and gone and arranged something he had specifically said he didn't want.

And without a word, he shoved past his brothers and out the door.

The icy winter air hit him in the face like hitting a brick wall, and in that instant, Ben knew he had over-reacted. Yes, he was frustrated, and yes, he was annoyed with this dog and pony show, but that didn't mean he had to take it out on Darcy.

Or his brothers.

He walked several feet away from the gallery entrance and let out a long, weary breath. How the hell had his life gotten so out of control? The book, this trip, his life... Nothing was going the way he wanted it to, and now he had pretty much screwed up royally.

"Want to explain what happened in there?"

Ben slowly turned around and faced Jack. "Where's Henry?"

"He's inside doing his best to charm Darcy so that maybe she'll forget what an asshole you are."

Yeah. He deserved that. Raking a hand through his

hair, he shivered from the cold. That's what he got for storming out without a coat. Jack clearly knew what he was thinking, because he was smirking.

"The adult thing to do is go back inside and apologize," Jack said, sticking his hands into his own coat pockets. "Or you can stay out here and pout."

"Jesus, Jack, give me a break already."

"Oh, I should give you a break? I drove for hours to get here, Ben. I left my fiancée at home so Henry and I could surprise you, and before we can say more than one word to you, in typical Ben fashion, you're pitching a fit about something."

"Typical Ben? What the hell does that mean?" Ben demanded.

"It means when things don't go your way, you walk away. Now, I don't know Darcy at all other than a brief phone conversation with her, but she seems like a nice woman. What the hell she's doing with you, I don't know." He paused. "But I'll give you this little bit of advice, and then I'm going inside, because it's freaking cold out here. Go in there and apologize. Even if you don't think you were wrong, apologize. You made a scene, you embarrassed her, and somehow, I doubt she was the problem."

"So you get a fiancée and suddenly you think you can dole out relationship advice?"

Jack snorted a laugh. "Dude, I know I can. I may not be an expert, but even I know not to be the guy who creates a scene that embarrasses my girl." He clapped Ben on the shoulder. "Think about that."

And then he turned and walked into the gallery.

"Well, shit," Ben murmured as another chill racked his body. Hanging his head, Ben turned and walked inside. He immediately spotted Darcy talking to Laura and his brothers on the far side of the room. With a sigh of resignation, he made his way over.

He didn't look at either of his brothers.

He didn't acknowledge Laura.

His gaze zeroed in on Darcy, and he saw the defiance in her eyes as he got closer. Good. He wanted her to be pissed off, wanted her to make him work at apologizing.

"Excuse us for a moment," he said as he wrapped an arm around her waist and pulled her toward the hallway that led to the gallery owner's office.

"That was rude," she griped as soon as they were alone. "But I guess I shouldn't be surprised. You know, you could've—"

But he didn't let her finish. Ben captured her lips with his and kissed her like his life depended on it.

And it did. Because without her, he didn't have one. At least, not one that was worth living.

He kissed her until they were both breathless and she melted against him.

Slowly, he maneuvered them until her back was against the wall and his forehead rested against hers. "I'm a complete and total jerk, and I'm sorry. I took my frustration out on you, and that wasn't right."

She sighed and looked up at him. "I get it. I know you're hating this, but it's not too much to ask for you to play nice. At least for a little while."

"You should have told me you invited my brothers," he said carefully.

"Then it wouldn't have been a surprise."

He couldn't help but smirk at her snarky comeback. "Maybe I don't like surprises."

One corner of her mouth twitched too. "Maybe you need to get over that."

He drank in the sight of her—her dark hair done up in a messy-yet-stylish bun, the smoky eyes, the red lips. If they were alone and in this position, his hands would be under her little black dress right now.

But they weren't.

But now he had definite plans for later.

"Maybe you need to stay close to me to make sure I don't screw up anymore," he said seriously.

Her smile grew. Just a little. "Maybe you need to behave and trust me when I tell you that you need to do something."

This game was kind of fun, he mused. "I don't know if I like having you in control. That's normally my role."

And her smile grew a little bit more. "You can have control anyplace else you want. But here? Let this be my turf."

Yeah, he had some plans for later.

"How much longer do we have to stay?" he murmured against her lips. "Because I can't wait to see what you're wearing under this dress, and I want to be in control of finding out."

She purred against him and made him go hard as a rock. "You're going to have to hold that thought, because we've got at least another hour here and then a late dinner with your brothers."

"Darcy," he whined. She was killing him.

Standing up on her tiptoes, she kissed him thoroughly. "You're totally not helping."

"I wanted to give you more to think about," she

whispered softly and then nipped at his earlobe. "Now let's go and be social and have a nice dinner with your brothers."

And as she pulled him out into the crowd of people, Ben did his best to paste on a smile and bide his time until they were alone.

---

When they finally walked into their hotel suite after midnight, Ben was mentally exhausted. The rest of the cocktail party had been fine—he had spoken to the HGTV rep, he'd talked to about a dozen other people, and he'd been polite to them all.

Of course, he'd let Darcy do most of the talking.

And dinner with his brothers had been fun. It had been a while since the three of them had gone out to dinner for the hell of it, and Ben hated to admit it but he'd had a good time. They were staying in the city tonight since the drive back to Boston was long, and they had all agreed to meet up for breakfast.

They'd caught him at a weak moment, and when Darcy had flashed him a beguiling smile, he would have agreed to anything.

Ben leaned against the door and watched as she made her way around the room—slipping off her shoes, taking off her earrings, and letting her hair down from that sexy little bun she'd had it up in all night. His fingers twitched with the need to go to her and help her remove all those items, but he was biding his time.

She stood by the window and stretched. The little black dress rode up her thighs, and his mouth began to water. He knew she was doing all this for his benefit,

and he'd give her a few more minutes to tease him
and then…

She was his.

"It's like Christmastown down there," she said softly.
"All the lights and displays, and I can see the tree at
Rockefeller Center from here." She looked over her
shoulder at him and smiled. "If it snowed—even a little
bit—it would be perfect."

"I thought you said you never wanted to see snow
again after the storm we had," he said, pushing off the
door and going to her.

With a throaty laugh, she watched his approach.
"That was said in the heat of the moment. Now that I've
had time to think about it, it wasn't so bad."

Ben wrapped her in his arms and kissed her. When
he lifted his head, he said, "I'm pretty damn thankful
for it myself."

Her cheeks turned a little red. "Me too."

Her voice was soft and breathless, and he felt as if
he'd been waiting forever to get her alone. "I have a
question for you."

Dark-green eyes looked up at him.

"What are you wearing under this dress?"

A slow smile played across those gloriously red lips.
Darcy took a step back and out of his arms. Ben thought
for sure she was going to tell him what she had on, but
instead, it looked like she was going to show him.

Reaching behind her, Darcy unzipped the dress and,
with a little shimmy, let it fall to the floor.

Ben forgot how to breathe.

There was so much and yet so little covering her.
A red satin bra that barely contained her breasts, an

impossibly tiny red lace thong, garters and stockings, and stilettos.

It was as if he had his own *Playboy* Playmate standing in front of him.

Taking a predatory step toward her, Ben reached out and placed a hand on her hip. "It's a good thing I didn't know about all this earlier."

"Really?" she asked, her expression going coy. "And why is that?"

"Because we would never have left the room." Pulling her flush against him, Ben heard her soft gasp. Part of him wanted to kiss her, to claim her lips and devour her. But her body called to him.

"I thought the red would be festive," she murmured. "A little holiday spice to celebrate the evening."

She was like a present he couldn't wait to unwrap.

Slowly, so slowly, his hands began to wander. He watched as Darcy's eyes drifted closed and her head fell back. She sighed his name as his hands gently squeezed her ass and then traveled up to do the same to her breasts.

"Ben," she sighed again, squirming against him, "please."

"Please what, baby?" he murmured against her throat, his tongue tracing the soft skin there.

"Take me inside. Take me."

Scooping her up in his arms, he walked them toward the bed. "Believe me, I will."

---

Breakfast with the Tanner brothers had been interesting. Darcy was intimately familiar with the bonds of brotherhood, but this wasn't like anything she'd ever witnessed before. There wasn't a lot of teasing and laughter; it was all very reserved. By the time they said goodbye, it seemed like they were happy, but it wasn't like watching her brothers, that was for sure.

They'd spent the rest of that day sightseeing, and that night, Ben had another small gallery to see. It had been nice but uneventful. Darcy had had a great conversation with the gallery owner, and they'd gone out for a late dinner with the head of a public relations firm. It had been a perfectly fine way to end the business portion of their trip.

Now as they were packing up and preparing to head to the airport, she felt that same overwhelming sense of sadness again.

"I can hear you sighing," Ben said from across the room.

"I can't help it. This has been another amazing week, and now it's going to be longer until we see each other again."

"Darcy, I need to get home and do some work, and you're going to be busy with work and then the holidays. It's not going to be so bad. You'll be too busy to miss me."

She straightened and stared at him as if he had grown a second head. "Somehow, I doubt that. I'm going to miss you because I love you and love being with you and spending time with you. And not having you with me for Christmas? It's killing me."

"We've been over this."

"I know," she snapped and then took a minute to compose herself. "We keep going over it. I want us to be together, Ben. I thought you wanted that too."

He sighed loudly and shut his suitcase before giving her his full attention. "You know I want that too, but it's not that simple, Darcy. I can't just drop everything and stay here and entertain you."

"Entertain me? You think I'm looking to be entertained?" she cried.

His head hung down. "Okay, that came out wrong."

"You think?"

When he looked at her this time, he looked mildly irritated. "You know, I flew to North Carolina to spend Thanksgiving with you, and then I flew here to New York and brought you with me so we could spend time together. Why don't you come back to Washington with me?"

For a minute, he almost sounded hopeful.

"Because I need to focus on finding a job," she said with annoyance.

"You can look for a job online from anywhere," he said mildly.

"I need to work, Ben. I know it's just for Aidan and it's a temp job, but I still need to make a living."

"So come later in the month."

"Then it's Christmas, and you don't do Christmas, remember?"

"Then come after Christmas." This time, it was said through clenched teeth.

They were at a standstill. She knew she was the one being difficult here—she knew that—but for some reason, she wanted to fight with him. It was ridiculous and childish and yet, there it was. She was used to pitching a fit and having people give in to her. But Ben didn't. He fought back and did his best to make her see how her way wasn't the only way.

But in this particular situation, there didn't seem to be *any* way.

"I guess we'll just have to play it by ear," she said and returned her attention to packing. "We'll talk about it again after New Year's."

And right then, the thought of spending the holidays without him hurt more than she'd ever thought possible.

---

He'd surprised her.

A week later, with less than a day's notice, he called and told her he was flying in for the weekend. It had been a flurry of activity to get herself together and ready. She warned him that there was a big family get-together this weekend because Riley was in town for a show, but he didn't care. He said he just needed to be with her.

That first kiss when she climbed out of the car at the airport was always the sweetest.

The drive to the apartment was always filled with the basics to pass the time.

The frantic way that they reached for each other as soon as they were behind closed doors was what Darcy lived for.

Now, breathless and a little sweaty, she curled up against Ben and sighed. So good. "I missed you."

He kissed her forehead. "I missed you too."

"You're sure you can only stay for the weekend?"

He nodded. "I've got a client coming to the studio on Tuesday for some work on a custom home he's building. So far, I've managed to put him off about three times. I can't do it again."

She sighed again. "I understand. But I hate it."

Hugging her close, he murmured, "Me too." He wished they could stay like this, tangled up together with nothing to do but catch their breath until they could start all over again. But they couldn't.

Family dinner.

Great.

He couldn't complain too much—she had warned him, and he figured he could give up an hour or two of having her to himself.

Just as long as they could come back to the apartment, be together, and be left alone for the rest of the weekend.

Two hours later, however, he began to wonder if he had completely miscalculated. It wasn't just a get-together; it was dinner. For twenty people. There was no way they were going to be in and out any time soon. With a sigh, he looked around. *How do people stand it?* Ben wondered, and not for the first time that evening.

Darcy looked up at him. "I can see that you're miserable and not having a good time—"

He immediately put a finger over her lips. "Don't. Whatever you're thinking, not today. Or tomorrow. We only have the weekend together, and I'm just happy to be with you," he said softly, and only when she nodded did he remove his finger. Then he kissed her, slowly and sweetly, on the lips. "I love you."

With a shaky sigh, she melted against him. "I love you too."

"It looks like dinner is being served," he commented as they walked toward the dining room. Everyone seemed to know where to sit, so he just followed Darcy's lead and was somewhat relieved to find them sitting next to Riley and Savannah.

The room was so loud. There were about ten different conversations going on and kids were crying—it was a lot to take in.

*I can do this for one meal*, he chided himself. *One meal and then we can go.*

"Ow!" he hissed and then looked over at Savannah. "Did you just stab me with a fork?"

With an evil smile, she nodded. "I did."

"Why? Why would you do that?" he asked quietly, doing his best to sound menacing.

"Because you're frowning. Now smile and relax, or next time, I won't be so gentle."

Unable to help himself, he laughed. Then, leaning back, he caught Riley's eye. "Is she this evil at home?"

Riley laughed. "Sometimes more. But I'm sure you're used to it. Savannah's a day at the beach compared to my sister."

"Hey!" Darcy chimed in. "Watch it! Just because there are two people separating us doesn't mean I can't get even with you."

Riley continued to laugh. "Bring it. Although I heard a rumor that someone was trying to be a little more mature," he taunted. "Ring any bells?"

Ben laughed at Darcy's muttered curse.

"Oh, just shut up," she warned her brother right before she took her first forkful of salad. "Jerk."

Leaning over, Ben kissed her on the temple. "That's my mature girl."

# Chapter 11

BEN WAS READY TO LOSE HIS MIND. IT WAS LATE MONDAY morning, and he was lying in bed while Darcy returned phone calls—some to her family, some about jobs. The job calls he could completely understand, but the family ones? How much more could these people want to be together? And on top of that, in two weeks, they were going to do it all again for Christmas. Didn't they ever take a break?

The dinner Friday night had gone on until almost midnight. Then Saturday, Aidan and Zoe had come over to hang out. And yesterday, Riley and Savannah stopped by before heading to the airport.

So much for a weekend for just the two of them. Next time they did this, it was going to be in Washington.

His flight home wasn't until the early evening, but he had hoped they would have some time alone—just the two of them, no family members—before he had to leave. Hopefully, her calls wouldn't take too long. Glancing over at the bedside clock, he frowned. She had already been out there for almost an hour.

Knowing that staying in bed wasn't helping anything, he got up and showered. When he came out of the bathroom—in just a towel in hopes of enticing her off the phone—he was mortified to find Aubrey and Brooke sitting in the kitchen.

"Holy shit!" he cried out and quickly went into the bedroom and shut the door.

Didn't this family *ever* stay in their own homes?

Darcy came in the room a minute later. "Oh my God, I'm so sorry! I didn't even think when they showed up. I thought you'd come out dressed!"

"Really?" he hissed. "In all the times we've stayed here, when have either of us come out of the bathroom fully dressed?"

At least she had the decency to look embarrassed. "Okay, fine. We never have, and that should have registered with me. I'm sorry." She came over and tried to hug him, but he was too wound up. "C'mon, Ben. It's not like they've never seen a man in a towel before."

That was *so* not the thing to say.

Ben quickly pulled on his jeans, grabbed a T-shirt out of his bag, and turned to glare at her. "All damn weekend, we had everyone around us. Is it too much to ask that on our last few hours together it be just us? What was so important that your family had to be here?" He did his best to keep his voice down, but it was a challenge.

"They were helping me prep for my last call," she said with a hint of defiance. "They waited until it was almost lunchtime to come over to give us some privacy. They had no idea you were in the shower."

"You could have told them," he countered. "Or better yet, you could have knocked on the damn door and said 'Hey, Ben. We have company.' Either of those would have worked."

She huffed. "I've apologized, Ben. What more do you possibly want?"

"I want some time alone with you, dammit! I leave here in a little more than four hours. I would have thought you wanted that too."

"I do! I just have to make this last call."

He let out a weary sigh and sat down on the corner of the bed. "And then what? Then you'll need to talk to Aubrey and Brooke. And then Zoe. And then Anna. And then who knows? And the one person who you *should* be talking to, the one whose life you supposedly want to share, when will you talk to him? Am I going to have to wait in line behind twenty freaking Shaughnessys before it's my turn? Because I have to tell you, Darce, that's not working for me."

Off in the distance, he heard the front door open and close.

"Great!" she cried. "Are you happy now? They left!"

Jumping to his feet, he yelled, "Oh yeah! I'm thrilled!"

"Oh good," she replied sarcastically. "Because we all know that *your* happiness is the only thing that matters!" And with that, she stormed out of the room.

Ben instantly followed and was a bit stumped when he saw her grab her purse and keys. "Where the hell are you going?"

"I'm going to follow them and apologize. Oh, and while I'm out, I'll make my last call since, thanks to you, I'm almost late for it."

And before he could say another word, she slammed out the door.

---

Ben was gone.

Darcy kept walking around the apartment as if he was hiding somewhere—along with his luggage—but he wasn't.

He was gone.

Throwing her purse across the room, she let loose a string of curses before collapsing on the sofa.

*Well, what did you expect?* she thought. *You walked out and stayed away for several hours.*

"I was trying to calm down," she said out loud, as if arguing the point that way was going to make a difference.

Aubrey, Brooke, and Zoe had told her she was being unreasonable and that she needed to go back and talk to him, but in typical fashion, she had been stubborn. "Okay, maybe I can fix this," she said to herself. Rising, she went to her purse and its scattered contents and prayed she hadn't broken her phone. Seeing it still intact, she picked it up and called him.

"Hey," he said gruffly.

"Hey." She had never been more relieved for someone to answer their phone. "So, um, I'm here at the apartment and you're—"

"At the airport."

"Your flight isn't for a while yet," she said softly, doing her best to stay calm and find a way to apologize.

"I found an earlier one."

"Ben, I...I'm sorry. I shouldn't have left like that."

"No. You shouldn't have."

Now she was done being meek and soft. "Need I remind you that you've done the exact same thing to me? You walked out of the gallery—"

"And I came back in ten minutes later and apologized," he reminded her. "You were gone for two hours before I left, Darcy. What the hell was I supposed to do?"

"Um, you could have come after me. You could have walked over to Aidan and Zoe's and found me. You could have—"

He let out a low growl of frustration. "The last thing I wanted was more time with your family. Look, they're all very nice—great, actually—but I was done. Don't you get it? I'm not like you. Sometimes, I don't want to have an audience around for every little thing. You and I needed to talk, and I wasn't going to go to your brother's house and do it there with everyone watching."

"It wouldn't have been that way."

"I can't do this with you right now," he said wearily. "They're calling my flight."

"Don't go," she begged. "Please. I made a mistake. I…that's how I've always done things—I run away. I can see now that it's wrong, and I'm sorry. I'll come and get you, and we'll go someplace and talk. Not here. Hell, we'll go and find someplace else to stay for a few days. Please, Ben. Don't go. Not like this."

He sighed. "I think it's better if I go."

Tears stung her eyes as she waited for him to continue.

"There are a lot of things that we both need to think about, and being apart for a while might not be a bad thing."

"You're…will you promise to think about coming back for Christmas?" she asked, her voice trembling.

"I need to go. We're boarding. I'll text you when I land."

"Ben—"

But he was gone.

Her body crumpled to the floor as she began to cry. Darcy was never one who fought crying. When she felt the need, she did it. But this cry was different. This was the kind of cry that shook her entire body and felt as if her soul was being ripped from her body.

How was she supposed to fix this? How could she make things right if he didn't want to talk to her?

But more important, how was she going to survive if this was the end?

There was a soft knock on the door, and she wanted to yell at whoever it was to go away. The last thing she wanted to do was talk to anyone.

"Hey, Brooke mentioned... Oh my God! Are you okay?"

Great. Owen was here.

Instantly, her brother was at her side, crouching down and gently pulling her to her feet. He led her over to the sofa, made her sit, and then went to the kitchen to get her a glass of water. Then he went and grabbed a box of tissues from the bathroom. Then he cleaned up the mess from her purse.

If nothing else, Owen was the king of waiting you out until you were ready to talk.

"Ben left," she finally said when Owen sat down beside her.

He nodded. "The girls mentioned that the two of you had fought earlier."

She nodded and explained it all to him. "I honestly didn't think it was all such a big deal. I really didn't. I mean, we'd talked about him wanting to turn over this new leaf, that he was going to stop hiding away and being such an introvert. So I don't understand what changed!" she cried.

For a long moment, Owen said nothing. Then he shifted so he could face her. "Life is very different for people like you," he began.

"People like me? What does that—"

He held up a hand to silence her. "You're comfortable in your own skin. You're social and confident, and even though you have your own insecurities, you never

let them show. And to the rest of us, you present yourself as someone who is fearless."

"But I'm not."

Owen went on as if she hadn't said a word. "For
people like Ben—who, by the way, I can totally relate
to—social interactions are difficult. Bordering on painful. It's one thing to want to change who we are, but it's
another to actually do it. When Ben said he wanted to
change that part of himself, he didn't mean overnight or
all at once. Things like that take time."

And that's when she realized what she'd done, what
she'd asked of him.

What she'd forced upon him.

"I didn't give him the time."

Owen shook his head. "No, you didn't. When Brooke
and I first met, she was far more social than I was. She
had an ease and grace about her that I envied. My whole
life, I wished I could be more like that, but she was the
one who finally drew it out of me."

"That's what I'm trying—"

"Brooke was patient. She didn't push."

Darcy sighed and flopped back on the couch to lie
down. "You know we're not patient people, Owen. Well,
you are. But not the rest of us. It's genetic or something."

"Studies have shown that—"

"Not the time for statistics!" she interrupted. "That's
not helpful right now."

With a sigh of his own, he leaned back against the
cushions. "It's all I've got," he said simply. "I'm not sure
what I'm supposed to do or say in this kind of situation."

"I know." She flung her arm over her eyes and wished
she could start the day over.

"You can't change who you are any more than Ben can change who he is. You are impulsive and excitable and passionate about the things you want and believe in. He's a private and intellectual person who is passionate about the things he wants and believes in. You have to find the right balance, and it's not something that just happens, Darcy. It takes work." He paused. "Can I make an observation?"

She lifted her arm and glared at him. "I thought that's what you were already doing."

"Well, this one might make you mad."

Again, she just glared as she watched him swallow hard and move away from her a bit.

"You have a tendency to not work."

Sitting straight up, she punched him in the arm. "I work! I have a job. I've always had a job."

"Ow!" Grabbing his arm, Owen got to his feet. "I wasn't referring to a job," he explained, and Darcy couldn't help but notice the annoyance in his voice.

Okay, *that* was new.

"I'm talking about in every other aspect of your life. You don't work, Darcy. You run away. You make a joke. You…you punch people in the arm!"

"Okay, that was wrong of me. I'm sorry."

"And you throw out apologies without really feeling them."

She got to her feet. "Now wait a minute…"

"I'm not scared of you!" he shouted even as he took a step back. "And that's another thing you do. You intimidate to get your way. You do everything except actually *work* at making things right. You look for the easy way out, and if you are serious about Ben, if you're in *love* with him and want to build a life with him, you're going to have to work for it. Do you understand that?"

Holy shit. Who was this man, and what happened to her mild-mannered scientist brother?

Owen took a tentative step toward her. "I am so relieved that Brooke didn't give up on me. She had every reason to. I was insecure and...and so comfortable in the safe life I had created for myself that I didn't realize how miserable I was. And Ben, well, he lives alone, works alone, and he's not close to his family. And that's not a crime, Darcy. Not all families are like ours."

"I know. I was just so excited that he was here and everyone liked him that I thought—"

"Brooke's not close with her parents, and she lost her only brother, and they weren't close growing up, either. It was hard for her to understand the dynamics of our family and feel comfortable with everyone. Don't you remember the first time she came here?"

Darcy chuckled. "Aidan and Hugh were jerks to her."

"Exactly. She flat-out told me she didn't want to be around my family. Ever. It was devastating to me because, well, you guys are everything to me. How was I supposed to choose?"

"And if you remember correctly, you chose her and left," Darcy said and then gasped. "I...oh shit."

He nodded. "Granted, I didn't stay away long, and everyone worked things out. I left because they were blatantly mean to Brooke. We all like Ben," he went on. "He just needs a little more time to get comfortable."

"But what if he doesn't? What if he never gets comfortable?"

Owen studied her for a long moment. "Then he's not the right man for you."

Well, damn. Those were not the words she wanted to hear.

Tears started to well up in her eyes again as she slowly sat back down. Owen was instantly at her side, taking her hand in his.

"All is not lost here, Darce. Don't be in such a rush. Sometimes it's okay to have time alone to get your head together and figure out what you want."

"And get a tattoo?" she teased, because it was either that or cry.

He chuckled and tucked her in beside him, kissing her on the temple. "It certainly took my mind off how much I missed Brooke and how much I'd screwed up."

"Physical pain can do that for you."

He laughed again. "Such a brat. And for your information, Brooke thinks my tattoo is sexy."

"Ew, please. I do *not* want to think about you being sexy. Just no."

"Too bad. You know I only speak the truth," he said with a grin. "So deal with it."

She swatted him away and then pulled him back for a hug. "Thanks, Owen. I needed that."

"So what are you going to do? Do you want to come back over to Aidan's? We're all talking about going out to dinner tonight."

"Dude, it's only two in the afternoon."

"Closer to three, but we have to coordinate babysitters, because Dad and Martha have plans tonight."

"I'm going to head back to Dad's, I think. First, I need to clean up around here, but after that, I'm going to take some time to think." She paused. "Besides, Ben said he'd text when he landed and maybe…maybe by then, he'll want to talk to me."

"Don't push," he reminded her.

Nodding, she replied, "I won't. It's not going to be easy, but I'm really going to try."

"Good girl." He stood and walked over to the kitchen table. "Brooke left her sunglasses here earlier, and she was afraid to come back over. That's why I came."

"So you drew the short straw?"

He laughed at the image. "Basically. But I'm glad I did."

"Me too."

---

It was good to be home.

That was what Ben kept telling himself as he settled back in. He texted Darcy when he landed and told her he'd call her tomorrow. Right now, all he wanted was to grab something to drink and head down to his workshop and just create.

The entire flight home, he had been picturing a design in his head—something for Anna's bar—and he was anxious to see if he could create it. At the same time, he had come up with some ideas for Connor's tree house.

Damn Shaughnessys. Even when he was away from them, they wouldn't leave him alone.

A couple of snow flurries were blowing around as he made his way across the property. He made a mental note to catch a forecast so he'd know what kind of weather to expect this week. Not that it mattered—he had no plans other than to hole up and work.

No distractions.

*Yeah, right.*

The truth was he had a feeling even if he didn't bring a phone with him, he was going to be distracted by his own damn thoughts. Of Darcy. Of family. Of jobs.

And what could have been his future.

Stepping into the workshop, he felt all the tension start to leave his body. The smell of the wood and oils was like a balm for him. Slowly, he walked around and touched several surfaces as he made his way back to the room where he kept some of his choice pieces of wood. He knew exactly what he was looking for—a long length of mahogany that would be perfect for what he was thinking for the bar. On the plane, he had sketched out the design, and he had it in his pocket, but he didn't need it. It was vividly playing in his mind.

Taking the wood, he carefully maneuvered it and brought it out to the workbench. It took a few minutes to clean it off, and then he picked up the nearest straight chisel and mallet, turned on the radio, and started to work. With every piece of wood he chipped away, Ben felt a sense of excitement. Song after song played on the radio as a plain, rectangular piece of wood transformed into something ornate and beautiful. He felt as if he was uncovering some sort of hidden treasure, and with every layer he carved away, he was closer to finding it.

God, how he loved the challenge!

His back ached, his hands were shaking, and his stomach growled noisily. Taking a step back from the bench, Ben looked up at the clock and was certain he was hallucinating. Three a.m.? How had that happened? Carefully, he put the tools down. More than half the piece was well on its way to being what he wanted it to be. He yawned and stretched and felt a great sense of satisfaction.

It was an incredible feeling. He couldn't wait to show Darcy and...

*Shit.*

Scrubbing a hand over his weary face, he made his way back to the house. The plan was to make himself something to eat and grab a couple of hours of sleep. Midway through his peanut butter and jelly sandwich, he could hardly keep his eyes open. Stumbling to the bedroom, he knew it was foolish to have stayed up so late, but he couldn't regret it.

Out of the corner of his eye, he saw his phone on the dresser and saw someone had texted him. He didn't doubt for one minute who it was, but he was too damn tired to respond.

He'd do it later.

Or at least that was his plan. When Ben woke up six hours later, he felt like hell. Six hours was about the norm for him, and yet he still felt like he could sleep for another ten. Unwilling to give in to that, he got up, showered, and made himself a real meal before heading out to the workshop.

He was anxious to look at the piece and see if it really was as good as he thought or if his tired brain had been playing tricks on him. By the time he realized he didn't have his phone with him, he was too engrossed in his work to stop.

Around four in the afternoon, he went back up to the house. His need for something to eat had him unable to work any further. With a bowl of chili heating in the microwave, he went and got his phone.

Four texts and three missed calls from Darcy, along with two missed calls from Henry.

In the background, the microwave beeped, alerting him his meal was ready, but Ben called Darcy first.

"Hey, you," she said breathlessly when she answered the phone. "Are you okay? I…I've been calling—"

"I was down in the workshop and forgot my phone," he said, quickly interrupting her. Doing his best to multitask, he went to the kitchen and grabbed the steaming bowl from the microwave and then added his toppings while they talked. "And then I got so involved in what I was doing that I lost track of time and…sorry."

He heard her soft sigh. "It's okay. I thought…I was kind of afraid you were avoiding me."

"When I get in the zone on a project, I tend to lose track of time," he said as he sat down. "I really am sorry."

They were silent, and Ben took a spoonful of the chili and almost cursed at how hot it was.

"So what are you working on? I didn't think you had any pieces scheduled until after the holidays."

Ben told her about his idea for Anna's bar. "I'll send you some pictures when I go back out there, but promise me you won't show them to Anna yet. I'd rather she see it when it's closer to completion."

"Ooh, she's going to be so excited! I can't wait to see it."

And he knew she was being sincere, not just saying it to make him feel good. Why? Because she understood him and his work, and that was a rare gift. Was he seriously going to let that slip through his fingers?

"What about you? What are you doing today?" With the time difference, he knew her work day was over, and he sat back and ate his dinner while listening to Darcy talk about her day—working with Aidan and how much she was ready to be done with it.

And as much as he hated to bring up the subject, he had to know. "How about the job search? Have you heard anything yet?"

She was silent, and with Darcy, that was rarely a good sign. "I did."

"And?" he prompted.

"I have an interview in Seattle next week," she said quietly, which surprised Ben. He thought for sure she'd sound more excited about it. His heart sank.

"That's great, right?" he said cautiously.

"Yes, of course. Of course it is. It's in retail, but…but that's okay for now."

And just like that, he knew. She was doing this for him, not because it was right for her.

Suddenly, his appetite was gone. Pushing the bowl away, he got up and walked to the wall of windows and looked out at his property. This was his home, where he wanted to be. And as much as he loved the glimpse of the life he could have with Darcy, it wasn't meant to be. They were too different. Too set to follow paths that were really never meant to meet.

What kind of man would he be if he stopped her from following her dream? He couldn't live with himself if he did that.

He loved Darcy too much to ask that of her.

"Look, Darcy, are you sure about this? Because you don't sound that way."

"Ben," she said, her voice going trembly, and he wanted nothing more than to wrap her in his arms and soothe her. "Yes, I want a job doing PR, but I want you more."

And with his heart in his throat, Ben did his best to block the image of her face from his mind.

"Darcy, listen to me. Sure, it would be great in the beginning if you came to live with me and we could be together all the time. But how long would it take for you to realize that you were miserable and start blaming me? If anyone had tried to stop me from pursuing my dream, I would have resented it."

"I don't understand. You said you wouldn't come to New York if I worked there, and we—"

"Darcy," he interrupted softly, then paused to consider his words. "I've learned a lot over the last two months, and I can't do this. My life is here and…and I don't want to keep traveling, and I enjoy my privacy. All that time with your family? It was exhausting. It's not something I can handle all the time. I'm sorry."

"Wait, you're breaking up with me? Seriously?"

"I barely tolerate my own brothers," he went on and then silently vowed to call his brothers because, well, he wanted to rectify that. "We're not close, and seeing them in New York was great, but that will tide me over for another six months or so."

"It shouldn't be like that!" she argued. "You seemed to have so much fun when we were together, and they want to be closer with you, but you keep fighting them on it."

"I'm not fighting them, Darcy," he said, trying to sound reasonable. "It's just different for me. We saw each other, and it was fun. What's wrong with that?"

"But family is…family is everything! I'm not saying you have to be joined at the hip with your brothers, but you should be a part of each other's lives. You should talk to them and share what's going on with you and care about what's going on with them. You're not alone in your grief, Ben. You need to make peace with it, with losing your parents. If you would just open your eyes, you'd see—"

"You're a fine one to talk about that," he snapped.

"What's that supposed to mean?"

"Tell me, have you made peace with your mom? Have you made peace with the fact that she's not here or that you have all kinds of family issues because of her?"

"I do not have—"

"Yes, you do!" he cried out. "You're still searching for some perfect family scenario, Darcy. You cling to your family like they're the key to everything in your life, and at the same time, you blame them for all that's wrong with it."

"That's just normal stuff, Ben," she said with exasperation. "We all have family issues to some degree. But you're cutting off a part of your life because your parents aren't here anymore."

"And I say you're afraid to be away from your family because you have abandonment issues because of your mom."

"How dare you? I enjoy being with my family, and you would enjoy being with yours if—"

He sighed with frustration. "I can't be like you and your family. I don't want to be."

"Then that's your loss," she said scornfully. "And it makes me sad. How could you not see that?"

"Because this is who I am!" he shouted. "That's what I'm trying to tell you! I thought I could change, thought I *wanted* to change. But I don't. I enjoy my solitude. I like not having to check in with anyone. I don't expect you to understand it, and I already know you don't like it, but it's not going to change. *I'm* not going to change. How long will it be before you resent me for that too?"

Silence.

"I'm sorry," he said. "More than you'll ever know. But this is for the best. You are going to do amazing things with your life. You're going to travel and prove to the world how brilliant you are. You don't need someone holding you back."

Still, she didn't speak.

"Go and take on the world, Darcy," he said softly. "Show them what you're made of."

He heard her sob, but she didn't respond.

"Someday, someone's going to appreciate all that makes you special. And you are." He stopped there, because his throat clogged with emotion, and he felt the unfamiliar sting of tears. "And he's never going to want to let you go."

Another sob.

"Take care of yourself."

And as he hung up the phone and watched the screen fade to black, it felt a lot like his own life.

All of it had just left him.

—◆—

"I know you didn't want to go out, but you needed to."

Looking at Anna, all Darcy could do was nod. It had been four days since Ben had ended things with her, and she still felt numb.

"What can we do? Tell me what we can do to help you."

They were sitting in a booth at Anna's pub along with Zoe, and as much as Darcy knew she should eat, all she could do was push the food around on her plate. "I don't know. I wish I did."

Anna studied her for a long moment. "Can I say something?"

Without looking up, she nodded again.

"Do you remember how much you used to wish you could move away from here?"

Another nod.

"It wasn't so bad, right?"

She sighed and looked up. "It's not about logistics, Anna. It's…it's about his heart. Ben is not a family-oriented person. I could have handled living in Washington. Hell, I actually *wanted* to move there. It's beautiful and peaceful, and I love his house. But to tell me that he can't handle my family?" She shrugged. "That's something that can't be overcome. I just…I can't."

Reaching across the table, Anna squeezed Darcy's hand. "I understand. I hate it for you, but I get it." She paused. "Although…"

"Although what?"

Anna waved her off. "You know what? It's nothing. Don't mind me."

"No, come on. You clearly had something to say there. Out with it."

"I don't know. Think of the whole situation. I mean, you already knew he wasn't close with his brothers. He doesn't hate them; he just doesn't feel the need to see them all the time. There's no crime in that. I love Bobby, but it's not like I'm counting the seconds until I see him again."

"Isn't he still here?"

Anna nodded. "If anything, I'm counting the seconds until he goes home."

Darcy couldn't help it. That made her laugh. "Anyway…"

"Anyway, it just seems odd to me that he had such a complete turnaround in how he felt about your family. Maybe there's something else going on."

"Like what?"

Zoe chimed in. "Okay, I know this is going to come out weird, but bear with me." She paused. "You have a very unique way of dealing with your family, Darce. A lot of it has to do with your mom, but maybe you're clinging too much to this sense of needing to be close together in order to be close."

"I don't…I don't understand." A small twinge of unease began in her belly, because she did understand, or she was trying to. This was eerily similar to what Ben had said to her.

Anna looked at Zoe and then back at Darcy. "You know that your family is closer than most, right?"

Darcy nodded.

"Not all families are like that. Living close together doesn't necessarily mean you're a close family. Does that make sense?"

"I guess, but…"

Zoe spoke up again. "In the time I've known you, you've been all over the place where your family is concerned. You hate living so close to them, then you hate being far away. You hate how everyone knows your business, but then you hate when people aren't involved in your life. You need to find some balance."

"Well, I hope we'll have some now. I mean, eventually Dad and Martha will get married, and everything will be balanced."

Anna and Zoe looked at each other and then back at her. "Balanced?" Anna asked. "How?"

"You know, because then we'll be a complete family. Honestly, I don't know if I would want to move away once we're finally all together."

"Um, I hate to say this, but we're not," Zoe said.

"What do you mean?"

"I mean, Riley and Savannah don't live here. They're firmly settled in California. And Hugh and Aubrey aren't exactly right around the corner," Zoe reminded her. "And lastly, Ian and Martha? *If* they get married, it will be about them. Not the family."

"I agree," Anna said. "Ian and Martha getting married would be to complete *them*. Martha's not a substitute for your mom or to make your family whole. It would be because he fell in love with her and she makes *his* life complete."

And in that instant, Darcy's heart squeezed so hard that she felt as if she couldn't breathe. All around her, voices became like a loud buzzing in her head. She felt hot and then cold. Her vision blurred, and she realized her eyes were filling with tears.

"Darcy? Sweetie, are you all right?" Anna asked, her voice laced with concern.

As hard as she tried, Darcy couldn't give her a verbal response, so she simply nodded. Then she reached for her purse and fumbled with it as she put money down on the table.

"I have to go," she whispered. "I…I'm sorry, but I have to go."

Zoe and Anna stood and called out to her, but she kept moving. Weaving through the lunch crowd, Darcy did her best to get out the door, to get air. Once she was outside, she wasn't sure where she wanted to go or what she was going to do. She gulped in the fresh air and tried her best to calm her rapidly beating heart.

What the hell was wrong with her?

But she knew.

Walking as fast as she could, she got to her car and quickly pulled out of the parking lot. She had driven with Zoe, but she'd apologize to her later.

Part of her was screaming to speed out of town, to put her foot to the floor and go. But another told her to be reasonable. She could barely see through the tears that had begun to fall, and the last thing she wanted to do was cause an accident. She drove aimlessly—and slowly—through the heart of town, and by the time she hit the back roads, she was able to wipe the tears away and see.

A shaky breath came out as everything came into focus. She wished she could just call Ben and get this all out. Share with him all her crazy fears and anxieties.

And to tell him that he was right. She was clinging to her family for all the wrong reasons.

He would listen, and she knew he'd make her feel better.

But he wouldn't understand.

Hell, she barely understood.

So where did that leave her?

Darcy slowed the car and realized that the answer was right in front of her.

Turning the car, she drove slowly up the single lane, past the large oak tree on the left and past the fountain surrounded by wildflowers on the right. She could drive this route with her eyes closed; she'd been here so many times.

But this was the first time she'd done it alone.

She parked and then sat for a minute and tried to figure out what it was she was supposed to do. Say.

"Only one way to find out," she murmured as she climbed from the car. It was twenty-seven steps. She'd counted them often enough. And she was counting them now. When she came to a stop, she turned, looked down, and smiled. "Hi, Mom."

It was weird saying those words out loud. She'd never done it before. Every time she'd come to the cemetery, she'd been with her father and brothers, and they all talked to her silently. Only her father spoke—he would share stories of what everyone was doing and how everyone was—but after that, it was silent prayer time. So to be standing here and talking? It felt strange.

With no one else around, Darcy slowly lowered herself to the grass and sat at what she guessed were where her mother's feet were. And that felt odd. Then she mentally yelled at herself to quit focusing on what was weird about this and simply talk.

"So this is new, huh?" she said, her voice small and trembling. "I bet you're wondering why I'm here. I think I am too. I can't believe I've never done this before. I'm

sure you're disappointed that I never did, and I'm sorry.
I should have. When I was little, I had an excuse—
couldn't drive. But once I got older, I should have
come." A sob came out before she could stop it. "I'm so
sorry that I didn't. I'm a terrible daughter, right?"

A light breeze blew, and Darcy pulled her sweater
tight around her. The weather had been unseasonably
warm, so there hadn't been a need for a winter coat, but
right now, she wished she had one.

"I know if you were here you'd probably be telling
me that I'm not terrible, but you'd be saying it because
that's the kind of thing moms say. You'd say something
to make me feel better, but you shouldn't. It was selfish
and inconsiderate of me. And if you asked any of your
sons, they'd tell you it was typical of me." She paused
and let herself cry some more. "I'm not someone you
would be proud of, Mom. I am selfish, and I've out-
grown being so inconsiderate, but I was for a long time.
And I didn't even realize that I was that way. No one
told me. No one tried to correct me."

Self-loathing filled her as she drew her knees up to
her chest.

This was so much harder than she'd imagined.

"I'm so lost right now. Just when I thought I was getting my life in order, it all fell apart again. I keep grasp-
ing for that one thing that's going to make it all right,
that's going to make everything fall into place and…and
it's always just out of my reach." She sighed. "I thought
if Dad got married, it would happen—like everything
would fall into place for me. For our family. And that was
so wrong. For starters, there was never anything *wrong*
with our family. You raised five amazing sons, and you

married an incredible man who held us all together when you were gone, and I don't think I ever appreciated that. I was so busy focusing on what I was missing that I didn't consider thanking him for all he was doing.

"He's so strong, Mom. And I know it's probably so weird for you to know that he's dating and all, but he's happy. He's really, really happy. It's so good to see him smiling and laughing, and I'm telling you, he looks ten years younger. Easily."

More tears fell as Darcy stared straight ahead and looked at her mother's headstone.

*Lillian Grace Shaughnessy. Beloved wife and mother.*

How many times had she stood here and read that and it hadn't really registered? How often had she talked about her mother without letting it sink in that she was a real person? That she was never going to see her, meet her, or talk to her?

"Please don't take this the wrong way, but I have to say this. Actually, I think I've needed to say this for a long time." She took a steadying breath and braced herself for…something. "I was mad at you. I was so damn mad at you for not being here." She sobbed loudly and didn't care who—if anyone—heard. "My whole life, I've been angry at you, and even though I know it's not your fault, I can't help the way I feel. I listen to Aidan and Hugh and everyone talk about these amazing things that you used to do, and I feel…cheated. Why did I have to be born so late? Why didn't I get to do any of those things with you?"

Off in the distance, Darcy saw another car driving down the road, saw other people bringing flowers to loved ones.

"I never admitted that to anyone," she said as she

furiously wiped away her tears. "I always knew it was wrong to feel that way and that people would think I'm a terrible person if I said it, but I needed to finally say it. I was afraid if I said it—if people really knew that I thought like that—they'd leave me. For a time, I thought it was why you left me—because you knew I was a bad daughter. I'm sorry. I'm so sorry for thinking like that. I know now, and I understand that you would be here if you could. And you need to know that I would give anything for that to happen."

She cried some more. She cried until there were no more tears left.

"I didn't bring you flowers," she said sadly. "In my defense, I didn't realize I was coming here, but I should have brought you flowers. Daisies. I know they're your favorite." Another pause.

"I met someone," she said, trying to sound cheery. "His name is Ben and he's...he's everything. He's an artist, and he does the most incredible things with wood. And he lives in this cabin in Washington state." She paused and let her mind wander to the cabin. "I would love to live there. Which I think is going to cause some major fights with everyone, but I really would. I spent so many years being forced to be close to home, and then I spent a couple of years wanting to be away, and here I am again. But to be with Ben? I'd live on the other side of the country. Pretty crazy, huh?"

Her head fell back, and she let the sun shine down on her for a minute. Straightening, she went on. "But that all fell apart, and I don't know how to move on from it. I don't know how to get over losing him. My heart...my heart is broken, and it hurts so much."

A strong wind blew, and she shivered with it.

It made her think about her time at Ben's cabin, how cold it had been and how she swore that she hated it, but right now she'd give anything to be there with him. Cold or no cold, she just wanted to be with him. She wanted to talk to him about her hopes, her dreams…and hopefully, their future. Darcy knew she was strong enough to fight for him, for them. She'd had time to think about everything he said to her, and coming here today to talk to her mother had been the right thing to do. She felt stronger, more at peace than she'd ever felt in her life. And as soon as she got home, she was going to call Ben and tell him.

But she needed to finish something first.

"I love you, Mom," she said and realized it felt good to say it out loud. "I miss you every single day, and I want you to know that I am going to do everything humanly possible to make you proud."

Slowly, she got to her feet and stepped in close to the marble headstone. She kissed her fingers and then laid them on the cold stone. "Thank you for being my mom. And I promise you, I'm going to come and visit more, and I'm really glad that I came here today." She paused and ran her hand along the top of the marble. "I'm not mad anymore. I wish I could take back all the years that I was, but I can't. I have to deal with that. But even when I was mad, I always loved you. And I always missed you. And I can only hope that you're looking down on me right now and know…" Tears welled up again, and her throat tightened. "I love you."

In a perfect world, there would be a response, a sign of some sort that Lillian heard her. The only thing that

Darcy knew was that her heart felt full and yet light for the first time in weeks.

Maybe that was her sign.

She smiled at the headstone and then smiled up at the sky.

And then slowly made her way back to her car.

# Chapter 12

"SON OF A BITCH!"

There was nothing worse than the sting of a sharp metal blade cutting through skin. And as he let out a string of curses, he made sure anyone within a five-mile radius knew it too.

He knew the drill. It happened often enough. Still cursing, he applied pressure to his hand and made his way across the dusty workshop to pull out the first aid kit. Within minutes, he had managed to slow down the bleeding even as he pulled out the supplies he needed to clean up and cover the wound.

Looking down at the newest cut, he grimaced. At this rate, he wasn't going to be able to finish any of the work that was strewn across his workshop. His focus was off, and he was making careless mistakes. Once his hand was bandaged, he put the supplies away and put the case back in the cabinet. Leaning against the workbench, he let out a shaky sigh.

Something had to give.

He was killing himself—barely eating, barely sleeping—and for what?

There was a simple solution to all of it. All he had to do was call Darcy and tell her he was wrong. That he needed her, wanted her, couldn't live without her. And while he knew it would help set things right, he knew he was still in the same predicament he was a week ago.

He was still someone who was hiding from his past, his family, his life. It would be wrong to ask her to make peace with her life when he couldn't do the same with his own.

Shaking his head, he turned and walked across the room, where he flipped off the light switch and walked out into the fading light. The cold Washington air hit him first, and it was such a contrast to the heat of the workshop that it felt as if he'd walked into a wall. It took the air right from his lungs, and he almost welcomed the sting.

Once he was in the house, he sat down on the bench and took off his coat, pulled off his shoes, and sighed. The quiet was killing him. When he stood, he looked around and saw all of the things that were familiar to him—pictures on the wall, the furniture—and sighed again. There were still traces of his grandparents here but nothing of his parents.

How was that possible?

Walking up to the main level, he looked around again. The afghan on his couch was made by his grandmother. The rocking chair in the corner was made by his grandfather. He had made sure to keep those things, because they reminded him of his childhood.

And yet he'd put everything that belonged to his parents in storage.

Out of sight.

Jack and Henry had taken a few things with them when they moved, but Ben had not wanted the reminders around him. His heart beat fast until it felt like he'd run a marathon. At the time, he'd thought it would be too painful to have things that belonged to his parents around him, thought that out of sight meant out of mind. But he was wrong. So, so wrong. All it had done was hold his emotions at bay. It kept him locked in a suspended sense of time.

And he knew that if he didn't do something about it, he was never going to move forward. He was never going to have peace.

He was never going to have a life.

Forcing himself to breathe, he pulled his phone from his pocket and stared at the screen. Christmas was in four days. He'd worked through the anniversary of his parents' death just like he had every year. What kind of son did that make him?

He swiped the screen, pulled up Jack's number, and hit Send.

"Hey, Ben!" Jack said, sounding pleasantly surprised. "What's up?"

Where did he even begin?

"I…I'm calling to say I'm sorry."

Jack was silent for a moment before slowly saying, "O-kay. For what?"

It was going to sound crazy, he was sure, but he needed to just jump in with both feet and get it all out. "For everything," he replied gruffly. "I've been a shitty brother, and I just want you to know that I thought I was being strong. I thought that if I just ignored all the memories that it would help me to keep going. I didn't realize how it was affecting all of us—our relationship. The times that I spend with you and Henry mean the world to me, and I'm always afraid to acknowledge that because—"

"Because it scares you," Jack said solemnly. "I know. Believe it or not, Ben, I feel the same way. I think I've tried to cling to you and Henry because you're all I had. I mean, not anymore—I have Donna now too—but you guys are my only tie to Mom and Dad. And it hurts when you refuse to talk about them or celebrate the holidays because of them."

"I know. I know...I need to work on that."

"It's not too late," Jack said, and Ben could hear the smile in his voice. "You still have four days until Christmas."

He couldn't help but chuckle. "I said I need to work on it, but I can't just jump in and do it on such short notice. Besides, I wouldn't even know where to begin."

"I'm sure Darcy could help."

And that's when he realized that he never even talked to anyone about breaking up with Darcy. "Uh, yeah. Not so much. At least, not this Christmas."

"Uh-oh. What did you do?"

Ben sat down on the sofa and told Jack all about the trips to North Carolina, the Shaughnessys, and his eventual fight with Darcy.

"So you purposely picked a fight with her?" Jack asked.

"Yup."

"And you haven't talked to her since?"

"Nope."

"You're an idiot. You realize that, right?"

"I've been telling myself that same thing for days."

"So what are you going to do about it?"

"I'm hoping to finally get my head out of my ass and convince her to take me back."

Jack laughed hysterically. "Damn! I don't think I've ever heard you like this—so honest! It's kind of cool. So how are you going to do it?"

"Honestly? I don't know. Calling you needed to come first. I love Darcy, but my relationship with you and Henry needs to be my top priority here." Then he smiled. "She helped me to understand that, and I know it's what she'd want me to do. Next, I'm going to call Henry. I miss you guys, and next time you're both here, I'd like us to go through Mom and Dad's stuff that's in storage. I think it's time that we dealt with it and everyone takes what they want and then…"

"We let the rest go," Jack said quietly. "Yeah. I know."

"But we need to do it together. Deal?"

"Deal."

Nodding, Ben realized that this was a good thing, a good first step.

"Can I make a suggestion?" Jack asked.

"Sure."

"Henry can wait. Hell, I'll call Henry and give him a heads-up that you're going to call. You need to call Darcy. Now," he added with a small laugh. "Don't wait, man. It's Christmas, and you both deserve to be happy."

"I…I want to. I really do. There's just no way to make it all work in time."

"No one says you have to be in the same place for Christmas—although that would be awesome. But at least talk to her and apologize and make sure she's all right. Then you can work out travel arrangements and all that crap. The important thing is that you take the first step."

And then an idea hit him.

One that—if he could make it work—would be the real proof that he was ready.

"There's actually another step I need to take first," Ben said cautiously.

"A step before the first step?"

"Yeah," he said with a low laugh. "Something like that." Taking a steadying breath, he said, "What if… what if we spent Christmas together here? Just the three of us, and celebrate a Christmas like we did when we were kids. We'll pull out the old ornaments and make some of Mom's recipes and all go together to the cemetery on Christmas Day. What do you think?" Jack was so quiet that Ben feared the line had gone dead. "Jack?"

Jack cleared his throat, and when he started speaking, Ben could hear the emotion there. "I think that would be amazing. I think Mom and Dad would really like that."

Ben let out a sigh of relief. "Darcy was always encouraging me to call you. You and Henry. And I didn't want to listen. I didn't believe that she knew what she was talking about. But you know what? She did. She was right." Then he laughed a little more. "Damn, I…I am really glad that I called you, Jack."

"Finally!" His brother laughed with him. "Things are going to get better, right? We're going to put in the effort to be more involved in each other's lives, right?"

"Absolutely," Ben agreed.

"Darcy's a pretty smart woman. You better not let her get away."

Her face popped into his mind, and he smiled. "Tell Henry I'll call him later," Ben said right before he said goodbye and hung up.

He had hope.

He felt good.

———

When she got in her car, her phone was ringing.

"Oh my God, where are you? Where did you go? Are you okay?"

Anna.

Darcy smiled, but she was too anxious to be on the phone with someone else. "I'm good. I really, really am," she said with a giddiness that had her feeling like anything was possible.

"You scared the hell out of us!"

"I know and I'm sorry, but I—" She stopped when her phone beeped with another call. "Hang on."

Zoe.

Switching the call over, she answered.

"Hey, Zoe! Listen, I—"

"Do you have any idea how you freaked us out? The whole family is out looking for you and—"

"Okay, okay, hang on. I've got Anna on the other line. I'm okay. Call off the dogs! I promise to call you back." With another laugh because this was her crazy life, she switched back over to Anna. "Sorry, that was Zoe."

"Now I've got Quinn on the other line. You sure you're okay?"

"I'm fine. I was about to call—" Her phone beeped with another incoming call. "Son of a bitch!" she yelled and then laughed. "Hang on again."

"I'm just gonna hang up..." Anna was saying, but Darcy wasn't really paying attention.

This time, she didn't even look at the screen. She simply swiped and answered. "I'm fine, okay? Everyone can stop freaking out, because I'm really okay. I freaked out, and I went for a long drive. I'm at the cemetery, but I'll be home soon. I promise."

"How soon?" a deep, male voice replied.

*Ben!*

"As soon as I can get a flight," she said as she sighed happily.

His rich, wonderful laugh only added to her happiness. "Hey, you," he said softly.

"Hey."

"Why are you answering the phone at the cemetery?"

Oh yeah…that.

"I was here visiting my mom after having a mini meltdown while out with Anna and Zoe. I left the phone in the car while I was…you know…and when I got back in here, it was ringing. First, it was Anna checking on me, then Zoe, and it turns out everyone's looking for me, so when you rang in, I thought it was someone else trying to find me."

"It was," he said, his voice serious, solemn. "I'm trying to find my girl so I can apologize and beg her to forgive me."

Turning on the car and the heat, Darcy couldn't help but smile. "You want to know something funny?"

"Right now?"

She laughed. "Especially right now."

"I…I guess."

"I was just getting in the car to call you to apologize. Funny, right?"

"Darcy, you have nothing to apologize for. What happened was…it was all my fault. I'm so sorry for the things I said."

"We both said things in the heat of the moment, but I think they were things that had to be said. That's why—"

"No," he interrupted. "I never should have lashed out at you the way that I did. Never. I was so stuck in my own head and thinking of how I want things to be, but that way? The way I was thinking? Was so wrong! You helped me to see that."

"I…I did?"

"Yes. God, Darcy, you have no idea," he began and then let out a dismal laugh. "For years, I've been living in my own little world with blinders on. I kept my focus on one thing and one thing only, because I didn't want to think about anything else. I didn't want to think about my parents or my family, because it hurt too much. And other than the occasional ribbing from my brothers, I was able to stay in my protective little bubble.

"Then you came along," he went on. "And you came into my life and my home, and you questioned every single thing that I did—"

"I wouldn't put it quite like that," she argued lightly.

"It was exactly like that," he said, but there was no condemnation there. "At first, it was because we were working together, but the more time we spent together, I came to realize that it's just who you are, and it's one of the things that I love about you. You push me, you challenge me, you make me feel. I had forgotten what it was like to let myself feel."

"Oh, Ben."

"Seeing you with your family? I realized that it bothered me so much because…because it was everything that I wouldn't allow myself to have. You were all there for and supported one another, and it was just a stark reminder of what I wasn't doing."

"But you said that we spent too much time together."

"Who am I to say what's too much time? My family dynamic is different than yours—of that, there's no doubt—but who's to say that if my parents were still alive that we wouldn't be more like yours?"

"Your family doesn't have to be like mine," she admitted. "Every family is different, and what I am really just coming to understand is you don't have to all be close logistically, as long as you're close emotionally. I'm hoping to put that theory to the test."

"Is that right?" he asked, and she knew he was teasing her.

"Oh, yeah. I've been looking at jobs in Seattle and—"

"Before you go any further, can I just say something?"

She sighed dramatically. "I kind of feel like you've been doing most of the talking."

"Let me just say this, and then it's your turn. I promise."

"Okay."

"I still don't want you taking a job that you hate just to be close to me. I want you here by me—more than you'll ever know—but it has to be right for you."

"And it will be—"

"Still talking," he interrupted with a small laugh. "Anyway, what you did for Brooke? Could you maybe do that sort of thing for me?"

That was completely not what she was thinking at all. "Seriously? Don't you already have a representative?"

"I do. But he hasn't come up with anything beyond the book deal. He's not thinking about other ways to get my name out there, and I think you know what I would do and what I wouldn't do. I want someone who understands me."

"Yeah, but you can share these ideas with him and see what he thinks." Then she paused. "Or honestly, at this stage of the game—at least where the book is concerned—that's your publicist's concern. You do have a publicist, right?"

"Yeah, through the publisher. But I'm thinking beyond the book. I mean, what am I going to do after it? I want to keep doing work for private clients, but I would also like to have a gallery or something in Seattle to showcase my work year-round. I have no idea how to make that happen."

Darcy's heart began to pound rapidly. Was he serious? This was exactly the kind of thing she would love to do. It was so much fun doing it for Brooke, and to have the chance to help Ben do what he wanted and start living the life that he wanted...

"Wait. You're not asking because you feel bad for me, are you?"

"What are you talking about?" he asked.

"Ben, I told you how I needed to find a job, and now you're offering me a job. You have to admit it sounds like you're doing the same thing."

"No, I'm not. I'm ready to start a new phase of my career, and I believe you can make that happen for me. You understand me. You get me. And you've seen the way I work around here. I seriously need your help."

It was like a dream come true. "You know this means you'd have to listen to me."

"I am aware."

"And I'm probably going to be bossy."

"I'm more than ready for it."

Her eyes stung a little with tears—happy ones this time. "And it means you're going to have to see me all the time, because we'll have to work *very* closely together."

"That's the part I'm looking forward to the most."

"Me too. You have no idea."

"I do. Come back to me, Darcy. Live with me. Work with me. Just love me."

"I do, so much, Ben. But in all fairness, I need to tell you some things."

"More than that you're going to boss me around?" he teased.

She knew he was trying to lighten the mood, but he had bared his soul, and she thought it was only right for her to do the same.

"I was mad at my mom," she said quietly, and she almost held her breath and waited for his reaction.

"O-kay."

"That's why I came here today. I mean, I've been coming to the cemetery my entire life, but I never came alone, and I never really talked to my mom."

He was silent for a moment. "Never?"

"Never," she repeated. "I thought it was weird, and I figured there was no point in it. But today I came here and talked to her. I actually yelled some and cried through a lot of it, but the point is, I made peace with myself about the whole thing."

"And how do you feel now?"

"So much better," she said with a shaky sigh. "I know that she would be here if she could. She didn't leave me on purpose, and it's not my fault that she's gone. I struggled with that for a long time."

"Why would it be your fault?"

"She was out getting a prescription for me," she replied. "And in the back of my mind, I always thought that if I hadn't been sick, then she never would have been out that day."

"Oh, sweetheart, you can't think like that."

"It felt so good to say all those things out loud. Of course, it would have been great to get some answers, but someday I will, right?"

"I'd like to think so," he said quietly.

If they were going to be okay, if they were going to be able to move forward, then she had to say what was in her heart. "You need to do it too, Ben. I'm not saying you need to go to the cemetery right now or at all, but you should talk to them. All of them."

He was quiet, and she feared that she had offended him again and that he was going to argue with her.

"You want to know something funny?" he asked after a minute.

She chuckled. "Right now?"

"Especially right now," he said, mimicking her earlier words.

"Go for it."

"Right before I called you, I called Jack."

"You did?" she asked excitedly. "How is he?"

"My brother is fine," he answered. "But we had a good talk. A really good talk. And I told him that I was wrong for cutting myself off from him and Henry. We decided to try and have them come here for Christmas—to celebrate together and to celebrate our parents." He told her of the plans he had just talked to his brother about.

"Oh, Ben, I love that. I think that is a wonderful idea."

She wanted to feel bad—especially since he had made this breakthrough with his family—but she was just so happy to hear his voice and know that things were on their way to becoming okay. But the selfish part of her was disappointed that they weren't going to be spending Christmas together. "I can't wait to hear all about it."

If it were up to her, she'd be driving to the airport right now while telling her father to just pack up her stuff and ship it. It wasn't possible, and if anything, it gave her a new outlook on this particular Christmas—it would be bittersweet.

It would be her last one alone.

Her last one as the odd-Shaughnessy-out.

Her last one without the man she loved.

# Chapter 13

I⊤ WAS AFTER MIDNIGHT ON CHRISTMAS EVE, AND THE entire house was quiet. Darcy sat on the sofa looking at the Christmas tree. All the lights in the house were out except for the multicolored ones adorning the tree. She was wearing her new Christmas pajamas and sipping a cup of hot chocolate.

"You know Santa can't come unless everyone's asleep."

Smiling, she turned her head and saw her father standing a few feet away. "I wasn't going to stay up all night," she teased softly.

Ian Shaughnessy came over and sat beside her. "What are you still doing up?"

She shrugged. "You know how much I love looking at the tree."

"That's why you have one up in your room," he reminded her. "Try again."

Leave it to her dad to call her out on the fib. "I couldn't sleep. And I could only toss and turn for so long. I thought maybe a warm drink and sitting down here for a little while would help."

"And has it?"

She shook her head. "Not yet."

They sat in companionable silence.

"I think tomorrow is going to be a bit of a zoo," Ian said after a few minutes.

"Why's that?"

"Look at all those presents! And that's not including the ones I still have to put out for the kids from Santa."

Laughing softly, Darcy turned her head and looked at her father. "Six grandkids," she said with a sigh. "Seems like life's come full circle, huh?"

Ian nodded. "And we're not done yet."

Her brows went up. "Do you know something that I don't know?" she asked curiously.

"Nope. Just know that none of you are going to stop at one baby."

"Technically, Owen's got two." The image of her twin nephews made her smile.

"So could you, sweet pea."

And she immediately began to choke.

Ian patted her on the back until she could breathe again. "Dad! What the heck?"

"What? What did I say?"

"Why would you even say that?"

He looked at her as if she were crazy. "Say what?"

"You cannot possibly put me in a conversation about everyone having babies!" she said adamantly.

"And why not?"

Her eyes went wide. "Seriously? Um, how about because I'm not married yet? Or how about because I don't even know if things are going to work out with Ben? And…and…"

Ian hugged his daughter close and waited for her to calm down.

"Sorry," she murmured.

"Darce, I know you're a little sad. And I know you're missing Ben, but don't sell yourself short. You're going to see him in a few days, and everything's going to be all right. And you know what I think?"

Looking up at him, she asked, "What?"

"I think that you, my sweet girl, are going to have the greatest love of them all."

Tears instantly filled her eyes. "You do?"

He nodded. "And do you know why?"

She shook her head, too overwhelmed to speak.

Tucking a finger under her chin, he said, "Because you have the biggest heart of anyone in this family. *You* were the one who held us all together when we would have fallen apart. Without you, Darcy, none of this would be possible." He motioned to the presents, the tree, the family photos. "You are the reason there is so much love and laughter here."

"Dad—"

"It's true. Now I'm not going to lie to you. It's not going to be easy to watch you leave here in a few days. I've sent you off to visit your brothers, I've sent you off to college…but I knew those were temporary visits."

Tears stung her eyes. "It's not like I'm never coming back."

"I know. I know." He paused. "I convinced your mom to move away from her parents," he said casually.

"Um, what?"

Ian nodded. "It's true. Granted, it wasn't very far— not like the other side of the country or anything—but still, she left her family to be with me."

"Wow."

"There isn't any place in the world that you can live that I'm not going to love you, Darcy. My only wish for you is that you be happy."

Tears welled up in her eyes as she reached out and hugged him. "Thanks, Dad," she whispered.

"I like Ben," he said, taking her cocoa from her and taking a sip. "I think you gave to him exactly what you gave to all of us." He paused. "And that makes him a lucky man."

She gave a quiet snort. "I don't know about that. All I know is that I don't ever want him to be alone again. It broke my heart thinking of him living the way he was."

Ian studied his daughter for a moment. "See? Such a big heart. I think Santa is going to be very pleased with you. Maybe he'll leave a little something extra for you under the tree."

Darcy couldn't help but laugh a little. "Dad, I'm a little old for that to work."

He hugged her back, and when they broke apart, he stood up. "You're a good daughter, and I am honored to be your dad. You are the greatest gift to this family. I have two things that I want to give you."

Ian walked over to the tree and looked around for a moment. Then he reached into the pile and pulled out a small box. Sitting back down beside her, he handed it to her.

"Dad, we're not supposed to open any more presents tonight," she chided playfully.

"I was trying to think of a way to give this to you when we were alone. So I'm actually glad you were up." He smiled lovingly at her. "Go ahead. Open it."

Putting her mug down, Darcy carefully opened the package. It was small, like the size of a box you'd put a pair of earrings in. But that's not what she found inside.

She looked down and then at her father. "It's a key," she said, feeling slightly confused.

Ian nodded. "Yes, it is."

"But to what?"

"That is the key to this house."

Maybe it was late, but clearly, one—or both—of them was more confused than the other. "Um, Dad, I already have a key to the house. I live here."

He smiled as he reached out and cupped her cheek. "That key is more symbolic," he began, and she heard the slight tremor in his voice. "That key is to let you know that you will always have a home here. Always. Whether you want to come home for a weekend, a week, or... well, you get the idea. I can't guarantee that your room will always look the same, but no matter what, there will always be a place for you."

It was one of the greatest gifts he'd ever given her. Putting the key down, she leaned in and grabbed him in a fierce hug. "Thank you," she whispered.

When they broke apart, Ian stood and walked back over to the tree. "And I know that Santa's about twenty years late with this, but I hope you know that he never forgot."

She looked at him oddly. "What? What are you talking about?"

He handed her another box. It looked to be the size of a hardcover book. With the paper off, she lifted the lid off the box and gasped.

And then smiled.

It was a bifold silver picture frame.

On one side was a picture of Darcy as an infant in her mother's arms. And on the other? A picture of her and Martha from Thanksgiving.

She knew what it meant, and it made her heart soar. Tears fell in earnest as she hugged her father close. There was no need for words.

———

It wasn't that Ben wasn't having a good time.

He was.

But he also wanted this particular good time to end so he could get back to his life and the things he needed to be doing. His brothers were leaving tomorrow, and as much as he didn't want to be a jerk, he was so ready for them to go. Because once they were gone, Darcy would be arriving the next day. They'd coordinated it that way because she didn't want to interfere with their visit.

Damn, but he loved his girl!

Christmas Eve had been amazing. They'd laughed a lot, they'd cried a lot, and more than anything, Ben remembered everything he had loved about the holiday. The giant tree looked good in his living room, and they had not only put all the family ornaments on the tree, but Ben had taken out all the ones he had made and had in storage and put them on it as well.

They looked good.

Really good.

"There's snow in the forecast," Jack said as he finished his cup of coffee. "Nothing major, but if we're going to do this, we should probably go now."

Ben agreed.

Thirty minutes later, they laid the wreath they'd made out of the tree trimmings in front of the headstone that read "Thomas and Julia Tanner— Beloved Parents." Just seeing those words had Ben getting choked up. But rather than turn it into something sad, they continued the celebration, taking turns telling a favorite Christmas memory as they laughed and remembered. When the snow began to fall and they made their way back to the car, Ben turned one last time and looked at his parents' plot.

"I promise to make you proud," he said softly.

That night, snow dusted the trees and the roads without accumulating too much, and the three of them shared one last dinner together before his brothers had to leave.

"Your flight is so damn early," Ben said. "You're going to have to leave here around four in the morning."

Henry nodded. "It wasn't ideal, but it was part of the great pricing I found."

"It's almost not worth going to sleep," Ben said. "We've yet to go to bed before two the entire time you've been here."

"Then we won't sleep," Jack said, raising his glass. "We'll spend this last night pulling a—relaxing—all-nighter, and then you'll get your peace and quiet back."

Ben chuckled. "It's highly overrated, I'm told."

"You got that right," Henry said before taking a pull of his beer.

They ate grilled salmon and mashed potatoes and salad and enjoyed one another's company as they did it.

"So what's next for you, Ben?" Jack asked. "What projects are on the horizon?"

"I have my choice of what I want to do," he began. "I have three clients who I'm always doing pieces for, and then I have the bar I've been working on." He stopped and smiled. "And then I may do a custom tree house."

His brothers just stared at him.

"I know. It's completely different from anything I've ever done, but I've watched some DIY shows on the subject, and I've been researching it, and I may give it a try."

"Who's the client? Do they have blueprints for you? That involves a lot more construction than you usually do, doesn't it?" Henry asked.

Ben nodded to all the questions. "The client is one of Darcy's brothers, and it's very different, but I think it could be challenging. I've been doing some drawings, and I've got an image in my mind of how I want it to look. I'll have to run it by Hugh and his wife and see if we're on the same page, but that's what I'd like to do next." He shrugged. "There's never a lack of something to do. And with any luck, Darcy will get things going on finding me a gallery and starting that phase of my career."

"It's about time you had a place for your art. The sheer amount of stuff you have in storage in the workshop will fill a gallery," Henry said.

"Well, it wouldn't only be my stuff on display. I'd like to showcase local artists and maybe even some students from our old high school. You know, pay it forward like what was done for me."

They all smiled and nodded in agreement, and Ben had to admit, he was going to miss this.

"So what about Easter in Boston? Is that something I'm going to enjoy?" he asked and almost burst out laughing at the surprised looks on his brothers' faces.

"You're really going to come and spend a holiday with us?" Jack asked.

"Yup. And remember, you asked for it."

"Oh lord."

"You'll be missing the days when you used to miss me," Ben added with a big grin. "And then I'm going to have to say I told you so."

"Just don't do the dance," Henry said with a groan.

"I have never done a dance," Ben said primly.

"Oh please! You were the worst at the 'I told you so' dance!" Jack said, laughing at the memory. Then he and Henry jumped out of their seats and acted out the ridiculous dance that included quite a few jumps and stomps. When they were done, they both looked at him blandly. "Bring back any memories?"

Doing his best to keep a straight face, he shook his head. "Mmm, nope. Sorry. Doesn't ring a bell." It wasn't until they both sat down that Ben started to laugh. "And just for the record, I never shook my hips quite like that."

The room erupted with laughter, and as they finished their meal and worked together to clean up, he knew for sure that he was going to miss them this time after they left. As anxious as he was to get back to work and back into his normal routine, he knew that this time they spent together was crucial on so many levels. More than anything, it helped him to feel a lot more grounded and back in touch with what was important in life.

He turned on the TV, and they argued over what to watch and found a hockey game that they could all agree on. When was the last time he'd done this? Watched a game—any game—with a group of guys?

Too long.

Far too long.

Hell, when was the last time he'd done anything social with anyone?

With the Shaughnessys.

With Darcy.

He missed her so damn much. She'd changed his life in so many ways, and he couldn't wait to have her back here with him—where she belonged.

———∿∿∿———

Ben was finishing his coffee and watching the clock in hopes of time moving faster so he could leave for the airport when his phone rang.

"Hey, beautiful."

"Hey, yourself," she said in the sexy voice that he couldn't wait to hear in person. "So, minor change of plans."

Uh-oh. "What's going on? Is your flight delayed? I was just on the website, and it said everything was on time."

She laughed softly. "No, no, no, nothing like that. I just got off the phone with a guy who owns a gallery in downtown Seattle. This is an amazing opportunity, but we have to act fast."

"Darcy, I thought we were going to wait a little while before we started doing that sort of thing."

"I know, I know, but I was just sort of looking around online and saw this and wanted to jump on it. You never know. It could be a great opportunity."

"Opportunity for what? What exactly are we talking about?"

"He has an opening for a show next month that I'd really like to get you into, and he's looking to sell the gallery. So if you go and meet with him on the way to the airport…"

It would be a good way to kill time, he thought.

"I wouldn't even know where to begin," he said honestly. "I have no idea what I should be asking or—"

"The only thing I need you to do is look at the space and talk to this guy about the show. I think you'll have an idea if it's something you want to buy after you've been there and checked out the space. So what do you say? Will you go? Will you look? And then when you pick me up, we can talk about it."

He chuckled. "Sweetheart, I had a much different idea for what we were going to do after I picked you up."

"Ooh, I like the sound of that. We can do both. I promise. I'll text you the address, and before you know it, I'll be there with you."

"And I definitely like the sound of that."

By the time they hung up, Ben was already at the back door putting on his boots.

Anticipation spurred him on. The sooner he got done with this meeting, the sooner he'd be on his way to the airport.

During the drive, he thought about all the plans he had for them for tonight. At first, he had planned on staying in the city for the night—getting a room at the Four Seasons and going out for a romantic dinner. In his mind, it would be wildly romantic. They had talked every day since that day he called her and she was at the cemetery, but they both agreed that there were some things they needed to talk about when they were face-to-face.

So he nixed the wild and romantic plans and opted to bring her home where they could simply reconnect and talk and just get anything and everything out of the way that they needed to before they could move on.

And that's what he wanted more than anything—
to put all the misunderstandings and hurt feelings
behind them so they could start their lives together the
right way.

And he had to admit, the thought of having her back
at his house and in his bed was better than any five-star
hotel image.

Making his way around the city, he followed the GPS
directions until he reached his destination. He parked his
truck and noted that the gallery was in a very desirable
part of the city—a very artsy part. He'd come to events
this way before, and they were always well-attended. It
would be a great location for a show.

Stepping inside, he saw a lot of boring art.

Disappointment swamped him. Ben wasn't sure what
he was expecting, but this bland assortment of water-
color wasn't it. Slowly, he walked around and took in
his surroundings. If he were to do a show here, he would
have to request that the gallery undergo some sort of
overhaul. Or at least strip down the walls and put away
these paintings until his show was over.

"Mr. Tanner?"

Ben turned and smiled as an older gentleman
approached him.

"I'm Stewart Ramsey," he said as they shook hands.
"It's nice to meet you. I was thrilled when Darcy told me
you were willing to come in and meet with me. So tell
me, what do you think of the space?"

Ugh. What was he supposed to say to that?

"Be honest," he prompted.

Oh well. If it was going to move this meeting along,
he'd be honest. Go big or go home, right? Better for him

to say exactly what he was looking for so there'd be no misunderstandings later.

"It's uninspiring, Mr. Ramsey," he began. "The art clashes in spots, the flow is awkward, and basically, there isn't anything here I'd want to hang in my home."

For a moment, Stewart Ramsey blinked at him. "Oh. Wow. I don't think I was quite expecting that."

Ben sighed. "Sorry. Maybe I could have been a little less blunt."

"No," he said immediately. "This is what I needed. For so long, I haven't been able to figure out why things weren't working, but no one would give me any advice. I really appreciate your bluntness."

"You're the first to say that," Ben said with a small laugh.

Stewart let out a small sigh and then seemed to collect himself. "Okay. Tell me what you'd like to see here that would make you want to hold a show with me."

They walked around the gallery as Ben mentioned removing the watercolors and suggested what kind of wall art and colors would complement his work. They made their way to a small back room that housed only two paintings.

One was of a house in the mountains.

The other was a house on the beach.

One was him. One was Darcy.

And just like that, the need to get in his truck and get to the airport was almost overwhelming. He pulled out his phone, looked at the clock, and saw that her plane wouldn't be landing for almost two more hours, and he groaned.

"Everything all right?" Stewart asked.

Ben nodded.

Behind them, the chime over the front door rang out, and Stewart excused himself. Ben stayed where he was and studied the paintings some more.

"I always wondered if the beach was anything like it's portrayed in pictures," a soft voice said from behind him.

And Ben's heart simply stopped.

"Portrayed how?" he asked softly, afraid to move.

"The sun is always shining, the sand looks pristine, and the sky is always this pink pastel color."

"Personally, I've never seen that."

"The sky or the pink?"

"The pink," he replied. "My sky is pretty gray."

"Seems about right."

"For a little while, I thought I saw some pink, but then it went away."

"Probably was forced to go away," she said mildly. "Some places are naturally gray like that."

"Mmm, maybe. But I'd be curious to see what all the fuss is about with the pink sky and the sand and all that."

She was standing beside him, and it took everything he had in him to not reach for her. His curiosity got the better of him and had him waiting to see what she was doing here.

With a shrug, she said, "Last I checked, Washington isn't known for its pink skies and white sand."

"Maybe I've been thinking of branching out."

She shrugged again. "Sure. Temporarily."

And then he was done with the banter. "What are you doing here? I thought your flight wasn't coming in for a few more hours."

"I got an earlier flight."

That totally took him by surprise. "Why didn't you tell me? I would have picked you up. Hell, I would have slept at the damn airport if that's what it took to get you to me sooner."

"I know you would have." She nodded, but her gaze stayed on the paintings. "But I wanted to surprise you. Oh, and I got a job."

"A job?" he asked.

"Yup."

"Where?"

"Here."

They were talking like polite strangers. Surprise him? Yes, she'd managed that. Infuriate him? Um, yeah. That's more like what he was feeling right now.

Now he was really done. Not only did he face her, but he gently grasped her by the shoulders and forced her to look at him. God, was she beautiful. That face, those eyes, everything about her just had him ready to drop to his knees.

"I don't understand."

"I'm going to be managing this gallery. At least temporarily. Stewart's looking to sell it, and I'm here to help him get things in order and find the right buyer. But a few things have to happen before we can get started. I'll need to figure out the commute and get a car and—"

He cut her off with a kiss.

Cupping her face in his hands, his lips covered hers, and for the first time in almost a month, Ben felt like he could finally breathe.

He could relax.

He could touch her.

And he could…

"I've been counting down the damn minutes until I could get to you," he said, lifting his head.

Darcy looked up at him with mild disbelief.

"It's true. My brothers left, and I haven't been able to do a damn thing work-wise because all I could think about was you. I almost got on a flight to North Carolina yesterday to come and get you."

"Get me?"

His hands were still on her face. "Yeah. Get you. You're mine, Darcy Shaughnessy. You showed up on my doorstep and turned my entire life upside down, and now you're stuck with me."

She took a step away, out of his arms, and gave him a stern look. "Oh really? You think it's just that easy? You just announce that you're ready to come and get me, and I'm supposed to, what? Get all swoony?"

"Swoony?"

She crossed her arms and tapped her foot sassily. "It's a word."

Ben couldn't help but laugh. He loved this—the banter, the teasing, the arguing…her. "Fine, it's a word. Any other questions?"

"Tons."

"Go for it," he said with a smirk.

She gave him that sassy pose—arms crossed, hip cocked, and confident smile that he loved.

"Well, my plan was to walk in here and surprise you," she replied. "Then I was going to talk to you about my ideas for the gallery."

"And what are they?"

"I was thinking it would be the perfect location

for you to set up a permanent display. It would be a place where you can showcase your art and other local artists—ones you approve of, of course. The space isn't huge, but it does come with a private loft apartment upstairs that you can use when you're in town for shows. That would cut down on commuting."

He nodded in agreement, because they had already talked about some of that being his vision. The loft? That was a definite perk.

"And then I was going to invite you to dinner to talk more about it."

"I see," he said after taking a moment to consider her words.

"And at the end of the night, I was going to kiss you and ask you to take me home with you. Beg you to, actually."

She was totally stealing his thunder.

He studied her for a long moment. "That's not going to work for me."

Her eyes, those big, beautiful green eyes, looked up at him and expressed her every emotion—disbelief, anger, sadness. "Oh." She stepped away from him, and he watched as she slowly sank to the floor and hugged her legs to her chest.

He crouched in front of her and placed his hands on her knees. "Don't get me wrong, I love your ideas for the gallery—this location is great, and other than it needing a major facelift, I think it has amazing potential."

"But?" she prompted.

He let out a long-suffering sigh. "But it's barely lunchtime, and I skipped breakfast. So if we can change dinner to lunch, I'd love to hear more about your plans for the gallery."

The relief on her face was instantaneous, but she didn't say anything.

"And after we're done talking business, we agreed that we have some other…business…to discuss. Personal business. I was going to tell you how much I missed you and need you in my life. Because without you, I have nothing. There's no light, there's no laughter, and"—he gave her a small smile—"everything's gray."

"Well," she said, fighting her own smile. "You do live in a very gray region of the country."

"I'd be willing to change that," he said, his voice sounding firm and confident and hopeful.

"Ben," she began, "you love your house. It's been in your family forever. You said you'd never leave there."

He shook his head. "I don't want to get rid of the house—it's too sentimental to me and my brothers. Mainly to me," he quickly corrected. "But it's a house. It's not a home. At least, it's not when you're not with me. I want to be where you are, Darcy. I want to make a home someplace with you. Anywhere you want. I just…I need you." Then he reached up and cupped her face again. "I love you."

His thumbs caressed her cheeks. "I thought I was doing the right thing. I thought by letting you go, you'd go and pursue your dreams and finally experience the life you wanted to live. The last thing I wanted to do was hold you back."

She shook her head but stayed quiet.

"And I would have held you back. Hell, I was holding myself back," he admitted. "I didn't realize how much I wasn't living until you were gone."

She sighed. "I missed you."

"I missed you too, and I promise I'm done with all that. It's not going to be easy, but I want to try. I really do. Will you help me? We can find a place closer to your family or anywhere you want. We'll make it work where I could have a workshop, and we could build a life together. Will you be there with me to remind me that I need to get out of my own way and live and laugh and be happy?"

"Ben—"

"Because that's what you do for me, Darcy. You do all that for me. And I'd like to think I do some of that for you too. That I make you laugh and smile and be happy. Not that you need me to do that—it's just who you are. But I hope some of what I do makes a difference in your life for the better."

And then she kissed him.

It was a kiss full of heat and promise, and if it were up to him, they'd never stop. But they were still in the back room of a gallery, and he had much bigger plans for them.

When she lifted her head, she sighed happily. "You do. You definitely do. You believe in me, and you encourage me in a way that no one else ever has. But if you ever push me away like that again, I will fight for you. I won't let you do that to me—to us—ever again. So know this now, Benjamin Tanner—you're stuck with me. I'm not going anywhere, and I'm going to love you and build a life with you, and we're going to be ridiculously happy."

She smiled and felt as if her world was righted when Ben smiled at her.

"There's no one else in the world for me but you, Darcy Shaughnessy. No one." He stood and pulled her to her feet.

And as soon as he got them home, he planned on proving it to her.

Repeatedly.

———~~~———

"Ben!" Darcy called out as she walked out of their bedroom.

It was New Year's Eve, and it was snowing. Not that they had plans to go anywhere, but she knew he had come in from his workshop over an hour ago, and she hadn't seen him since. Smoothing her hands over her dress, she went into the kitchen to check on their dinner. Ben had put their roast in the oven when he came in, and it smelled delicious. Peeking into the oven, she saw that it looked amazing too.

Everything else—their side dishes and appetizers— were all prepped and ready to go too. All she needed was her man.

Granted, she'd been in their en suite getting ready, but where would he have gone to? There was a bottle of wine on the counter that she had taken out earlier to go with their first course. She opened it and placed it back down on the counter to breathe. Calling out his name again, she walked around setting the table and getting candles lit. She dropped a spoon on the floor and bent over to pick it up.

That's when she heard a sharp hiss behind her.

"Don't move," he ordered, his voice deep and commanding.

She was bent at the waist, and no doubt he had quite the view of what she had on under her dress.

"Ben—"

"Shh," he said as he walked up behind her and put his hands on her hips. "Damn. This is almost better than the apron and stilettos fantasy."

Shaking her head—which was hanging upside down—she laughed. "I can't believe we haven't fully done that one yet. Clearly, I have the shoes here now."

"Baby, we have a lifetime of getting to that. But this? I am really enjoying it."

"All the blood is rushing to my head."

Rubbing up against her bottom made them both moan. "That looks like very skimpy underwear, Darce."

"It is," she agreed. "And if I don't pass out, I'd be happy to show it to you properly."

Laughing, Ben stepped back and helped her straighten. His eyes raked over her, and he let out another hiss of breath. "Darcy Shaughnessy, you take my breath away."

She was wearing the dress she had bought with the girls back in November—the green strapless one with the beading. She struck a pose for him. "You like it?"

He shook his head. "I love it. It looks like it was made just for you."

The compliment pleased her immensely.

Stepping in close to him, she wrapped her arms around him and kissed him softly on the lips. "Good. I was hoping you would. Maybe it's silly to wear it when it's just the two of us, but I thought since it was New Year's Eve, we could dress up." Then she noticed that Ben had showered—obviously in one of the other bathrooms—and was dressed casually in his usual attire of jeans and a flannel shirt. "Or I can change."

"No," he said and put a finger over her lips. "Give me

a few minutes, and I'll be back." And without another word, he went into their bedroom and closed the door behind him.

Darcy thought that was a little odd but shrugged it off and went back to setting the table. When she was done, she stepped back and admired it. With the soft lighting overhead, the candlelight, and watching the snow fall through the giant window behind the table, it was perfect. Pleased with her handiwork, she went about putting their salads out and the fresh bread she'd baked earlier. Next came the stuffed mushrooms and the shrimp cocktails. The roast still had some time left, and they had decided on the assortment of appetizers to hold them over.

She startled when music began to play over the sound system. Turning, she saw Ben standing in their bedroom doorway wearing a suit. The sight of him simply floored her. She always knew he was handsome and sexy, but none of that prepared her for how devastating he'd look dressed up.

Slowly, he began to walk toward her, and between the dim lighting, the soft music, and him, Darcy almost felt light-headed. When he was in front of her, she let out a small sigh. "Damn."

He smiled. "I clean up pretty nice, don't I?"

She knew he was teasing, but unable to help herself, she ran her hands up over the lapels of his jacket to his shoulders and then looked up at the face that she loved most of all. "That you do. But I have to admit, I like you dirty too."

He groaned and gently wrapped his arm around her waist to pull her close. "This coming from the girl in the barely there panties? I believe it."

It would be so easy to just say the hell with the food and be dirty right there in the middle of the kitchen, but there was no rush. Time was finally on their side, and Darcy knew that not only did they have all night, but they had all the time in the world. She kissed him on the cheek. "Come on, let's have something to eat."

She stepped out of his arms and went to grab the bottle of wine she'd opened earlier to pour them each a glass. At the table, Ben held her chair out for her, and together, they sat and enjoyed the start of their celebration.

As they ate, they talked more about the possibility of buying the gallery in Seattle. Darcy would manage it and also work as Ben's representative from this point forward. They talked about having their families come for the big grand opening—should they decide to do it— and how they'd deal with all that logistically.

They worked together to clean up and then reset the table for dinner. While they waited, Ben led her to the living room and asked her to dance with him.

It was perfect.

Who needed a night out in a loud and crowded restaurant when they could have this?

Swaying to the music, pressed together from head to toe, Darcy thought that life couldn't possibly be more perfect than this. Ben's body was so warm and hard and wonderful. He smelled so damn good, and she loved that he had gone along with her crazy idea of dressing up for a night at home.

"Darcy?" he murmured against her ear as he placed tiny kisses there.

"Hmm?"

"I love you."

She smiled and kissed his cheek. "Mmm, I love you too."

"I can't think of a better way to celebrate the start of the new year than being here with you."

"Me too." And it was true. This was better than any party or anything else she could have imagined.

They continued to dance in silence for a few minutes, and then he spun her around and dipped her at the end of the song. She laughed with delight at the surprise move, and when they straightened, she saw something on his face that she was beginning to see more of lately— peace. Benjamin Tanner finally looked like a man who was at peace.

And she loved that for him.

"Actually," he began, "I'm lying."

Wait, what?

"Um, what?" she asked in confusion, leaning back from him slightly.

"I mean, don't get me wrong. This is great. The dinner, the dancing, this dress on you…it's all very nice."

Her eyes went wide. "Nice?"

Ben seemed to ignore her shocked expression. "Mmm-hmm. It is. But maybe it's not…let's just say that maybe I can think of a better way to start the new year."

"I swear, if you say that it would be better to be naked right now, I'm going to slug you," she said with just a hint of snark.

He laughed softly and kissed the tip of her nose. "No. But that would be nice too."

"Ben—"

He took a step back and looked at her. "Darcy Shaughnessy, you were the first person who really understood me. You understood my work. You accepted me. I love working with you. I love playing with you. And I especially love loving you."

Her heart began to pound, because this was beginning to sound like a whole lot more than just romantic conversation during a dance.

"You are my hope, you are my muse, you are my life. When I think of my future now, there isn't one minute of it where I don't see you by my side."

Swallowing hard, she nodded. "I feel that way too."

His smile was slow and sweet, and when he reached out and ran one rough finger along her cheek, she couldn't help but sigh.

"There is nothing I want more in this world than to spend every day of my life with you."

And just as she was about to respond, he dropped to one knee in front of her and pulled a ring from his pocket. Holding it up to her, he took her hand in his. "Promise to always be by my side. Promise to love me when I'm unlovable and to accept me when I make mistakes. Promise to laugh with me, smile with me, and dance with me forever." He paused, and as his dark gaze held hers, he slipped the ring onto her finger. "Marry me, Darcy, and promise me we'll have our perfect forever."

Nodding, she felt the sting of tears and didn't care. When Ben stood and kissed her, she tasted him along with the tears that she couldn't hold back.

And it was okay.

Because they were the best kind of tears—the ones that were happy and shed for all the right reasons.

And knowing that she was going to have her perfect forever with Ben?

It was the best reason.

# Epilogue

*Six months later*

IT WAS A BEAUTIFUL SUMMER DAY. SOME PEOPLE would say the weather was perfect.

Ian Shaughnessy was one of those people.

As he made his way across the lawn, he felt something he'd never felt before on this particular trip.

Peace.

Stopping at the seventh headstone, he paused. Taking a handkerchief from his pocket, he wiped away the dust and pollen that coated the marble, and then removed the old flowers someone had placed there probably a week or so earlier. Once the area was neat and clean, he took the bouquet he'd brought with him and placed it in the holder.

"She was the most beautiful bride," he said quietly. "I'm telling you, Lily, when she turned around and faced me for the first time after she put your gown on, I swore it was forty years ago, and I was looking at you." He paused and let that imagery fill his mind and smiled. "Of course, she wasn't as calm as you were. Nope. Our girl is a bundle of energy at all times, and if I find out who let her have coffee yesterday morning, I'm going to smack them in the head."

He chuckled, and for a moment, he swore he heard Lily's laugh too.

"I knew this day would come," he went on. "Eventually. I've known for a long time that Darcy was a grown woman, but something about seeing her in a wedding gown—your wedding gown—made it seem like it was only yesterday that we were bringing her home from the hospital. Where did the time go?" He shook his head.

A flock of birds flew noisily overhead. Several cars drove down the lane on their way to visit loved ones as well.

"Oh, I almost forgot to tell you. We're expecting more babies." He chuckled. "I'm telling you, I wish these kids of ours would time these things a little bit better. I swear, it seems like they're either having babies one right after the other or several at once." He shook his head again and tried to see if he could get them all straight.

"Hugh and Aubrey started the process to adopt. After consulting with all her doctors, they decided it wouldn't be the best thing for Aubrey to try to get pregnant again. They also didn't want Connor to be an only child." He laughed again. "Although between that boy and the three dogs that they treat like children, I don't see how they can possibly handle any more than that.

"Aidan and Zoe just found out that they are expecting, and I think they're also going to have their hands full. No dogs, but your namesake is a handful. Always into mischief, that one. But, oh, Lily, is she beautiful. I'm telling you, there is nothing that sweet girl can't get from me when she looks at me with those big blue eyes. She has Aidan wrapped around her little finger too, so I don't think she's going to give up the throne so easily."

There were some stray weeds around the base of the

headstone, and he crouched to pull them as he continued his one-sided conversation.

"Oh, Anna and Quinn are expecting as well. They are due about a week after Aidan and Zoe. The girls are tickled about that, of course. Quinn's already a nervous wreck and demanding that they have a son this time because he wants his Little League team. Not that Kaitlyn can't play baseball, as we all reminded him." He laughed softly. "I think it would be hysterical if he ended up with an all-girls team. Can you imagine?"

A gentle breeze blew around him, and he took that to be her laughing with him.

"Lily, I'm telling you, the most amazing thing I think I've seen through all this—watching our kids become parents—is Owen. Well, first let me say Riley and Savannah are doing well, and Aislynn is a little angel, and they're trying to get pregnant again but nothing's happened yet. Savannah's anxious for Riley to get on the road or in the studio so he'll get off this baby kick. Riley's such a great father, and he's so confident, not that I expected anything else from him. He's always been confident. But back to Owen."

Picking up the weeds, he placed them off to the side to take with him when he left.

"When Brooke found out they were having twins, I swear to you we all thought Owen was going to freak out. But he never did. And now that the boys are mobile and running around, he and Brooke are talking about trying to get pregnant again too. It's crazy! Our little boy who was afraid of his own shadow and didn't want to be around people is hoping for a large family!"

Sighing, he fiddled with the bouquet.

"And then there's our baby girl. Oh, Lily, what I wouldn't give for you to see her. She wanted to bring these flowers here herself, but she and Ben had an early morning flight. They're going to Hawaii. She was so excited about it—I think she talked more about the trip than she did about the wedding," he said with a laugh. "She was the most low-maintenance bride out of the group, and that's saying something! But it was important to her for you to have her bouquet." Reaching out, he touched one of the flowers and rubbed it between his fingers.

A lily.

Clearing his throat, he felt the telltale swell of emotion coming when it was time to leave.

"We did something right, Lily. We were two kids in love who spent a lot of time trying to figure out how to be good parents. It looks like we succeeded, because we have some amazing kids who grew up to be incredible adults, and now they're all happily married with families of their own." He paused. "I know, I know, Darcy got married less than twenty-four hours ago, but trust me. She and Ben will be starting a family soon. I know it. She's already talking about it. I can't even let myself imagine that day. It was too hard walking her down the aisle and knowing she's not my little girl anymore. Well, she'll always be my little girl, but you know what I mean."

Ian crouched one last time, picked up the weeds he'd put to the side, and held them in his hands.

"I miss you every single day," he said softly, placing a hand on the cool marble. "Every. Single. Day. It wasn't easy to let go of you and ask Martha to marry me. I love her, and she's wonderful, but it didn't seem right—or fair—that I got to be happy and find love again. I wish like hell it was you who was here. You'd be so much better at all of this than I am. If we're being honest, I wish it was us here together like we'd always planned."

Smoothing his hand one last time over the stone, Ian took a step back. "I love you, Lillian Shaughnessy. And thank you for giving me six of the greatest gifts a man could ever ask for." He smiled sadly. "I'll see you next week."

And as he walked away, he looked up at the clear blue sky and felt almost as if he could see all the way to heaven. Sometimes, he wished he could.

But sometimes, you had to have faith that those who were watching over you knew how much they were loved.

And missed.

And all the ways just having them for a short time made your life better.

# About the Author

Samantha Chase is a *New York Times* and *USA Today* bestseller of contemporary romance. She released her debut novel in 2011 and currently has more than forty titles under her belt! When she's not working on a new story, she spends her time reading romances, playing way too many games of Scrabble or Solitaire on Facebook, wearing a tiara while playing with her sassy pug, Maylene...oh, and spending time with her husband of twenty-five years and their two sons in North Carolina.

# THE WINDHAMS

**Award-winning historical romance by *New York Times* and *USA Today* Bestselling author Grace Burrowes**

## Lady Jenny's Christmas Portrait

Lady Jenny Windham pursues her artistic ambition only to find she must choose between true love and fulfilling a lifelong dream.

## Lady Louisa's Christmas Knight

No one would guess that Lady Louisa Windham hides a scandalous secret—except perhaps family friend Sir Joseph Carrington, a man with secrets of his own.

## Lady Sophie's Christmas Wish

Trapped by a London snowstorm, Lady Sophie Windham finds herself with an abandoned baby and only the assistance of a kind, handsome stranger standing between her and complete disaster.

RITA nominated and winner of *RT Book Reviews* 2011 Reviewers' Choice Award for Best Historical Romance

# *SPEND CHRISTMAS IN OUR CASA!*

However you like your romance, Sourcebooks Casablanca has got a holiday tale for you!

**By Terry Spear, *USA Today* Bestselling Author**

---

"A holiday treat...romance that sizzles and entertains."
**—Fresh Fiction for *A Highland Wolf Christmas***

### *Dreaming of a White Wolf Christmas*

A romance writer's life is changed forever when a nip from a playful white pup...turns her into an Arctic wolf shifter.

### *A Very Jaguar Christmas.*

An orphaned werewolf cub brings two fiercely independent jaguar shifters together under the mistletoe.

### A Silver Wolf Christmas

Old mysteries, Victorian mansions, and some new shifters in town... It's a Silver Town Christmas, and the wolves are ready to howl!

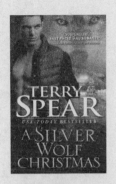

### A Highland Wolf Christmas

Sexy Highland shapeshifters in kilts. Who says Christmas dreams don't come true?

### A SEAL Wolf Christmas

Can an alpha wolf who's met his match...survive the holidays with her?

# WHO DOESN'T WANT A COWBOY FOR CHRISTMAS?

Fill your holidays with love, laughter, and plenty of down-home Texas flavor

**By Carolyn Brown, *New York Times* Bestselling Author**

*"'Tis the season for hunky cowboys...
A holiday treat to be savored."*

**—RT Book Reviews for Mistletoe Cowboy, 4 Stars**

### A Cowboy Christmas Miracle

It will take a miracle bigger than the state of Texas for these two feuding families to survive the holidays! **Burnt Boot, Texas series**

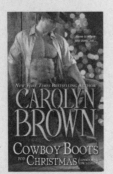

### Cowboy Boots for Christmas

An Army veteran and a woman on the run find love and healing in Burnt Boot, Texas. **Burnt Boot, Texas series**